SERVUS CAPAX

JERRY AUTIERI

1

Rome 194 BC

∼

Rome was not as Varro remembered it, but perhaps it never had been. It had become both larger and smaller in the six years he had been at war. Larger in that the breadth of its sprawl seemed limitless. No matter how far he pushed through the streets, they never ended. Yet once snared within, the city was dark and brooding. Buildings shoved together like thugs determined to prevent his passing. Enormous columns and statues threw shadows even into the widest plazas. He seemed never able to place his foot in the light. Someone or something always eclipsed it. It left him feeling as if he had squeezed into a box.

"You one of Flamus's heroes?"

The voice of the woman who had stopped them sounded raw and aged, but it she could not be much older than Varro. She had a strange accent and a Greek look to match. She might have been more attractive were he as drunk as Falco and Curio. But he carried far more worries back to Rome than either of them. Despite the triumph celebrations, he could not let himself celebrate as hard as the others. So he stared soberly at the woman with sagging white breasts barely contained in her dirty gray stola. She snatched Falco's arm and pulled it toward her chest.

"I've got a special price for heroes."

"You do?" Falco seemed astounded, as if he had just kicked over a rock and found a precious gem beneath it. "I didn't think the day could get any better."

He laughed and Curio did as well.

"Oh, it will get much better. I can do things you can't even imagine." She pulled Falco out of the flow of street traffic, which comprised of drunken soldiers just released from service and their drunken civilian friends who only needed the barest excuse to fill up with drink. The whole city smelled of sweat, garbage, and wine so sour that Varro would have poured it into a ditch were he on the march rather than pay top coin for it as they all had.

"What's the price for the two of us?" Curio asked, then hiccuped. He had drank so much, Varro wondered how he had managed to follow the transaction. He had spent most of the day dozing or if alert asking when they would eat dinner.

The woman's thin lips flattened out in a smile. "Well, for both of you being heroes who marched to victory with Flamus's army—"

"Wait!" Falco shouted in his centurion's voice, causing the woman to wince and turn the heads of men on the street still used to listening for shouted orders. "How much for the three of us?"

The woman's smile straightened out and she narrowed her eyes at Varro, obviously unhappy to do business with a mark who wasn't staggeringly drunk.

"Six denarii."

"What?" Falco recoiled from the woman. "That's... that's... that's how many for each of us?"

"It's a bargain," the woman said. "The three of you at once. That's a bit of work, especially to serve Flamus's heroes right."

"She's fucking mad." Falco's bleary eyes widened and he looked to Varro to corroborate his assessment. "Well, then, how much for us one at a time?"

"Two denarii each." The woman recaptured Falco's arm and began to pull him toward the shabby buildings behind them. "That's a special rate for you heroes."

"Well, alright. That's fairer. But six denarii? Fucking mad."

Varro grabbed Falco by the shoulder, the left side without the horrific burn scars he had taken in Sparta. He yanked him out of the prostitute's grasp.

"Come on. We've wasted enough time here. She'll put a bag over your head then rob you blind. That's her special service."

The woman gasped and glared at Varro.

"I cannot believe one of Flamus's heroes could make such an accusation." She turned a smile back to Falco and tugged at his arm. "Now, just follow me."

"It's Flamininus," Varro said. "At least get his name right."

"That's right! Respect the Consul," Falco said, suddenly persuaded to Varro's side. "She'd put a bag over my head, like they tried to do in Boeotia?"

"Or worse," Varro added, pulling Falco free of the woman who appeared to finally understand she had wasted effort on the wrong mark. She was already smiling past Falco at the throng of men squeezing through the narrow, shadowed street.

"Don't worry. I think I have enough denarii for all of us."

As Falco stepped back from the prostitute, Varro saw Curio holding open a pouch heavy with silver coins. The thin light reflecting off the silver cast a pale reflection under his idyllic smile.

As fast as if he were saving Curio from an enemy pike, he interposed himself between the pouch and the prostitute. She had only glimpsed what Curio had offered, but her puffy, jaded eyes were alight with greed. Varro shoved the purse against Curio's chest, then he turned to the prostitute.

He drove his palm into her shoulder, knocking her back and causing her to stumble. She went down onto the dirt road with an exaggerated scream more like she was being trampled by a chariot than just having slid onto her posterior.

But her call drew the attention of shadowy men lurking around the building she had wanted to take Falco to.

"Alright, time to go," Varro said. "We're not looking for a fight."

"He hit me!" The woman screamed, pointing up at him. "Some hero of Flabinisus, that one!"

"You just threw yourself on the ground," Falco said.

"I don't see the problem," Curio added. "I can pay for all of us."

He again held forward his coin purse and Varro ripped it from his grip, whispering to him as he did.

"I told you not to flash your wealth, you fool."

But Curio had done sufficient advertising to draw the rough men who must work with the prostitute, who continued screaming her indignation as she backed up into the crowd like a crab scuttling under a rock.

"What's with them?" Falco asked. He raised a wavering arm at the men drawing through a rapidly thinning crowd.

"You boys are wrecking our merchandise. That's a problem."

The lead thug was a large as Falco, with a matching heavy brown interrupted with a thick white scar over his left eye. The other two seemed the sort who would happily kick a downed man, but not take the risk to down one on their own. They hovered close to their strongman's side.

"That's the one that hit me," the prostitute said pointing up at

Varro. Then, in a hushed, eager voice she shifted to Curio. "And he's the one with the purse."

"We don't want trouble." Varro said, slipping Curio's purse into his tunic.

"Well, you found it," the leader said.

Falco, now straightening up as he seemed to understand a fight was in the offering, looked to Varro. "Let me handle the big, dumb one. You and Curio can pick off those pieces of shit dangling from his ass."

The crowd instinctively flowed around them, with just as many pedestrians stopping to watch as continued on their way without a second glance at the brewing fight.

Falco turned back to the three men.

The club came out of nowhere and slammed over Falco's head, staggering him backward. The crowd erupted into cheers, the prostitute's being the most shrill and gleeful. Falco roared and held his head as if it might fall off his shoulders.

Varro's hand flexed for the gladius that was not at his side. They had entrusted their armor and weapons to the quartermasters encamped outside the city, where all of Flamininus's victorious legions had either deposited their gear or else sold back their weapons in the naive belief they would not be needed again. In any case, Varro's hand swished through open air.

He felt the comforting pressure of his pugio hidden against his leg, under his tunic. But rather than try to draw it, he leaped forward at the two other men who charged him and Curio.

They lurched forward with raised clubs, and one had an iron nail set into it. Varro knew to get inside their reach, where his training and conditioning would win the fight. But the thugs knew this as well and struck fast.

The spiked club clipped Varro's shoulder, tearing the fabric of his tunic but otherwise doing no harm. The prostitute, however, cheered as if Varro had been decapitated.

Both Falco and Curio squared off with their enemies. The crowd stretched and bent with the fight, men and women cheering and calling out for blood. Behind them, the disinterested rushed by as if this sort of deadly street fighting was a common sight.

Varro skid to the side, and landed a punch to his enemy's ribs. The solid blow drove out his breath in a pained gasp and sent him crashing forward into the road. A quick glance to his left showed Curio had his man doubled over while he drove his knee into his face.

Falco, however, covered his head and face with both arms against a flurry of blows from the strongman. Despite his size, he was fast and each strike landed with a meaty thud followed by delighted cheers from the spectators.

Varro ran at the thug, who turned to meet him. But he had been too happy to beat Falco into submission and turned too late.

He jumped the final distance and drove his foot into the side of the strongman's knee. It was one of the weakest points in the body, as Varro had learned through scores of combats. Collapse a man's knee and he was finished. No amount of muscle or armor could protect from such a blow.

The giant screamed as his leg bent sideways. His club clattered to the ground as his arms flailed around to catch his balance. But with his knee destroyed, he simply toppled into a pile.

Falco popped up as if he had merely been sitting out the beating. He then snatched the club off the ground.

"I'll do the world a favor," he shouted. "And smash your fucking brains out."

The crowded street shuddered with the cheering and clapping of the spectators. But as Falco raised the club, Varro seized his arm.

"You can't kill him. We're in Rome, not on the battlefield."

Falco's rage-red eyes met his. Varro saw in them the reflection of a old battles and the ghostly ranks of enemies framed against flaming anger. He could taste the bitter bile of hatred in his own mouth, and knew Falco's swam with it as well. He shoved his friend's arm down.

"But he was beating me."

"Some one had to." Varro shoved Falco's arm down and he relented. The crowd hissed and jeered, laughing and angry faces all smearing into a haze surrounding them. The strongman wriggled away like a worm, dragging his leg which had turned at an ugly angle.

Curio stood over his enemy, kicking him any time he moved.

Varro's assailant had fled into the crowd along with the cajoling prostitute.

"We really need to go before someone figures out who we are."

The crowd seemed unwilling to let them escape. But as Varro encountered resistance he made his best imitation of his old Centurion Drusus and shouted to clear the way. Whenever he needed to be fierce and intimidating, he called on the shade of his favorite leader and mentor. It never failed to get the reaction he desired, and the crowd of men and women of every age parted for him. Soon, they were on the other side of the throng and the spectators had once more melted into the endless stream of traffic on these dark side streets.

They let the procession drunks and hurried citizens guide them. It was the final day of the thanksgiving celebration for Flamininus's victorious return to Rome. While the great man himself had gone to reunite with his family and thus vanish from the public eye, the public carried on the celebrations as vigorously as if it were the first hour of the first day. Scipio's thanksgiving might have been greater, but this event was unlike anything Varro had ever experienced. Scipio's triumph was a vague memory to him in any case. He had not been allowed to accompany his parents to Rome and had remained with Yasha, the household slave who watched after him and his sister.

As he bounced from one stranger's shoulder to another's he wondered what remained of his old home. What of his mother and sister? He knew where they were, but did he want to see them? What was the point? Then he thought of Falco, laughing and staggering beside him, and his hands went cold. He reconsidered having a strong drink before telling him all he had to say.

It was going to be harder than any fight they had been in yet.

"The One-Horned Bull?"

Falco's arm bolted out and stopped Varro's wandering, hitting him across the chest. He looked up to the sign over a gray, sagging building and true to Falco's words a sign with the a massive black bull sporting a single horn hung over a doorway.

"With a name like that, we have to go in and try their wine." Falco looped his strong arms around Varro and Curio's necks. "I'll get this round, since you boys helped me out back there. Say, am I bleeding?"

A thin streak of blood was already drying on Falco's left ear and he scratched at it.

"I think so," Curio said."You got some blood on your back too."

"Bah, it was just a lucky hit."

"More like a lucky dozen hits," Varro said. "You were doing a great job blocking his club with your head. So let's go inside and you buy us that wine before you realize that you should be knocked out."

"I had to use my own since your rock-head wasn't handy." Falco tightened his arm around his neck. "Come on. It's almost evening and I can still see straight. That's not right."

They filed inside to yet another crowded room where servants flitted between scores of patrons leaning over their mugs in laughter in booming talk. A vague smoke filled the room and something savory carried on it that made Varro's mouth water. In truth, after six years of eating army rations he could hardly handle the rich food on offer in the city and he spent the first day with a sour stomach after gorging himself.

They frowned for a time by the entrance, looking for a place to sit and seeing none. But one of the serving women noticed them and waved them off to a corner where a barrel had been overturned as a makeshift table.

"It's still better than what we've had the last six years," Falco said. "Let's grab it before someone else does."

They sat on old crates that had been intended as chairs. Curio nearly fell off his, laughing as he did. But Falco held him upright, and when a servant came he ordered a jug of the best wine. The woman cocked her brow at their appearance, particularly Falco's bloodied tunic and the tear on Varro's sleeve.

"We've got the coin for it, woman." Falco slapped two denarii on the table with a bright chime. "If that's not enough, I've got it covered. Now, a jug of your best. Don't sell me anything less or I'll know."

The woman left the coins on the table and went to fetch their jug. Curio picked up the coins and flipped them over in his fingers.

"I never saw a coin until I joined the army."

"Me neither," Falco said. "But now we're seeing plenty of coins."

Curio dropped the denarii back on the barrel top and the servant returned with a red clay jug and mugs. She set them down without a word and swept the coins away. Varro was waiting for Falco to comment on her looks or else grab her. But instead he just smiled warmly at the jug and let her go.

"You really are drunk," Varro said. "For once, you didn't torment the serving girl."

"She seemed like a nice girl," he said. "I wonder if this is their best? You know I was talking shit about knowing if it wasn't. I wouldn't know good wine if Bacchus himself poured it for me."

"It'll be good enough," Varro said. He shifted on his crate, feeling Curio's purse move with him. He pulled it from his tunic fold and set it on the barrel, keeping his hand covering it. "Take care with your money. If you go flashing it everywhere you're going to end up losing it and probably your life as well."

"That's right," Falco added, rapping the barrel for emphasis. "It'd be a fucking shame to have lived through all that army bullshit to have some rat cut your throat right here in Rome."

Curio took back the purse, slipping his hand over it and secreting it back into his tunic.

"Is it really all over? We're out?"

He stared between them like a child. But he was not the fresh-faced lad Varro had met years ago. He carried the scars of war and of fears no man should have had to face. The touch of death had dug creases in his brow and hollows in his cheeks that no passing of time would ever heal.

Falco lowered his head and grabbed the jug. He splashed wine into the three mugs, then paused a moment before speaking.

"Let's have a drink, boys. After six long and bloody years, we came home. All our limbs, fingers, and toes, too. Let's drink to keeping our eyeballs in their sockets and blades out of our hearts. Let's drink for those who never came home. Those we hardly knew yet loved like brothers."

Varro and Curio raised their mugs to Falco's and touched them together before downing the wine. It was sweet and smooth, a match to some of the finest that his commanders had shared out for special occasions. He gulped it all down then set his mug to the table.

"Now that was good," Falco said, wiping his mouth with the back of his wrist. "We'll have another jug of it when this one is empty."

"That was a good toast," Curio said. "I can't believe we're all done with the army. How many times did it seem like I would die?"

"Forget those times," Falco said, grabbing the jug to pour another round. "Nothing good can come from thinking of that shit. Say, are you going back home, Curio? I don't even know where you live. You should buy a farm next to me and Varro. You know, rich people stick together, right?"

Falco and Curio burst into drunken laughter and Curio slapped the barrel.

"I'll buy all the farms around yours. You'll have to work for me!"

"I don't think so. Varro and I will have the area stitched up before you even figure out where we live. You'll be working for me, more like it."

"You're not a centurion now. You can't order me about anymore."

"We'll see about that. Plus I've got a grass crown and enough commendations for bravery to choke an ox. I'm still senior to you."

"I got the same commendations. But I'm not stupid enough to run through a fire and burn my ears off just to get a grass crown."

Falco kicked the table, making the mugs and jug wobble. "I didn't do it for a crown. I did it to save my life, and it worked well enough, didn't it?"

Their back and forth continued while Varro looked on, his stomach filling with cold water.

It was late in the day, at least for someone with duties in the morning like himself.

He had waited long enough, and maybe it would be better to tell them in this loud, crowded room.

They both settled down, realizing Varro remained outside of their playful teasing. Falco's heavy brows drew together and he frowned at him.

"You look like you just got sentenced to a flogging. What's with that face?"

"You look pale," Curio added. "You feeling sick?"

He hid his cold hands at his lap behind the barrel and tried to smile.

"There are some important things I need to tell both of you. I've been meaning to for some time, but it was never the right moment. Now, there's no time left."

Falco and Curio both leaned forward, and the drunken haze that seemed to smudge their features suddenly vanished.

"What do you mean no time left? "Falco asked. "It's not like we've got roll call at dawn tomorrow."

"Maybe not you two." Varro smiled and balled his hands out of view. "But I do."

2

The main room of the One-Horned Bull dimmed and the crush of patrons laughing, spilling wine, and shouting with full mouths faded into the black rim encircling Varro's vision. A thin man in a faded blue tunic shot to his feet then grabbed a serving girl and kissed her. She smashed an empty mug on his head with a hollow thud and the drunk collapsed into the circle of his laughing friends. The serving girl moved out of Varro's field of view like nothing had happened.

But Falco and Curio both seemed to grow in size, like they had suddenly become titans and were expanding to push out everything from the One-Horned Bull back into the evening streets where revelers still sang songs of tribute to Consul Flamininus and his great victories in Greece.

His mouth was hot and his saliva had dried up. He held his hands balled up against the cold and hidden behind the barrel. His fear shamed him, especially since he knew he deserved all the blame he was about to receive.

This dreadful fear was all his own making, and now he had to confront it.

"What the fuck are you saying, Varro?"

Falco's voice was soft and in reality, must have been lost amid the general racket of the drinking room, but to Varro it sounded booming.

"You're drunk," Curio said. "That's why you look like you're going to vomit."

"I'm going to vomit alright." Varro could taste the bitter bile at the back of his tongue. "But not because I'm drunk. I've been taking it easy, as you've teased me for all day. I wanted to be clear when I told you this. I'm just sorry it couldn't be a better time."

"Listen, Varro, I'm having memories of beating your face in back on the farm. Get to your point before I relive my best years with your face today."

"There's a lot to say." Varro dragged a heavy breath, and let his shoulders sag. He had to be braver than this. He owed it to his friends to be as straight as he could under the current circumstances. "You both need to listen and let me finish. Especially you, Falco. Keep your fists at your sides until I'm done."

Falco nodded, his frown deepening, and Curio leaned forward with an expression of grave concern, again making him look far older than his years.

"A year ago, after Sparta and King Nabis, you'll remember I was summoned to the Consul's command tent."

"I remember," Falco said, then nodded at Varro's leg. "That's when you got your pugio back. How can I forget? That thing keeps getting lost and finding you again."

"Well, it's not really my pugio. Not the one my mother gave me, anyway, but one much like it. You see, I was only summoned by the Consul, but I did not go to meet him. Instead, I was sent to meet with a senator, our old Consul Galba in fact."

Falco and Curio did not react with more than a raised brow. Everyone knew Galba was among the senators who had come from Rome to join Flamininus in making his treaties. That he would meet with Varro was only shocking in that the senator would remember his name.

"At the time, I was surprised he wanted to meet with me. He had news from home to share, and an offer to make me."

"News from home?" Falco leaned closer. "My home is close to your home. Was there something you should've told me but didn't? That's why you're twisting aside like you'd rather run into the street than finish this conversation."

He hadn't realized Falco was right, and he squared himself to their front again.

"Yes, Falco, there are some things I learned. Galba left it for me to tell you, and I just could never do it. I've been a coward."

"Look, it has been almost a year since," Falco said, leaning back and folding his hands on the barrel top. "Whatever news you had, if it was really serious I'd have heard it by now."

"Really?" Varro asked. "In all the years we served, did we ever get more than a single letter from Old Man Pius to say he was managing the farms after our fathers died? That was nearly five years ago. No letters from our mothers. No word at all."

"Are you so fucking stupid, Varro? My mother can't read or write. She wasn't as fancy as your mother."

Varro tilted his head in acceptance.

"Old Man Pius could have written but never did. And we were so concerned with our own survival we never thought to enquire after him. We just thought he'd handle things. Well, Falco, he died the winter following that last letter from him."

Curio looked between him and Falco, his face creased with confusion. But Falco straightened up again, dragging his hands off the barrel top and folding them under arm. As he considered the implications, raucous laughter from the patrons filled the silence. Varro broke into it, continuing his explanation.

"So when Pius died, someone had to inherit his farm. That would be his eldest son, right? But he lives somewhere in this giant city and has no interest in running a bunch of farms. But he had a mind to profit from their sale."

"What does that mean?" Falco's voice grew threatening. "Our mothers were still living there."

"Women can't own property. You know that. My father had designated Old Man Pius to manage business affairs until he returned. I guess my father was optimistic about surviving as a triarii. He only had a year left to serve. So I guess he did not designate me. Besides I was away and my mother needed a man to retain the property. So Old Man Pius got the farm when my father died, and when he died his son got it."

"Varro, that is terrible." Falco let a long sigh out. "So, his son sold off your farm? What happened to your mother and sister?"

Varro swallowed and looked Falco in the eye.

"He sold our farms. Not mine alone."

"How did he do that? I own that farm. My father is dead and as are all my other brothers and sisters. I'm all there is to inherit that farm."

Varro drew another long breath before continuing.

"Well, I knew this from a long time back. Seems like your father didn't run the business side of his farm so well. In fact, he was running the family into the ground. So he sold it to my father, or they had some sort of partnership. I don't really understand their arrangement. In any case, my father was the primary owner. So it would be part of my inheritance. Of course, I'd always planned to sell it back to you for an obol. But I guess it was all part of the deal Old Man Pius's son made. Both our farms are not only gone, but gone years ago. One family bought both, along with the Pius estate and some of the other nearby farms. A senator or someone in his family, as far as I know."

Falco stared at Varro and blinked.

"But it doesn't matter," Curio said, smiling as he reached a hand toward each of them. "We're all rich now. We've got our silver in a bank. Didn't the Consul say we should invest it in land? So, maybe you can buy back your farms. Or buy bigger and better farms. See, Falco? It's not a big deal."

But Falco pushed Curio's hand aside and glared at Varro.

"You've known all these years that my family is just a tenant on your land? You didn't think to tell me?"

"What would that achieve? I told you I was never going to keep it. I knew when my father died, and decided then that I would sell it back to you for less than a week's pay. I'd just give it back if that would be legal. How did I know this would happen?"

"That's right," Curio said, again reaching out his hands across the barrel to both of them. "It's just a bad deal for everyone. No harm, Falco. Knowing earlier wouldn't change anything."

Falco narrowed his eyes at Varro, and to his great relief it seemed his anger ebbed as his shoulders relaxed and frown softened.

"What happened to my mother?"

"Same as my mother," Varro said. "Remarried to someone here in the city. My sister was married off in a hurry. But I guess not fast enough for her husband to put a claim on the farm."

"Wait," Falco asked. "Who gave our women to these men? Our grandfathers are dead. So it can't have been them. It certainly wasn't us. So was it Pilus's son? That wouldn't be legal."

Varro shrugged. "I don't know what happens to a woman in this situation. Does it matter? They've started new lives. I don't even want to see my mother. If you want to find yours, you have the money to pay someone to look into it."

Falco scrubbed his hands through his hair and stared at the barrel top. Someone burst into laughter behind them while the three sat in sulky silence.

"You got a room at your home, Curio? Seems like I'll need a place to stay while I figure out where I'm going to live."

Curio drew his hands back and blushed.

"Well, I'll try to figure out something. I don't come from wealth."

"Neither did I," Falco said, letting his hands fall to his lap. "I'll be fine with anything."

Both seemed to realize the story was not finished yet, and simultaneously looked to Varro.

"You said you had roll call in the morning," Falco said, the frown resurfacing. "What did you mean?"

"Remember that pugio I got?" Varro's hand slipped over the hard lump of the sheathed weapon at his leg. Weapons were strictly forbidden in the city, but he was also strictly forbidden from ever being without his new pugio.

"I thought the Consul had found it for you, and that Greek woman who aided you sent it back."

"She sent it back," Varro nodded, recalling Ione, if that had been her real name. He had thought her a goddess, but now he could hardly remember he face. Those days were filled with so much pain that he might never remember anything from them. "But Galba did not return it to me. I should not have had it in the first place."

Falco looked to Curio, who shrugged.

"Listen, Lily, I saw you carry that weapon from your house to the recruiting station."

"My mother passed me something that I was never really meant to have. I hadn't earned it, but for her own reasons I guess she wanted me to inherit it. In any case, it is given only to those who serve Rome and the one I had was inlaid with gold."

"We served Rome," Curio said. "Why aren't our pugiones special?"

Falco mocked Varro as he answered, "Because ours weren't inlaid with gold. You make it sound like it shined with the sun. It was just a fucking speck of gold with some sort of design. Not even worth stealing."

"Well, this is special." Varro patted the hidden weapon. "And it marks me as a member of Servus Capax."

"Useful Servants?" Falco leaned back as if disgusted. "What are you, some sort of housekeeper? Aren't there slaves for that work?"

Curio chortled, reminding Varro that both he and Falco were still intoxicated. He decided to cut to the point, rather than drag out any more explanations while they might only have foggy memories the next day.

"It'd take me the rest of the night to explain. But it's an organization that serves the Senate, and therefore the citizens of Rome. They do things to advance the reach of Roman power. I guess I've been watched all these years, and a lot of the missions I received tested my abilities. In the end, Galba told me what had happened to my family and what my future looked like. I could return to Rome and spend my money, or I could really earn back the pugio my mother had pressed on me. I could continue to serve. And so I have chosen to do so."

Falco and Curio's mouths gaped and they stared at him. Varro felt his face warming, and he had to look aside.

"Yesterday Flamininus summoned me and gave my orders. I'm leaving for Numidia tomorrow morning."

"I thought you were with a whore like the rest of us," Curio said, sitting back with his face draining of color. "But you were signing up again?"

"I'd already signed up. It's a lifetime commitment. I'll still have to serve in my regular military duties like any other citizen. But in between and during service, I'll probably have a lot of irregular missions assigned."

"Numidia?"

Falco shot up from his crate, bumping the barrel and nearly toppling the half empty jug of fine wine.

"Don't shout it," Varro said, waving him down. "I'm not sure if anyone else is supposed to know where I'm going."

"Where you're going?" Falco kicked the barrel and sent the jug and mugs crashing to the floor. The jug ejected wine onto the legs of men seated nearby. They shouted in protest, but when they turned to see Falco with his chest heaving and veins standing out on his neck, they instead turned their backs again.

"I leave at first light with a merchant ship headed for Numidia. I don't know much more than that."

In fact, Flamininus had been explicit in his orders but Varro knew now was not the time to say more.

Falco kicked the overturned barrel again. "You're leaving me? After all the shit we survived together? You're getting a on ship tomorrow morning and leaving." He slapped both hands to his head. "This can't be you, Varro. Not at all. The Varro I know would've done better than to get me drunk and then say 'Hey fuck you brother, I'm leaving forever tomorrow. Enjoy your fucking life.'"

"That's not what I—"

"You can't sign up again!" Curio joined Falco in lurching to his feet. He swayed a moment then pointed at him. "We're out. You said so yourself. It's all done and now we just go off to buy a farm and marry a good woman. We could've all been together. But your going to someplace I've never heard of and leaving us."

"It's a lifetime commitment," Varro said weakly. "I couldn't sign you up for that."

"And you couldn't say anything?" Falco remained with his hands on his head. "Since when have we kept such secrets from each other? Ah, but I supposed I'm wrong there too. You didn't tell me about my farm. I guess it's all secrets with you, Varro. I don't even fucking know you."

Varro stood up. "It's not like I'm leaving forever. I'll be back in Rome on leave within the year, and probably done with whatever they need me to do in Numida the year after that."

"Great," Falco said with a false smile. "I'm familiar with the missions you get, seeing that you couldn't have done a single one without me or Curio. I think your chances of coming back next year are low. Think of how many you've seen killed in these six years. Then add to that all the men who didn't take home their whole bodies. That'll be you, Varro. Either fucking dead or wishing that you were."

He lowered his head in shame. Falco was not wrong in his assessment, particularly when this Kingdom of Numidia was a new kingdom recently aligned with Rome. He guessed only more violence lay ahead of him. But this was what his mother had chosen for him, wasn't it? Yet in his deepest heart he relished the chance to do more for Rome, to dare more, and to live on the edge of death.

"So what now? You're just leaving?"

"The orders were clear. I'm to board the trading ship and take the Tiber down to the coast, and from there onto Numidia."

The three of them stared at each other. Patrons looked askance at them, possibly expecting a fight to break out. Those closest to Varro picked up their drinks and left. Across the crowded room, a large man worked his way toward them.

"Well, then, good luck Varro. Have a nice fucking life." Falco slapped his hands to his side, his face as red as a tomato.

"Why not come with me? I didn't have any orders against you two joining me."

"I just got out." Curio slapped his palm to his forehead. "I don't ever want to go through that again. Six years of almost dying every day."

"I agree," Falco. "You can enjoy your special club with your special pugio. But count me out. We were fucking lucky to come home at all. You want to go back to it and throw yourself on a pike, then I'm not stopping you. But I'm not joining you either. In fact, we're done here, Varro. I don't even know you, and I don't like sharing a drink with strangers."

He tapped Curio's shoulder, who gave Varro a sneer and nodded in agreement.

Both of them pushed past Varro as he hung his head in shame. He did not look up from the jug and mugs spilled on the floor. Two of the mugs had shattered, leaking the dark wine-like heart-blood onto the wooden floor.

"Your friends broke our stuff. You got to pay for it."

Varro looked up to find the burly man who had pushed through the crowd to confront him. He had ugly white burn scars on his neck and under his chin and his right ear was a red, curled stump where it had been cut off.

"How'd you get the scars?"

"Does it fucking matter?" The man's deep voice penetrated the volume of the crowded room. "Got it years ago at Zama. Some fucking victory, eh? But that's history. Today, we're talking about how you broke our mugs and table."

"I'll pay for damages. Hold out your hand."

The man did not seem especially smart, and just another citizen who had done his duty. He sacrificed his ear and his skin for Rome, and now he worked an overcrowded drinking hole in the darkest streets of the city.

Varro shook out the dozens of denarii in his pouch into the waiting palm. The man lurched to cup his hands to catch it all.

"That'll pay for it, and keep some for yourself."

He left the man stammering his thanks. But he exited into the darkening streets alone and saddened.

"I'm sorry," he mumbled to himself, imagining Falco and Curio could hear him. "I couldn't drag you into this."

3

A year ago Varro had been summoned in the early morning to meet with an unnamed senator who awaited him in a tent beside Flamininus's. His body still ached with the pain of his broken ribs and the scores of cuts over his hands and feet. Yet he was instructed to wear a toga, and it flowed comfortably around his wounded body as he raced across the headquarters parade ground to the grandiose tent of the mysterious senator.

He had glimpsed both Falco and Curio across the field, dressed in simple tunics and staring at him as if they could not be sure what they saw. Hoping they did not realize it was him, he vanished into the tent where the morning light diffused through the immaculate cloth to bathe the interior with cream-colored light.

Screens had been placed strategically to create private spaces, florid with decorative patterns and pastoral landscapes. A small table had been set up with two couches. A gray-haired man in a white toga reclined on one, a plate of fruits and a silver goblet of wine set out before him. He was older now, but Varro recognized him immediately.

He snapped straight and at attention.

"Consul Galba, sir! Centurion Marcus Varro present, sir."

His former consul smiled indulgently. "Ah, thank you for the reminder of old times. But please, I am only a senator now. Let us forget military rank for the moment. Be at ease."

"Thank you, sir." But Varro hardly relaxed.

Galba chuckled and waved him toward the vacant couch.

"Centurion? You have had quite a rapid rise. But of course, I always expected you would."

"Thank you, sir." Varro moved toward the couch, but he stopped when he saw what rested on the table before it.

It was a pugio in a plain leather case, a deep divot on the sheath, and a stylized owl's head in gold inlay on its pommel.

He froze, staring at it. Then he looked to Senator Galba, who chewed on a handful of grapes while smiling.

"Please, Varro, be seated. We have important matters to discuss."

He acknowledged the offer with an incline of his head, then rested on his side beside the low table. A plate of grapes and a silver cup filled with wine had also been placed just above his pugio, but the dagger filled his vision.

"You're wondering how it came to my possession," Galba said as he finished chewing his grapes. "That is not nearly as important as how it came into your possession to begin with. I was astounded to find a young recruit in my legion carrying that specific pugio. So I've been watching you ever since, and you've surprised me."

"Watching me, sir?" Varro's hands itched to reclaim his dagger, but he held them at his side. Nor did he dare eat anything placed before him without the senator's permission. He suspected he had just stepped into some sort of test but was not sure why or what was to be tested.

"I observed your progress while I was your Consul, and through intermediaries afterward. It was obvious you were unaware of the meaning of your pugio. At first, I believed you had acquired it through thievery. But of course, I learned your background and understood perfectly what had happened."

"What had happened?" Varro repeated, looking at the dagger on the table. He had carried it against his flesh for years, and its powerful blessing had protected him from death too often to count. It should feel like part of him, but now it seemed alien and remote even when he needed only to reach out his hand to grasp it.

"Eat a bit first," Galba said. His white hair glowed in the diffuse light, wreathing his head in silver. "You've not had any breakfast yet."

He thanked the senator and reached his hand across the pugio to collect fat, dark grapes into his hand. An irrational fear that the dagger would somehow cut him as he stretched across it flashed through his mind. Galba continued to smile at him and reached for his own silver cup.

The thick skin of the grapes resisted his bite, and then sweet juice and pulpy flesh filled his mouth. He had not tasted something as exquisite as this since he was a child visiting a market in Rome. The seeds provided a delightful crunch and he momentarily forgot all his worries. This fruit was astounding in its flavor. Galba laughed.

"You've grown used to puls and army rations. You are a dedicated soldier, Varro. A true hero of the Republic. It is a shame some of your greatest victories cannot be known more widely."

Varro swallowed the grapes and nodded. Galba likely referred to his recovery of the stolen war indemnity and the recovery of

Macedonia's royal hostage. That all had to remain a secret to ensure Flamininus's reputation. Yet Galba knew of the disaster.

"I do my duty, sir. No more than any other man."

Galba leaned back and laughed.

"Do not be falsely modest with me. Look at this latest adventure. You helped bring a swift conclusion to the situation in Sparta, even if Nabis remains in power. In fact, it is good he remains in place. For now, Rome will have cause to ward against future aggression. We will garrison the region, something we could not have done had he been completely eliminated. You have advanced Rome's higher purpose, which line up with the purposes of those who carry that pugio."

"I'm sorry, sir. But according to my orders, I failed. I did not create an uprising or kill King Nabis. I made a mess of it all and in the end was thrown from a mountain peak."

"An amazing story," Galba said. "And I would not have believed it had Ione not reported it herself."

Varro felt his eyes widen at her name. He thought of her and Castor, then looked once more to the pugio.

"Who was she and why did she take my pugio? Why did Castor come to bury me once he had seen my pugio among my captured belongings? None of it makes sense, sir."

"It would not make sense to you, but it does to the members of Servus Capax."

He looked down to the pommel pointed toward him and the gold inlay of a stylized owl's head. He thought it a simple tribute to Minevera, the owl being her symbol. He had never considered it could indicate membership in a group.

Galba cleared his throat after sipping more wine and nodded to where Varro stared. "The gold inlay means this particular pugio was awarded by both Consuls for service involving heroic sacrifice and enormous risk to advance the overall plan to spread the Roman way of life to the world. The man who carried this pugio would be a hero worthy of his own thanksgiving day, were it not for the need for discretion."

Varro felt his throat tighten as he stared at the dagger before him. He shook his head in denial.

"Sir, this was given to me by my mother. She had it blessed at the Temple of Mars to protect me in battle. It was my uncle's pugio."

"No it was not," Galba said. The smile left his face and he stared gravely at Varro. At last, he sat up from his couch and so prompted Varro to do the same. The old senator's eyes narrowed behind pads of fat, and when he spoke his voice was low and stern.

"What uncle, Varro? Did you ever meet the man? Of course, you must have been told he had died before your memory of him, or some other excuse. Because I assure you that I know who carried that pugio, and it was no uncle of yours. I have had the time to learn the rightful owner. It was not hard to do, since he was a legend of his day. That man would be known to you as your great grandfather."

"Papa?" He sat back in shock, speaking the endearing name for his great grandfather. No one had shaped him as deeply as he had, not even his own father.

Galba flashed a brief smile at the name and nodded.

"He lived to an amazing age, and was quite close to you as his only male descendant. I had the honor of meeting him in my younger days. He later came to regret much of what he did. But all he did was in service to the citizens of Rome, and in a time of great peril to our way of life."

"Sir," Varro's voice was strained and dry. "This is a bit much to accept. My grandfather was in a secret society, undertaking risky work to advance Rome in the world?"

"Is it so hard to accept?" Galba raised his brow. "It sounds very much like what you have been doing all along."

Then it resolved for Varro in a staggering, bright flash. He recalled his grandfather's final admonition to him. His sweaty, wasted face and wild eyes staring into his own. The icy grip on his young arm, so potent even in the moment before death.

He heard the words again, rolling through his mind like thunder.

"Promise me, Marcus, swear to it before all the gods and all our ancestors. You will not live the life of violence that I have lived. You must not, cannot, become what I was. Learn and keep the ways of non-violence. Make an offering to Pax, and ask her to remember you. Swear this now."

And so he had sworn. But it was not what his Papa had really wanted to say after all. Even in his dying moments, he couched his words in secrecy.

"Of all my blood, you are most like me. But you are also unlike anyone else in our family. You can break this chain. You can become what I failed to be. Marcus, you can know greatness."

His great-grandfather had also said this in the same breath. Even as his eyes glowed with the madness of his tremendous age, behind all of it was the concern for his legacy and what his descendants would become.

He did not want his descendants to work in the shadows, hands slick with blood, and take no glory for it. Without a doubt, Papa had regretted much of what he had done, but it seemed that he regretted not earning a place in history even more.

"So you see that you have already taken up your ancestor's path," Galba said with a satisfied smile.

"No, my grandfather did not want me to follow his footsteps. He wanted me to stand out from the shadows, and wash all blood from my hands. He hoped in so doing I would achieve a greatness that he never reached."

Galba gave a short sigh and shook his head. "But your great ancestor was wrong about that. For he did earn glory and renown with those who knew his work. It is out of that deep respect that Castor came to find you, even without knowing exactly who you were. He knew that to carry that pugio, you were a man worthy of honor and respect."

"How did he know it was mine, and that I hadn't stolen it? You said it yourself, sir."

With a patient smile, Galba nodded his head.

"Because you were doing the work of Servus Capax. You carry the pugio, and so you have done the work needed. Some missions were small, such as rescuing that fool Pallus, and others like Sparta were of great importance to Rome. Each time a victory for you."

Varro blinked. "But not just me, sir. Falco and Curio both have always been at my side. Any victory is because the three of us worked as a team."

"A generous claim, but without your leadership the two of them would be lost. They did have a good showing in this last mission. So there is hope for them to develop independence. But you have been tested and tried, and have succeeded over and again. You are the true inheritor of your great-grandfather's abilities. And so, in discussion with Flamininus, we confirm your membership in Servus Capax."

"There is no choice, sir?"

Galba paused in reaching for his wine cup, then withdrew his hand back to his side.

"There is a choice, but I would not imagine your declining. Think on your future, Varro. You believe yourself a wealthy man now, free of worry and ready to settle into a fine life in the countryside. But I've news from home. We can speak of it in detail later, but you should know that your farm has been sold long ago, your mother remarried, and your sister wed. You have nowhere to call home."

Varro straightened up at the news, but before he could ask more, Galba continued.

"Not to mention the failings of your father will come to haunt you. You did not think killing Decius Oceanus would cut that thread out of your life? No, there are peers of mine who make their fortunes through the disasters of others. Those who snatch up farms of deceased legionnaires, buying those farms under value from the desperate survivors. Your father and even your grandfather had both tried to walk the shadowy path between good and evil and fell on the wrong side. Those peers of mine do not leave loose ends and remain your enemies even if you choose to withdraw from society."

"Sir, I never knew anything of my father's dealings. He wanted to do the right thing in the end."

"And he died for that," Galba said. "As did his father, and as you will. There are too many farms to be had, and great wealth to be made in accumulating all of them into a few hands."

Galba again reached for his wine cup, sipped from it while staring over its rim at Varro, then leaned forward on his elbows.

"You are either with them or against them. And you are newly rich with no rich friends. You will never be in more danger than when you are discharged from the army. At least in the battle line you see where the enemies are."

"I would not murder my fellow soldiers and steal their farms. That is the most despicable thing imaginable. That my father had a hand it it fills me with disgust."

"Of course it does. And do you think your mother did not know the manner of man she married? She was supposed to be marrying into the family of a great war hero, your Papa as you call him. Instead, she found him in denial of how far his sons and grandsons had fallen. He forsook his past and turned his eyes aside from his present. But your mother is a smart woman, and worked out the truth for herself. She discovered through your great-grandfather what Servus Capax is and what it means to be in its service. It brings the protection of the Consuls and Senate, even if some senators might otherwise want a member eliminated."

"So she stole Papa's pugio and gave it to me," Varro said, piecing together the final parts of the puzzle. "So I would be protected from my father's enemies."

Galba sat and folded his arms in satisfaction.

"Yes. Your own father was oblivious to all that happened around him. His head was too deep into the worries of a criminal life to consider anything more. Your mother knew one day those troubles would find you. I believe she worked out how your father would die long ago, and realized that by simple possession of that pugio you would be placed among powerful men capable of ensuring your safety, at least from hidden enemies."

Varro at last reached for the pugio, taking it into his hands and enjoying its familiar grip.

"How many times did I almost lose this?"

"Well, at least once when you left it at the scene of my slave's murder. You have enough silver now to pay me back for that loss. She was a favorite."

"You knew all along?"

"Of course," Galba said with a smile. "No one else in my legions had such a dagger. But it was a good test of Centurion Fidelis and Tribune Sabellius. I was ending my time as Consul, in any case. I had one last mission in mind for you, and that was a good enough excuse to send you on it."

"I was nearly killed, sir."

"Yes," Galba said. Then he drank from his cup once more. "Varro, I cannot let you keep that pugio. You have done much, but not enough as a member of Servus Capax. One day, I would be glad to award it to you. Of course, given my age and your youth, it might be another Consul to bestow it on you again. But before we speak further, I must know if you will accept your membership in Servus Capax. You will always be in danger and your work will be never-ending. But it is not all such a dire prospect.

"You will have a brotherhood among any who carry a pugio bearing that owl head you see in gold. There are men, and a few women, all over the world working toward the great plan. You will aid them as you would your own kin, and they will aid you. You will not worry for the hidden enemies your father has earned for you, but only for the enemies of Rome. And your wealth will not only be protected, but will grow, and property will be awarded for certain achievements. We can even help find you a profitable marriage. You can refuse to join, of course, and I will mourn your passing. For soon after you are discharged you will be found out, murdered, and your wealth stolen. So if you do go your own path, spend a good portion of that silver on bodyguards."

"That doesn't sound like a choice. I don't suppose I have time to consider this, sir?"

"None at all," Galba said. "Flamininus is a busy man, and I offered to make this proposal on his behalf. He will have his answer today, so he knows how to prepare. If you accept, you will spend the remainder of your enlistment on garrison duty, and then be furloughed to Rome for a rest before your next assignment. If you refuse, you'll continue as you are and be expected to participate in patrols and any action that may arise before the legion's general withdrawal. On discharge, you return to the life of an ordinary citizen."

"What about Falco and Curio?"

"The offer is to you," Galba said. "But we know your history with them. So we are prepared to accept them into service along with you, if you will take charge of them. We will not offer it to them directly. The fewer people who know, the better. And I'll require you to not speak of our discussion to anyone else, no matter your decision."

"And how long is my service?"

Galba unfolded his arms and his shoulders seemed to sag. "For as long as it takes for Rome to achieve our highest aims. This is not likely to happen in your lifetime."

"So it's service for life?"

"I think your strengths lie in a martial capacity, as your great grandfather's did. After a certain age a man cannot fight. You could consider retirement at that time, or take on a different, less physical role. But certainly, such choices are many years hence."

He looked to the pugio in his hands, then set it back to the table. He could not sign up Falco and Curio for a lifetime of service in something none of them really understood. If he did this, it would be his own decision and his own fate. His friends would be free to make their own lives. They did not have the same threats facing them as he did.

"I accept the offer."

Galba collected his old pugio, but a genuine smile spread on his face.

"A wise choice, Centurion Varro. A lifetime of adventure and riches awaits you."

4

Varro wandered the streets following the flow of ever-thinning crowds until nightfall. He then returned to the room he had rented together with Falco and Curio. He climbed the creaking stairs into he darkened hall, then counted down the doors to the room where they had been living for the past two days. The door hung open into darkness and he knew what it meant.

Standing in the frame, he stared into the black and empty room. It had been so small that they had slept side by side on the floor in their army bedrolls. Despite their wealth, they had been following Flamininus's advice to not reveal the extent of their riches at least until they could be secured. So they had done as most infantrymen had and taken a cheap room in a shabby corner of Rome.

Now the room was too big.

His own gear and bedroll remained stacked to the left of the entrance. Falco and Curio had collected their gear and left. The stained and spotted floorboards seemed to expand forever into he shadowed corners. A crust of bread still damp with wine was all that marked either of them had been here.

He sighed and entered the room. Wherever they had gone, he could not go searching for them at night. Tomorrow he would have no time to find them either. So he closed the door, leaving himself in complete darkness. He had not thought to fetch a lamp to light his way, and had expected to find the lamp in the room lit. But now he knelt down, feeling blindly for his bedding.

As he lay facing up into the dark, stuffy room his mind repeated the scene from earlier in the evening. Now that it was over, he realized how poorly he had handled it. For the last year he had kept his promise to not mention Servus Capax to anyone, yet in the end he had said too much. Had he put Falco and Curio in danger by doing this? He still did not understand what this organization did, other than work for Rome's advancement as a great power.

He rolled onto his side, feeling the hard floorboards press against his hip.

"With Carthage defeated, we look east to Greece and find endless sources of trouble," Galba had said later in their meeting. "One day, it must be pacified and brought under Roman control. But it is a long process requiring a careful setup, which has been taking place since the days we first pacified Illyria."

How could he drag Falco and Curio into something like this, where plans worked on a timeline of decades? No matter how he thought of it, they would be better off enjoying the wealth they had earned. While Galba's words hinted at wars to come, it seemed such a distant future. Falco and Curio would be older and their wealth could buy them less dangerous ranks than infantrymen. But life with Servus Capax seemed forever fraught with danger.

Sleep would not find him as he replayed his confrontation with Falco and Curio. He wished he had said something earlier, but then they might have tried to join him or else convince him to renege on his oath to both Galba and Flamininus, who had him swear loyalty and secrecy before awarding him a new pugio with the same owl's head in silver inlay. Flamininus claimed to have prepared it just for him. In any case, he had ended the best friendships he ever had or ever would likely have with a drunken argument. It was all his fault and he wondered how anyone could see him as a "useful servant." He was a fool, and nothing more.

Somewhere in the lonely night of turning over and over on is bedroll sleep did overtake him. After six years of relentless discipline he awakened at dawn. He still expected to hear the sounds of a camp or garrison surrounding him. Instead, he heard the bass voices of men speaking in the room next to his. A dim light entered from the window that faced an alleyway, enough for him to see by and prepare.

Every time he heard voices in the hall his heart fluttered, expecting Falco and Curio to return. But the footfalls continued past, and he returned to preparing himself for a long journey ahead. His armor and weapons awaited him outside of Rome, where he would catch his ship down the Tiber and then to the sea. He was not even certain where Numida was other than west of what remained of Carthage. It seemed a long way from here.

He carried a locked box of denarii, with the key to it held on a strap about his neck. For convenience he counted out enough coins to a purse so he could pay for what he needed while traveling. Otherwise, he was instructed to present himself to the King of Numidia, Masinissa. He would be taken care of from there and his coin was needed only for discretionary purchases while he lived in Numidia.

A wooden tube contained the papyrus with his letter of introduction from Flamininus to King Masinissa, who was said to be expecting him. It was sealed with wax impressed with Flamininus's family signet ring. Only the King was to break the seal.

As far as his mission, Flamininus had been as vague as usual. When they met that second morning of the thanksgiving, it was in a small garden in the Flamininus estate. He stood at attention while his former Consul sat in a toga, reading over papyri and wax slates stacked beside his wine and fish breakfast.

"Your first mission will be your easiest yet, Varro. Nothing like the last one, eh?"

"Thank you, sir," It was all he could think to say. He wasn't sure if Servus Capax was military or not, so he just continued with the consul as he always had.

"In fact, it's more of a training for you. King Masinissa was an enemy of Rome once. Did you know that?"

"Sir, I was only a boy for the war with Carthage. My parents did not keep me informed of current news. I wouldn't have paid attention even if they had."

Flamininus paused and his soulful eyes creased with a smile.

"I supposed neither did I. We're not so far apart in age, are we? Well, in any case, Masinissa was a canny opponent. He defeated Scipio in Hispania and he was but seventeen years old. After he joined our side, I dare say his famous Numidian cavalry carried the day at Zama. Since it is just we two here this morning, I'll dare further to say he must be one of the greatest living commanders after Scipio and myself."

"Only Scipio can claim to be greater than you, sir, and I've heard debates on that as well."

"Centurion Varro," Flamininus said chidingly. "You are a poor study at flattery. But I admit the sentiment works on me. In any case, don't try it on others. You'll fail miserably. Just be who you are and don't speak if you've nothing to say. In fact, when it comes to kings and their ilk it's best to not speak except at their invitation."

He inclined his head in acknowledgement and Flamininus continued.

"Here's a letter you will present to Masinissa. Those he claims kingship over may be little more than barbarians, but he is an erudite and cultured man. He has already been made aware someone from Rome with your special capacities will be sent to his court. With this letter and your dagger, you have all you need."

Accepting the sealed wooden tube, Varro asked, "Sir, what will I be doing for Rome while I am there.'"

"Learning how to be useful." Flamininus did not look up from the wax tablet he now reviewed, but a sly smile creased his face. "Masinissa is a master of hit-and-run, guerrilla warfare. He about drove Scipio to the brink of madness with it. The Roman army does not fight like this, but we will soon be fighting enemies who do. How better to counteract this than being able to deliver the same problems in kind? The king has ample opportunities in his new kingdom for you to learn and lead these kinds of actions against his enemies."

"Sir, it seems quite a long way to go to learn some new formations."

"It's not a formation drill." Flamininus put down the wax tablet and frowned. "You'll be learning more than just formations. If I wished you to learn something so commonplace I'd just have you train with the regular army. But you will not only learn how to fight as Masinissa does. You will learn how to lead men without the direct authority to do so. You will lead them because you are worthy of becoming their leader. You will get free men to do your will because your will brings them victory and glory. There is much more to what you will do in Numidia than just learning some fighting techniques."

"I see. Thank you, sir." But he was not sure he fully understood, and Flamininus seemed equally unconvinced as he let go a long sigh.

"There is a difference between being shown how to do something and doing it. When you return from Numidia I will not be

Consul. But I can already tell you we will be back in Greece and looking for a fight. The Selucids are not going to remain idle. The Achean League is going to start trouble. We will need a man in Greece, someone who can gather locals to a cause and lead them to fight for our ends. If such a need arose, then you could be that man."

Varro could not see himself in such a capacity. He had struggled to get to grips with being a centurion in the regular army. Becoming some sort of rebel leader was just outlandish to him.

"And there's another thing, Varro." Now Flamininus leaned forward with a crafty smile. "The Carthaginians are still around. Weakened and beaten, but still here. Eventually, their city must be destroyed if Rome is to have any peace. Numidia shares a border with them. So use your time and new training to make trouble for Carthage. They are not allowed to go to war without permission of the Roman Senate, even in their own defense. So use that against them, Varro. Look for ways to get them tripped up between their actions and their obligations. Then maybe we will have cause to stomp Carthage from the face of the earth while they are still weak."

"Sir, it sounds as if you want me to start a third Punic war?"

"Don't credit yourself too far," Flamininus said, now returning to sort through his tablets and papyri. "But there may be opportunities to weaken and humiliate Carthage. I suppose if you do have the great fortune of being able to bring all of Carthage to war once again, then please send word back to the Senate before taking any action. The people are weary of war, and one so soon against a defeated enemy might not sit well with them. We would have to lay the groundwork for that."

"If war is the eventual aim, then why not start the groundwork now, sir?"

Flamininus paused and his wry smile returned.

"A good thought, one which I've had for a while. We are

working on it, be assured. Just do your part. That will be all, Varro. You will return here in a year for a rest and to report on your progress. Fortuna go with you."

Varro saluted but lingered long enough for Flamininus to raise his brow and ask why he delayed.

"Sir, I've not said anything to Falco and Curio. But I've got to tell them something. I can't just leave them."

"I'm sure you'll think of what to say. Just remember your oath. You do not plan to invite them along?"

"I had no choice in accepting your offer, sir. But they don't have the same worries I have. They should be free to do as they will with their wealth."

Flamininus shrugged. "It seems you give them no choice either. In any case, be careful in how much you reveal. If they should come with you, then they must be brought into service as well. This is a serious commitment, which you will soon come to understand if you don't already."

That last exchange with Flamininus continued to echo in his head as he prepared this morning to leave Rome. He had accused Varro of giving them no choice. Well, it was a better thing that they not be brought into something he could not explain until they were bound to a lifetime of service. He had always assumed he was doing the best for them by leaving them out, even if they did not realize it.

But as he slung his pack over his shoulders and bounced down the creaking stairs into the common room below, he wondered if he had done the right thing. People shuffled to their tables through the early dawn light filtering into the room, speaking in sleepy voices. He scanned the faces for Falco and Curio, and of course found only strangers. He pushed through them to the exit, suddenly doubting he had made the correct choice. Worse still, in his heart he had known he was wrong all along.

He should have given them a choice, at least when they were not drunk and enraged.

Then he paused outside the inn and considered what would've become of him had he declined. Galba seemed absolutely convinced he would end up dead, but would it actually be by his enemy's deeds or another member of Servus Capax? Putting such thoughts aside, he set out.

He flowed down the hills with the already thickening crowds of men and women. Daylight had not reached the streets yet, and most were still coated in blue shadows. He had not even thought to eat and did not feel hungry. Perhaps he might eat on the boat while heading for the sea.

Outside the city, he retrieved his armor and gear from quartermasters there. He strapped on his weapons, including the Servus Capax pugio, and hung his helmet from his neck, but did not wear his greaves, mail shirt, or carry his shield. The bulk and weight of so much would've staggered a civilian. But he was still conditioned to carrying heavy loads on long marches. So he headed off toward the riverside without any loss in his stride.

The Tiber was filled with ships moored along the shore. None were exceedingly large. He was searching for a trading ship of medium size whose captain was a man called Sextus. This had all been arranged with Varro after meeting Flamininus and getting details from one of his aides. He would take the merchant ship downriver the short distance to the port at Ostia, and then depart for Numidia. As a simple passenger, he had no real duties other than to stay out of the way of the crew.

After asking around for a captain named Sextus and receiving directions of various accuracy, he at last found the trader and his crew.

Sextus was a barrel-shaped man whose flesh had been weathered by sun and wind into brown leather. His curly beard was thick and gray and his eyes a surprising black that held their sparkle despite his age. His crew were of various sorts, all sturdy and young and busy loading in the last of their wares. Being a trading ship, all the men were armed with swords, not gladii but similar in design and suited for close actions on deck.

Varro introduced himself to the captain, who checked his pugio hilt then nodded.

"They said you'd have a dagger like that. Get aboard and stay out of the way." Sextus looked over his heavy bags. "And keep all that junk out of the way, too. Don't need a man tripping on that and going overboard."

No one helped him board, but he clumsily made his way up the gangplank. He found an open corner of the deck to stow his gear and settle himself. Leaning across the rails of the trading ship, he watched the crew rolling casks up onto the deck where teams of men secured them under netting.

Sextus supervised all of this with a deep frown. It all seemed completely ordinary, and nothing like a covert mission to a foreign kingdom. In fact, Varro's lack of sleep began to tell on him and he settled his head on his palm to let his eyes droop.

Then suddenly Sextus was shouting for everyone to shove off.

"Looks like they've found us," he shouted as he bounded up the plank, shoving the men there ahead. "Get us into the current and hurry!"

Varro stood back from the rails as men used long poles to shove off as others jumped into the muddy banks to help slip the vessel into the Tiber current. Across the distance Varro saw a group of men in brown or green tunics armed with clubs and spears. They shouted at Sextus, but Varro couldn't understand the words from this distance.

The intensity of the crew grew palpable. Even though they were better armed and higher than their would-be attackers, it seemed Sextus and his men were eager to escape. Of course, a trader could hardly afford to cause bloodshed right on the major waterway into Rome. Even if justified, it would bring Sextus troubles and lost profits.

"Can't you dogs get us launched any faster?" Sextus yelled over the rails at the men below. Those on deck groaned as they leaned on long poles. Across the way the gang drew closer.

Then Varro noticed another group heading for the ship.

Two men actually, carrying their gear on their shoulders and the familiar outlines of scutum shields in their traveling bags at their backs. Their helmets hung on their chests, just as Varro's.

"Falco! Curio! Hurry!"

Varro's heart slammed against the bottom of his throat. Seeing them ready to travel, he realized how desperately he needed their companionship. It was a rush of selfish joy to see them coming but in this instant he knew no matter what riches lay ahead nothing was as valuable as their friendship. His life would be poorer for their absence.

But Sextus's ship slid from the shore into the current. Men below splashed through the water and were helped aboard by their fellows. Sextus let out a cry of victory.

"You've got to land downriver," Varro said. "Those two men need to join me."

Sextus made obscene gestures as the men now running along the shore. His sails caught the breeze and the helmsman steered them out into the main current.

"Neptune's balls, I do. The payment was for one man with a dagger like yours. Not three."

"I can pay you more," Varro said. "I have…"

He reconsidered admitting to carrying enough silver to tempt any honest man into dumping in the Mediterranean Sea, never mind greedy sailors. Fortunately, Sextus did not pay attention to him.

"You can't pay me enough, son. Those men are going to send word to Ostia and follow me. I might have accidentally compromised one of their women if you take my meaning. Rather important fellows, those bastards, and they get testy about a common sea dog thrashing the bedsheets with one of their precious flowers. So, until I can negotiate a better price for the damages, I've got to stay away. Right now it seems the price is either my head or liver, depending on which one of them you listen to. Meaning, your two friends can find another passage. Ships are sailing to Numidia all the time."

Falco and Curio ran as fast as their burdens permitted and waved after Varro's ship. They had also noticed the angry mob and to Varro's relief, they fell back from pursuit. If they identified too much with Sextus's ship, they would probably become unlucky victims themselves.

Varro waved to them, mimicking the rise and fall of waves, and then pointed toward the southeast. He had told them he was going to Numidia to meet its king. That would be enough information for them to follow. If Sextus was right, they would be behind him in a few days.

So he watched them recede into the distance as they leaned on their knees to catch their breaths. Sextus's angry mob continued to follow along the shore in a comical pantomime of rage until they too broke off.

Sextus leaned on the rails and let go a long sigh.

"Well, that probably means no provisioning in Ostia."

"What does that mean?" Varro asked as he watched Falco and Curio's shadows turn back from the shore.

"A long, hungry voyage to Numidia, provided we're not caught before we even get to sea."

"We've got a head start," Varro said. "And the voyage isn't that long. Surely you have some provisions aboard."

"True," Sextus admitted. "But as I said, they are rather important fellows in the shipping business. If we're not lucky, they'll close the port just to catch me. Let's pray they're not that organized."

Varro looked back up the river and at the muddy, churning wake of the ship. If Ostia closed to catch Sextus, then Varro might be caught up with his troubles.

"Yes," he agreed. "I'll pray for a fast current."

5

Ostia remained open to Sextus's ship, and it passed through the port without stopping except to allow inspectors aboard to assess taxes on wares. Sextus had held his breath during the entire inspection and Varro believed him about to pass out. Yet he paid his taxes without complaint, and while this satisfied the authorities his civility seemed to have been more vexing to them than if he had resisted. After all, Varro knew no one who liked a tax collector.

Once out to sea, the tension among the crew eased and they began to sing as they performed their duties. Varro kept out of their way and passed the afternoon watching the coastline vanish into haze. A thin smile formed on his lips as he thought of Falco and Curio trying to secure their own passage to Numidia. With their resources, they could each buy a trading ship if they had to. It seemed strange to him that they all should be so wealthy but have no way to enjoy it. Until they had done what Flamininus called necessary preparations, it was better to hide their money in a bank and slowly invest in land and men to hold it for them.

The idle thoughts faded away with the coast. Sextus and his crew were competent sailors, or so it appeared to Varro. The intricacies of sailing were beyond him. Sailors seemed to spend most of their time tying down one thing or another, pulling on ropes, and looking at the sky. Somehow, it all added up to making the ship travel to a specific destination. He could look at the sun and generally determine a direction. But men like Sextus and his crew could look at the sky or stars and know precisely where they traveled.

So he endured the rocking deck with its creaking and popping. He watched the seabirds following and losing interest to wheel back toward land. This was about as lazy as his future days would be for a long while, and so he enjoyed being a passenger with nothing to do but enjoy the natural beauty of the sea. Even on the return passage to Rome from Greece, he had been too busy as a Centurion to admire much of the ocean's beauty.

But admiration turned to boredom and he soon found himself restless. Six years of constant work with only fleeting moments to sit back had left him unable to indulge in idleness. But the crew were irritated at his attempts to join in. In the end, he had to content himself with sitting out the journey as little more than another piece of cargo packed onto this ship.

As he was the only passenger, he was largely forgotten. Sextus checked on him by evening, telling him they would continue throughout the night with different crew on shift and that they would make port the following morning.

"The crossing isn't actually so long," he said. "It only takes this long since we still avoid Carthage. We're not at war but that doesn't mean they can't give us grief, or pretend to accidentally damage our ship. We're small fish to them, and could get plucked off the water without anyone in Rome caring too much."

They passed the rugged, purple coast of Sicilia before the sun set, and once it rose again Varro found the crew readying for arrival in Numidia.

"You sleep like an old seaman," Sextus said. "I took you for one of those army-types that would hang over the rails the whole trip."

"I used to," he said, wiping sleep from his eyes. "But I've been through too much to let some rocking waves bother me."

Sextus laughed. "I don't think it's a choice for most men. But those scars on your face tell the story, don't they? You're a hard one, I bet. All that armor and that shield of yours, I'm sure you've seen a good amount of fighting. You have my respect and gratitude. I don't know why you're going to a place like this but I wish you luck. The tribes I've dealt with over the years are filled with hard men, too. And they're barbarians to their core. You can't change them if that's what you're here to do."

"I can't tell you why I'm here. Mostly because I'm not even sure myself."

He craned his neck to see past the rails and rigging to the shoreline ahead. The land rose up into hills and was stained green. A city sat safely in the shadows and flowed down to the port. The sign of green surprised him.

"I thought the land here was all rock and sand."

"Depends on where you go," Sextus said. "I'm never far from a coastline. I've seen some places that are nothing but sand, but that's to the west. I can't say what's deeper inland here. The port is where I do my business then return to sea."

Varro studied the brightening image of the coast and the port. Pleasant columns of hearth smoke rose to its rear as white stains against the hilly backdrop. Bright sails were already catching the dawn light as ships slid into the harbor, some towed by smaller boats. He searched for the palace where he was to present himself to King Masinissa. But the only thing that looked like a king's palace to him was a tall stack of buildings of plain yellow stone.

Compared to what he had seen in Greece, this seemed utterly barbaric.

"I see you weren't wrong about these Numidians," Varro said. "Their king's palace looks like a pile of stones."

"King's palace?" Sextus followed his gaze. "That's the garrison, I expect. This isn't where their king lives. This is Russicada, the port that serves the capital at Cirta. That's where you'll find the king's palace."

"But I'm to present myself to King Masinissa." He winced at the whining note in his voice. But he had not anticipated an overland journey. "How am I supposed to get to Cirta if this is not it?"

Sextus laughed. "That'll curb my admiration of you, boy. Isn't it your affair? A few servants of a rich man asked me to take you across the Mediterranean to here. What you do here and how you travel is hardly my business."

"But I know no one here. Do they even speak Latin?"

"Of course they do!" Sextus slapped Varro's shoulder. "This is the port for Cirta. You'll find all types here and someone to take you inland. Just offer to add your sword to someone's caravan. You'll be at Cirta in no time, I'm sure."

Varro's bright mood had soured, but it seemed to have an inverse effect on Sextus and his crew, who learned from their captain that their passenger was lost even before he stepped off the ship. It would avail him nothing to be angry with these men, so he tried to ignore their smirks as he watched Russicada grow in size and clarity as they made their final approach.

Their ship was just large enough to need towing to the dock. Varro collected his gear as this proceeded and when everything was settled, he prepared to disembark.

"Don't be so gloomy," Sextus said, still smiling and wiping his hands on his pants. "Listen, go see if a merchant by the name of Spurius Antius has any work to take you to Cirta. Tell him I sent you. That'll get you in right shape."

He thanked the old captain and left him and his amiable crew at the docks.

Once off the water and into the city of Russicada, he discovered a city populated with a mix of all types, from clear Romans to dark-skinned men who draped themselves in light robes head to toe. While he stared in wonder at them, he was in turn ignored. Though his gear should mark him as a Roman legionary, it drew no reaction from others.

His first few interactions failed as the people he met did not seem to speak Latin or else pretended they did not understand. This was a city of commerce, and unless one had specific business he could expect no time from the busy inhabitants.

Varro wandered streets looking for anyone who could direct him to Sextus's recommended merchant. Uneasy with the twisting and shaded streets crowded with ancient rock buildings and strange inhabitants, he always kept the docks in view. He had traversed a wide area but had not penetrated into the city.

"Hello, a fellow Roman at last!"

A man in a native outfit of cream-colored cloth sat in the shade of a white awning outside of what must be a small inn or tavern. He seemed incredibly pale compared to the natives, several of whom sat near him in quiet conversations of their own. Of note was his bright smile and boyish face. He seemed to glow with the best part of youth, and it made Varro think of Curio.

"Come here, my friend. Please!" The man stood and pulled a stool to his small table. "Share a drink with me. It has been too long."

Even though only an hour into his exploration of the city, Varro felt instant relief at finding a fellow Roman among so much strangeness. He crossed the dirt-packed street to the Roman, who extended his hand to point to a small clay decanter.

"It is date wine," he said. "Nothing like it back home. Share a sample with me, if you have the time."

Varro thanked the man and accepted the offered stool. Both sat in the shade. The dark and creased faces of the older natives around them spared only a moment's glance at the two Romans in their midst.

"I am Kaeso Bellus." The young man called out in a strange language into the darkness of the tavern. "They'll bring a cup along for you in a moment. I am so happy to meet a fellow citizen here."

He had a warm and smooth voice, betraying his boyish looks. Varro immediately liked him and introduced himself. A reed-thin man with skin like old leather emerged from the shadow with another small clay cup that he set beside Bellus's.

"You speak the local language," Varro said. "So you live here?"

"Yes to both," Bellus said. He pulled back the sleeve of his long robe and then poured the wine into both cups. "I would think this costume would give that away. You're fine to laugh, as I know I did when I first arrived here. But these robes are necessary for living in this climate, even so close to the sea."

The wine trickled into both cups and Bellus tapped it against Varro's to ensure no drop was missed. He then lifted his cup and offered a fresh smile.

"We've only just met. What shall we drink to? Rome, fortune, or health?"

"Why not all three?" Varro suggested. Bellus laughed and they touched their cups together. The date wine was more viscous than he expected and sweet enough to raise his eyebrows.

"Ah, you've not tasted anything like that before," Bellus said. "A treat to be found only in these lands."

They fell to a brief silence and then idle chatter about the weather in the region. But soon Bellus nodded to the bronze helmet stacked atop the gear Varro set beside feet.

"Don't tell me they're sending the legions here? I've just heard word yesterday that we've finally departed Greece."

"No," Varro said with a shy smile. "I've got a diplomatic assignment to King Masinissa's court."

Bellus leaned his head back and looked at Varro through narrowed eyes.

"All by yourself? You were looking quite lost a moment ago, but maybe you were just searching for your friends."

"I am friendless here," Varro said. "And I am lost. In fact, I hoped you might be able to assist me."

"Well, do not say you have no friends here," Bellus said with an easy smile. "We've just shared a drink, and for a legionary, I would do all that I can to help. You have some bitter scars, my friend. I wonder what kind of diplomatic work you do? You don't seem the type to enjoy a debate."

Varro touched the scar over his eye, conscious of all the attention it had garnered him since leaving Greece. In the army, everyone but the recruits had such scars.

"Well, nor am I one who looks to his sword to solve all problems. But it does seem the problems I'm given need a sword above all else. Listen, I was recommended to a merchant by the name of Spurius Antius. I hoped to work out an arrangement with him to travel onto Cirta."

Bellus leaped out of his chair and put his hand to his chest. The sudden motion made Varro reach for his pugio, but he stayed his hand. The old men around them cast rheumy-eyed gazes at him before returning to their conversations.

"Fortuna is kind to you, Varro. For I am an agent working with Antius."

"That is incredible," Varro said, a warmth spreading through his chest. "I couldn't get anyone to talk to me and thought I'd never find him. And now I've met you."

"This calls for another round of date wine." Bellus adjusted his stool, smiling as he called to the reed-thin man.

"What do you mean you are an agent?" Varro asked as he waited for the fresh decanter of wine.

"Merchants throughout the region come here to move their goods." Bellus spread his hands wide. "And they need intermediaries to make deals and connections for them. I learn what is coming into port, and what is ready to leave. I connect the right parties and collect a fee. It is honest but easy work. In fact, it makes me feel like a thief to do it."

"How did you come into that line of work?"

The reed-thin man appeared with a new jug of wine. Bellus snapped a silver coin onto the table and the server snatched it into his sleeve before turning away.

"After the war with Carthage ended, I had nowhere to go. No place to call home back in Rome. When it was time to return, I ended my service here. I know you may think it is desertion. But I worked it out with my Centurion and Tribune, both of whom could see the profit in this arrangement. They actually helped me get started. Now it has been a decade since, and I'm on my own here."

Bellus poured out more wine and they again raised their cups.

"So, here is to your safe and happy journey to Cirta."

They both laughed as they touched cups, and Varro merrily downed the date wine.

"I don't know if I can get used to something so sweet." He set the cup down. "But it leaves a pleasant aftertaste."

"That it does," Bellus agreed. "Now, I will arrange your trip with Antius. My work is all done by early morning. So I only have to catch him before he sets out. That is where fortune will have another role to play. He is here still, but I'm certain he will be leaving either today or dawn tomorrow. It is a few days of travel by camel. If you miss him, he won't be back until he has goods to port again and I cannot say when that will be."

"If I do miss him. Then there must be other merchants coming and going. Anyone will do."

"True!" Bellus downed his cup and then stood. "I'm off to speak with Antius, then."

Varro began to gather his gear, but Bellus stopped him.

"You don't mean to drag all that gear around Russicada, do you? Wait here for me. Besides, I have some other business to attend on the way to his offices. I will arrange your trip, conclude my business, and return here to guide you to the right caravan."

"I'd rather go with you. Besides, it's no trouble to carry the gear with me. I'm used to it."

Bellus's smile faded and he drew closer.

"I'll be honest, Varro. I know you are new here, but you've already noticed that people won't speak to you because you're clearly Roman. It's another reason I dress like the natives. It just makes it easier to pass unnoticed. Now Antius is a Roman himself, and he has plenty of local slaves in his service. I shouldn't have to tell you the locals aren't fond of us, even if Numidia is Rome's great ally of the moment. This is a decidedly Roman section of the city. You'll be fine to wait here and enjoy a good breakfast. In fact, I shall order it and pay for it myself. I know just the right dishes."

Varro looked to the frowning old men involved with their own conversations. Bellus had not been wrong, for until now he had met no one willing to help him.

"Trust me," Bellus said, closing his eyes and nodding his head. "I've been here long enough to know the best way to get things done."

"Well, I suppose all I might be doing is wasting a bit of time. I'm under no time pressure to get to Cirta. But I can't let you pay for my meal."

"Nonsense," Bellus said, his youthful smile returned. "I am your host, strange as it may be. I shall pay. And if you have enjoyed my services, you can repay me at some future date. You will be a diplomat in Cirta. How good is it for me to have a friend among the court? Merchants trade in rumor as well."

He smiled knowingly and winked. Varro returned the smile, but did not think of himself as a diplomat. Nor did he want to be indebted to someone who would use him to gather rumors. Yet he was not going to cast aside good luck.

He let Bellus order his breakfast then head off into the city. The reed-thin server eventually brought out several plates of meat and fish that Varro found either too bland or pungent for his tastes. The date wine helped cut the displeasing flavors, and he wondered at Bellus's sense of taste. He had drank nearly to the bottom of the jug when he realized he should not let himself go in a strange city.

Hours passed and Varro had grown worried within the first of them. No one seemed to mind or care that he sat in the shade and watched men in their long robes crossing back and forth across the narrow streets. He listened to the babble of the local language and then tried to figure out what sort of game the two old men played on a small board set between them. Another man with a white beard looked on, offering advice to both sides.

Bellus returned at the very moment he expected his newly made friend had forgotten him. It was late afternoon, and the sun bounced off his cream-colored robes as he fluttered into the light.

"It's all arranged," he called from across the street. He clapped his hands together as he returned to where Varro now stood. "You can join the caravan tonight."

"That is great news!" Varro clasped arms with Bellus and then guided him to his stool. "So he had no problem taking on another traveler?"

"None at all," Bellus said with an easy smile. "And why would he not? I told him you were from the legions and properly armed. He's glad to have another traveler interested in a safe passage to Cirta."

That made Varro pause.

"I know merchant caravans are always under threat from bandits. But is that really a problem so close to the capital? I would think the king keeps his roads safe."

Bellus tilted his head. "Nothing is ever completely safe. Peace of mind is all Spurius wants. Guards just keep the opportunists away. You'll have nothing to worry about for the entire trip. It'll be as if they are escorting you, I swear it."

6

Bellus kept Varro enthralled all afternoon with stories of his time in the legions and the battles that brought Carthage to defeat. He did not seem old enough to have participated in the fights, yet his details were vivid and compelling. Varro recognized an old veteran when he met one. His complaints of the enlisted life were his exactly. In fact, as they lounged the day away drinking date wine beneath the awning of Bellus's favorite inn, Varro forgot he was the officer in so many of his shared complaints with Bellus.

"Damned Centurions!"

Both of them cursed the officers for their iron discipline and relentless drive. It seemed no other type of man could survive the role. Drink might have played a part of Varro's spirited disrespect for the very rank he held. In fact, he realized he had finished a third jug of date wine plus eaten another salty meal that only made him want to drink more. His great friend Bellus covered all the costs.

"You'll soon pay me back," he said as Varro tried to force his coin on him. Bellus shoved it away so often that Varro spilled the pouch of denarii and had to gather them up from the dust. As he did the key to his strongbox hung from his neck and bounced against his face.

"Take care of your money," Bellus said. "Or you'll be relieved of it. Russicada is a port city, after all. Not exactly a home to pirates, but many who might be inclined to that life."

Varro's face warmed and he recalled Curio flashing his coins around. He was not as drunk as that, or so he believed. Still, Bellus had chastened him and he stuffed the purse away into his tunic.

When the sun drew down to the horizon, Bellus stood up and clapped his hands together.

"Let's get you off to Antius. You'll camp with his caravan tonight and by dawn, you'll be setting out."

"I can't thank you enough," Varro said as he gathered his gear. "I was expecting this city to be the capital. I had no idea where I was going."

"I'm glad I could help, and you've been a fine drinking companion. I've not had so much fun in months."

Varro found his load harder to bear when his balance had been compromised. His foggy mind wondered if maybe he had taken too much of that date wine and was no better than Curio had been. But he dismissed the thought with a sniff. Curio had been staggering. He was as stable as a marble statue.

He tripped over something in the road and ended up beneath the pile of his gear. Bellus laughed and helped him up.

"Oh dear, I should not have let you get to this condition. If Antius sees I've brought him a drunk, he'll kick you out of his caravan."

"I'm fine," Varro said as he steadied himself. "I can drink as good as any infantryman."

"I'm sure you have an iron gut, Centurion Varro. But you are a bit too red-faced to introduce to Antius. It's my reputation as well.

You must understand. I promised him a strong, upright legionary and here you are falling over shadows in the road."

"I told you, I'm fine." Varro slapped Bellus's back, nearly causing him to fall over as well.

"That does it," he said, regaining his footing. "They'll be no harm if you go to Antius before sunrise tomorrow. You're a legionary. So you should be fine to get up before the dawn."

"That's how it goes in the legions." Varro saluted and smiled.

"Then you'll sleep the drink off in my place. It's a modest apartment, but you'll find space on the floor. It's better you sober up a bit. It's entirely my fault. I am so sorry."

"Don't be sorry," Varro slapped him again, and Bellus stepped forward with the impact. "I loved that date wine. The sweet gets better as you drink it. Besides, I only had two small jugs of it."

"Now I know you're drunk," Bellus said as he spun Varro in the opposite direction. "Two was just the start of it."

"But you don't look drunk!" Varro pointed at him as he let Bellus prodded him along the road.

"That's because I paced myself. Listen, you'll be better for a few hours of sleep and then you can curse me tomorrow on the march."

So Varro tottered along the darkening streets into narrower and darker alleys. He began to smell urine and a vague sour scent in the air. Doors and windows here were closed and the natives seemed to have all vanished, leaving only faint echoes in the distance to mark that anyone lived in the city.

"Where do you live, Bellus? This place looks like a refuse pit."

"It's only a little ahead now. Keep walking, Varro. Just take that right corner and we'll be up some stairs to my place."

"I hope upstairs is better than this. I've marched behind mules that have smelled better."

"That's right," Bellus said soothingly guiding him by the shoulder. "Just around the corner."

He rounded the corner, aware of the last light of the sun vanishing as he did. This path was utterly black with shadow and he could not see a way forward.

With a shove from behind, he staggered ahead with the weight of his load pushing at his shoulders. He crashed into something soft that pushed him back.

Then a heavy object smashed over his head and he crumpled to the ground.

"Fuck! You broke his neck!"

Varro lolled on the ground, his head swimming and his gear slid forward onto his shoulders, pressing him down. The voice sounded like Bellus's.

Then the weight of his gear lifted and someone hauled his head up. He had only a moment to see vague shapes in the darkness before a heavy bag slipped over his head and cinched closed.

"He's fine," said a deeper voice. "You said he was strong. So I hit him good."

"That you did," Bellus said. "But he's still awake. You were supposed to gag him first, you fool."

"I'll just do this, instead."

The weighty crack against Varro's temple bounced his skull off the ground and he blacked out.

When he awakened, he felt a wetness on his face and the scent of vomit filled his nose. A piece of leather jammed between his teeth and the bag remained on his head. The fog of drink vanished and he tried to reach for his pugio only to find his hands bound at his back and his feet tied at the ankles.

He lay on his side against wood planking that vibrated against his cheek. He did not move while he tried to ascertain what had happened. His head still felt like it wobbled on his shoulders but he did not hear the sounds of the city around him. Instead, he heard the wheels of a cart squealing in time with the vibrations against his face. Someone shifted on the floor next to him and he heard a sigh.

The cart he was in rolled steadily and without any sense of speed. Wherever he was being taken, his captors were in no rush.

"He's moving again," said the deep-voiced man, who was the one seated in the cart.

"Just in time," Bellus said from ahead of the cart. "We're here. Take him down carefully."

"I'm careful." Deep-Voice seemed irritated at Bellus's warning. The cart rolled to a stop and the man beside him slid past Varro to land heavily on the ground.

Then strong hands grabbed him by his shoulders and dragged him out of the cart. He staggered around as his handler got him in position to haul over the shoulder.

"Set him inside," Bellus said. "In the cage for good measure. Then bring out his bags. I want to go through them."

"I know what to do."

The deep voice rumbled in his ear and Varro detected a slowness to the speech. Sandals crunched on gritty rock as he bounced along the man's shoulder. Tied at the wrists and ankles, he had no way to escape. They paused a moment, then he felt rock scrape against his legs as his carrier turned sideways. It was as if they squeezed into a place.

"It's dark in here," the deep voice said.

"We'll light a lamp." Bellus said. He was closer behind than Varro thought.

Deep-voice dropped him into the cage, which Varro felt as heavy iron bars against his back. But he did not hear a door slam shut. Instead, Bellus and his man left him alone for a long while. He was not sure of the duration, as his head still swam and he felt like closing his eyes. In fact, he might have, for suddenly he felt a hot hand at his neck.

"Here it is," Bellus said. "I got a look at this earlier. Now to see what he has in that box, as if I don't know."

Varro felt he was directing the words to him, but he could not reply with the leather strap in his mouth. All he could do was drool and moan through it.

The cord at his neck snapped away to release the key he held against his chest.

"That's for the box," said Deep-Voice.

"Yes, and all of Centurion Varro's silver, I expect. Isn't that so, Centurion?"

He did not respond but listened to the lock jigger then click. He carried hundreds of denarii in that chest, having expected to live off it over the next two years. Bellus whistled.

"That story about being a diplomat to Masinissa must be true. Look at all this."

He heard the merry chime of silver as Bellus must have run his hands through the coins.

"We're rich," said deep-voice. "We don't even got to sell him now."

"Don't be stupid, Lars. Of course we do.'"

"Don't call me that!" The deep-voiced Lars shouting echoed sharply, making Varro believe he was in a cave.

"I'm sorry, brother. That was thoughtless of me," Bellus's voice was as smooth and assuring as it had been when he lulled Varro with drinks and lies earlier in the day. "It's just an expression. But I think Centurion Varro might have some actual value to the king."

He heard more clanking and shifting as they tore through the rest of his belongings. At last, Bellus grunted.

"You do seem prepared for war. I don't know what sort of diplomacy you're bringing with all this armor and war gear. But it doesn't matter now, does it?"

"He's not answering," Lars said.

"I noticed. Maybe it's because you tied his gag too tight."

"But you said to make it tight 'cause he might bring his friends."

"He has no friends."

Bellus's voice was just in front of his face. He dragged the tie around Varro's neck, loosening it and then tearing the bag from his head. The fresh air rushed over his skin and he looked into Bellus's youthful, trustworthy face.

"Look at that," he said with a frown. "He's vomited and drooled all over himself. He can't possibly speak with this."

"You said make it tight."

The man called Lars was a large dark shape behind Bellus, who eclipsed almost everything else in the darkness. The yellow, wavering glow of a lamp shined behind him. He could not see any other detail as Bellus worked at the leather strap in his mouth.

"You can shout all you like out here, Centurion Varro. You'll just bring more enemies to yourself if you do. I'm trusting you to behave, or I'll let my brother retie this gag."

When the strap came free, Varro felt instant relief in his jaw. He sucked a breath and rolled his head to relieve pressure. Bellus leaned back, smiling patiently.

"Feels better, doesn't it?"

When Varro's eyes were finally able to focus on the shapes before him, he gave an appreciative nod.

"Much better, thank you."

"So polite? I thought you'd spit in my face and promise me death."

"To what end? I'm tied up and your prisoner. We'll get to that moment eventually, but not now."

Bellus chuckled and the bulk of Lars moved closer behind him.

"What does that mean? Is he threatening us?"

"Yes he is," Bellus said, holding up a hand to stay the massive shape of his brother. He would make Falco seem like a child, and Curio seem like a baby.

"I hold all the power," Bellus said. "And you'd do well to obey me."

Varro did not answer but tried to see his surroundings. He was in a cage of black iron bars, like so many he had been imprisoned in before. Bellus sat in the cage door with Lars behind him. All of them were in a low-ceilinged cave where a crack to the outside revealed starlight.

"You're going to sell me to local slavers?" He asked, finally settling on Bellus again.

"I was thinking of ransoming you to the king. What would he pay for you?"

Varro shrugged. "If I were him, I'd pay nothing. Until I assume my post with him, I'm just any Roman traveler. You're better off selling me to slavers."

Bellus's smile faded.

"I know what you're thinking. You don't want to be seen as a failure before the king. But if you carry a box of silver like that, then you must be important. In any case, you could be sold to the local slave trade. If you think escape from it will be simple then you are an even bigger fool than I thought. In fact, Centurion Varro, they'd probably do nothing to prevent it. The desert is a prison for those like you, and you'd be dead in a few days on your own. Long before you get anywhere useful. Slaves here do not need chains to bind them to their masters."

Varro sneered and looked aside, his face burning. Was he such a simple man that Bellus could read his thoughts, or was Bellus more perceptive than he seemed?

"The only mystery to unlock is why you are traveling alone with so much money. You have to be better than a diplomat. You're here to fight, and you bring enough silver to raise your own army. I think if your king won't pay your ransom, there are those in

Carthage who would enjoy learning what you're really about. I imagine they're as expert at torture as any Roman, maybe even better since they hate your kind."

"Your kind?" Varro tilted his head. "You're not Roman?"

"Want me to shut him up?" Lars asked as Bellus simply smirked. He shook his head.

Lars now loomed closer, and the light caught the side of his head.

He was bald and had a terribly deep and wide red scar at the top of his head that drove down to a point above his left eyebrow. It was as if his skull had once been chopped open. But a blow like that would have spilled out all his brains. The other eye faced the wrong way, making it impossible for Varro to determine where he looked.

"How do I prove to King Masinissa that I have you?" Bellus crept closer, adjusting his cream-colored robe. "We both know he will pay and that he's the one you want to go to. Any other plan is going to get far worse for you, Centurion Varro. Especially since I'm keeping all this fine war gear you have. That'll sell nicely, except maybe the chain shirt. It's not practical in the desert."

Varro held Bellus's eyes, and to his surprise, his captor was the first to look aside. He judged Bellus to be a crafty opportunist and skilled liar, but he was no fighter.

"Where did you learn to lie like that? I honestly believed you were older and a real veteran."

"What makes you think I lied?"

"You're no soldier. You're a coward. Take me out of these bonds and you'll have your idiot brother fight me while you hide."

Lars roared his anger and slammed his fist against the cage, shaking it and causing Bellus to stand up.

"Let me tear his head off!"

But Bellus put a calming hand on his brother's chest. "Go wait outside, Lars. He's not a danger and just trying to make you mad.

Let me talk to him for a moment. Then we'll count the coins. What do you say?"

Lars glared at Varro, and in that moment of rage both his dull eyes seemed to focus. But then they drifted apart and he turned with a low growl. Bellus watched him go before returning to Varro, crouching down again.

"He does what I say. So you can't provoke him into a fight in hopes you can exploit it to escape."

Again Bellus had seen through him, and Varro decided that until his head cleared completely he had better remain quiet and not plan anything more.

"But I'll warn you, Centurion Varro. If I ask Lars to tear you to pieces, he will do exactly that. And he has the strength to do so."

Varro narrowed his eyes at Bellus.

"Save the threats. You just provided a list of all the ways you can make money off of me alive. If you drop a broken, half-dead man on any of them you'll be the one on the run. But I expect you've done that plenty of times before. You have a fucking cage in a cave, for the love of Jupiter. You spend your days kidnapping new arrivals and selling them off. So you have a reputation to uphold. No broken, half-dead castaways from you, eh?"

Bellus gave a sheepish smile and shrugged. "I've been known to take advantage of any situation I'm presented."

"There's a sealed wooden tube with my letters of appointment to the king. If you show him that and my pugio, then he'll know you've captured me."

"Fair enough," Bellus said. "It's nothing personal, Centurion Varro. You were just the innocent butterfly that flew into the spider's web. It happens all the time. Now, you just have to see if your king cuts you free, of if you'll hang on that web until you die."

7

By the sunset of the second day Varro heard the cart being loaded outside the cave. The idiot Lars hummed a tune as he worked and shadows of both him and Bellus flitted across the opening. He sat against the back of the cage, feeling it press his shoulders like the pinch of a tutor angered with his student. Varro was that that foolish student. Now that he had sobered up and had a full day to review all the naive actions that led him to this cage, he hoped King Masinissa denied his ransom. He would rather face death than the shame of having been so easily duped.

Bellus shouted something indistinct, but it did not sound Latin. He heard other voices answer with a sharp call. Over the last day he had met and spoken with a half dozen natives, or so Varro assumed from their foreign speech. No one ever came inside the cave except Bellus, and only once to leave him a half-empty skin of water.

"It's only refilled once a day," he warned. "So make it last. Oh, and you don't need to eat but once every three days. A hardy centurion like you could probably endure much longer. But we'll start at three."

Despite no food, he had eaten too well before his capture. He had relieved himself in a corner of the cage. The native foods had not agreed with him, making the misery of the stench even worse. Flies clamored around the cage all day, multiplying his torment.

"A tidy profit," Bellus said as he ducked into the cave. "Roman gear sells nicely, especially the swords. I think every tribal chief wants to claim he took one in battle."

Bellus stood by the door, a glowing smile on his boyish face. Yet there was a falseness revealed in his eyes, which lacked any sign of a conscience. Varro wondered how he could have ever seen good-hearted Curio in such a creature.

"They cost me quite a bit," Varro said, feigning coolness when he was eager for news. "I hope you got a fair deal for them."

"Always do. I've got a reputation for bringing only the best. Now, put this bag on your head, then come to the door. We've got some traveling to do."

He thrust through the bars what must have been the same bag used when bringing him here. It landed with a puff on the stone floor. Varro gathered it to himself.

"Which is it? Ransom, slavers, or the spider's web?"

"Put it on. Then you'll find out, Centurion Varro. Be fast about it, or Lars will do it the hard way. Please don't be a fool and run. There are a dozen Massylii tribesmen out there who will cut your legs out if you try."

Bellus's fake smile vanished and he nodded again to the sack on the floor. Varro looked into the black opening, catching a waft of his day-old vomit. Even leaving the cave, he would not be freed of the foul odors.

But anything that took him out of the cage presented an opportunity for escape. He was not certain how much of Bellus's depiction of the landscape was a bluff. He remembered Russicada being nestled into wooded hills by the sea. Trapped inside a cave filled with billowing filth, he could not smell salt in the air even if it was present. He did not know how far they had traveled when he was unconscious. It could not be far, not if he was in a cave. That suggested he was closer to the port city and its hills than Bellus led him to believe.

He fit the sack over his head and stepped forward. Bellus seized him suddenly and pulled the cinch closed before tying it off. When finished, Varro noticed he let his breath go. Maybe he was bluffing about everything. It could be all his gear was being loaded onto the cart and it was just him and Lars, neither of which would pose any trouble for him in a fight. The other voices of these so-called Massylii tribesmen were distant when Bellus called out. Maybe they were only passing by.

"Now turn around and put your hands behind your back," Bellus said. "Press up to the cage so I can tie you off. Your legs will remain free this time."

The decision to fight or surrender came at this moment. Once his hands were bound, he would forfeit any chance to save himself.

He did not respond to the command and instead stepped back from the cage.

"I'll return with a spear," Bellus said in a tired voice. "And Lars, too. Really, Centurion, you're in a cage. What do you think you can achieve by giving me a hard time?"

It was a fair question and Varro was not sure he could achieve anything. But he knew Bellus had either ransomed or sold him. If he wanted to kill him, then he could do it any other way from denying him water to sticking him with a spear to starting a fire in the cave. Therefore he had value for being alive and unharmed, particularly if he were being sold as a slave. The interactions with native tribesmen suggested this was so.

"You have one last chance before I fetch my brother." Bellus's voice again sounded collected and in command. "Turn around and put your hands behind your back, then come to the bars."

As hopeful as he felt, Varro still had the bag on his head. Moreover, he was in a locked cage. Ideas of escape melted away.

Then Fortuna showed him her sign.

He turned to comply with Bellus and as he did, the corner of the bag on his head revealed a tear in the seam large enough to fit two thumbs and the stitching itself revealed gaps. The hole and the spaces flashed the setting sun into the darkness as he turned.

If Bellus was preparing him for travel, then he would have the key to open the cage lock.

With a smile hidden beneath the sewn leather sack, he turned and put his hands behind his back, then slowly stepped backward toward the bars.

"That's better," Bellus said in his patronizing voice. "No need to make this—"

Varro suddenly smashed against the cage bars and drove his right hand like a claw directly into Bellus's crotch. Finding the soft flesh, he crushed down with all the strength of his training and rage.

Bellus gasped with the pain and while he was frozen in surprise, Varro used his other free hand to tear open the sack down the broken seam. It peeled around his head like the skin of a rotten fruit.

Keeping his grip, he twisted to face Bellus, who now let out a shrill scream of pain.

With his other hand, he reached through the bars and clasped the back of Bellus's head, then slammed it into the bars.

Releasing his grip on hapless Bellus's privates, he searched for the dagger that must be at his belt. It only took two pats to lay his hands on the familiar shape of a pugio hilt. It nearly leaped into his palm as he drew it out.

Keeping his head pressed to the bar, he then drove the blade between Bellus's ribs to puncture his lungs. Hot blood gushed over his hand and Bellus's mouth opened to expel a breathless gasp. Varro had seen this so many times in battle and used to wonder why some men screamed in death and others simply opened their mouths without a sound. Now he turned this gruesome knowledge to his own benefit, slaying Bellus in near-soundless execution.

He held Bellus to the cage as he slid down its length to finally reach the stone floor. The yellow light of the setting sun stretched far enough into the small cave to touch his cream-colored robe and turn it into deep amber. It deflated around him as he settled into death.

Varro worked his hands around the belt, his heart beating so fast it seemed he would faint. There was no key. Panic flared and he sat back. He was still trapped and even armed with a pugio he was helpless against anyone wanting to kill him.

He thought of Lars. Bellus's scream had been missed, brief as it was, and Lars still hummed tunelessly. None of the other voices he heard earlier gave any sound. Yet even if Lars was alone he imagined his vengeance would be terrible. He was a simpleton and hadn't the wits to survive without his brother. But Varro did not doubt his raw strength which would be tripled by his sorrow and rage.

"His neck." Varro leaped back up and felt around Bellus's neck, his fingers sliding along slick blood from where it had flowed up from his chest now that he lay on the floor. He grabbed the cord and pulled it along until he found two iron keys. Using the pugio he cut the cord and fed the keys into his other palm.

Both looked much the same, and he could not immediately figure which one was for his lockbox and which for the cage. The teeth of one were far more worn than the other and this he judged to be for the cage. His own lockbox had been a new acquisition and the key had no wear.

Stuffing the lockbox key into his tunic, he then cut away the remnants of the bag from his neck. He went to the cage door but found the bars here were too tight together. While Curio might fit his arms through, Varro could not. It was as if the door were not part of the original cage. Perhaps it was a replacement, and so the bars were spaced differently. However, he could stretch to reach the lock from the cage and not the door.

The keyhole was large, but the angle was difficult and he could not fit it on the first try. Bellus's dead eyes looked up at him from beneath the door as Varro scratched and slid the key around the hole.

"Brother, it's all ready."

Lars's deep voice carried ahead of him as his shadow eclipsed the amber light of sunset flowing in from the cave.

Varro cursed and struggled to fit the key. The angle defied him and Bellus's dead-eyed stare seemed to mock his attempts. He grunted in frustration.

Then he dropped the key.

His hands were slick with blood and as he caught the edge of the lock, he shoved it home. But it entered at an angle and sprung out of his grip, falling to bounce off Bellus's chest and flip to the opposite side of his body and out of reach.

Varro's scream of frustration and shock could not defeat the same cry from Lars.

"Brother! What happened?"

The giant barely fit into the small cave. Tears flooded his eyes and he rushed to gather Bellus's corpse. He was like a child's doll in Lar's arms.

"No! Wake up!" Lars stroked Bellus's head as sobs overwhelmed him.

Varro had backed away from the door.

But in lifting Bellus off the floor, Lars had inadvertently

knocked the key to the edge of the cage. The dull iron glinted with a shard of sunlight striking its teeth.

While Lars rocked back and forth, holding Bellus to his massive chest, Varro snatched the key. He couldn't possibly open the door to escape. Even if unlocked, Lars blocked the way.

But he had an inspiration.

He exchanged his lockbox key for the cage key, setting it in the same spot while Lars bawled and shook his brother's corpse.

"I need you! We were going to count the coins. This was our big chance! No!"

Lars seemed to remind himself of Varro's presence. He hung over his brother's corpse and his sobbing slowed to a sniffle. He then purposefully set the body aside, and when he turned his miserably scarred head toward Varro, both his eyes were focused and bulging with rage.

"I'm going to tear you to bits!"

He crashed into the cage, rocking it backward and rattling the bars. Varro kicked back out of instinct.

"He died like a pig," he shouted at Lars. "Like the piece of shit he was."

"I'll kill you!" Lars hammered at the cage with his fists, heedless of the iron bars defying him.

"Your brother was scum," Varro said, hoping to drive Lars past any shred of coherence. He wanted him delirious with anger. "His robe is not fit to wipe my asshole."

"I'll pull out your eyes!"

Spittle sprayed over Varro, even at the back of the cage. And Lars continued to rage against the bars as if he were the one imprisoned. In fact, he seemed incapable of any thought other than destruction. So Varro had to provide him with the inspiration.

"Seems more like you'll ruin your fists on the iron bars. What can you do to me out there?"

More spittle and curses blasted from Lars's mouth, and then he suddenly pulled back. Tears shined on his red cheeks and he glared at Varro. The cratered red scar over his bald head seemed to pulse. Varro's stomach churned just to look at it. But the enraged giant knelt beside his brother and began to feel around his neck.

"Where is the key, brother? I want to tear him to pieces. You should've let me." His thick hands searched over his body, finding nothing. "This would've never happened if you let me tear him up."

Despite his rage, Lars patiently felt around the corpse in search of the key. Varro's patience was so strained he nearly pointed it out to him. But soon Lars expanded his search to the area around his dead brother and soon grasped the key.

He held it up with a look of delight, presenting it for Varro to see. He grinned to reveal blackened teeth and a large gap between them. He looked even more ghoulish in the deep shadows thrown by the retreating sun beyond the cave.

"Here it is, Centurion. Now I'm going to tear you apart. First all your fingers, then your hands, then your arms, then your toes."

He continued to enumerate all the appendages and protrusions one could tear from a body as he tried to fit the key into the lock. The key slid in easily enough, but when he turned it made jamming click. He frowned and grunted, then turned again to the same result.

"You're too stupid to work a key," Varro said. "How many ways can it turn? Can you count so high, you idiot?"

"Don't fucking say that!"

He slammed the cage with his fist, sending sharp vibrations down Varro's spine. Then he turned his attention to making the key work.

Varro had kept his pugio hidden beneath his leg, hand clamped over its hilt. Now that Lars was at the door, pressing against it in a useless attempt to make the wrong key work, Varro struck.

There was one place on a man that guaranteed death. He had seen it happen scores of times in battle, both to his enemies and companions.

He sprung from the floor for Lars, who remained fixated on turning the key. While the bars could not fit his full arm, he did not need to. Only the blade needed to slip between the iron.

With a triumphant shout, the pugio blade slid between the bars, sweeping up into Lars's inner thigh to tear open a gash in his crotch.

The giant rocked back, roaring in agony and dropping to the floor as he grabbed at the jagged line Varro had carved into his inner thigh. A cut to the artery there ensured a man would bleed out in minutes. Lars, for all his stupidity, seemed to understand this as well.

The giant man thrashed in agony, but suddenly stilled. He now lay beside his brother, pumping his blood into a mutual pool of gore.

Wasting no time, Varro reached around and tore out the lockbox key then exchanged it with the correct one. This time, he took a long breath and held it as he inserted the key. Now it slid in and gently turned to the side, clicking through the tumblers and releasing the lock mechanism. He left the key in it as he pulled the cage door open to the inside.

"You both got what you deserved."

Varro spoke to Lars, who lay frozen on the ground with both hands clamped over his massive thigh. He wore a tunic, unlike his brother, and Varro saw the blood spreading everywhere beneath him. His eyes were closed and teeth barred. If he had not died yet, he would soon.

Stepping over Bellus's corpse, he carefully padded to the exit and listened. He heard only the wind and caught the scent of salt in the air. As expected, they were not far out of Russicada. If there were a dozen Massaylii tribesmen waiting for him beyond, they were too quiet. A group so large would have to make noise unless they were lying in ambush, which made no sense in this situation.

Nevertheless, he carefully made his way to the exit and looked out on the small camp he found beyond. A campfire had been recently extinguished and a small horse was tethered to a cart that held Varro's lockbox and gear.

The horse shied at Varro's approach, likely smelling blood. While he was no expert in handling animals, he had learned some skills from watching the cavalry all these years. He also had farming experience from his youth. So he gave the animal some room and did not move suddenly. If the horse bolted, he might lose all his gear again.

All his possessions remained piled in the cart. His letter to King Masinissa had the seal broken and had been extracted from the tube. It lay held by a rock on the cart bed, and black fingerprints showed where Bellus touched it. Whether or not Bellus could read the letter, Varro could. But he decided it best if he did not know what Flamininus had to say. He rolled it up and replaced it in the tube.

The promised tribesmen might have been the riders he saw in the far distance, a long line of carts and horses headed toward the hills where there must be a road to follow into Russicada.

"A liar to the end," he said to himself as he gathered his gear back. He opened his lockbox and it seemed most of his coins remained. If Bellus had stolen any, the amount was insignificant.

Among Bellus's stowed equipment he found wine and some dried fish and cheeses. He helped himself, eating on the back of the cart and staring at the crack in the hill face where Bellus and Lars lay dead.

"All in all, a hard lesson," he said to himself. But he had only lost time and suffered some indignity and a nasty lump on his head. In the process, he had rid the world of two leeches.

He offered a prayer of thanks to Fortuna, cleaned his pugio which now lacked a sheath as he refused to return to the cave to fetch it, then took up the driver's switch to goad the horse toward the distant road. It was a complaint beast, small but hardy, and it knew its work.

By the final light of the day, he came along to an encamped caravan, where he hailed the guards and asked if he could join them.

"We travel to Cirta, and would be glad for another guard," said the spear-armed guard who met him at the outskirts of the camp. "You look ... dirty, my friend. Are you alright?"

Varro regarded his bloodied hands and tunic.

"Just a bit of travel dust and a small run-in with slavers. I'll be happy to surrender my weapons to your captain if that makes you feel safer about me. I just need to get to Cirta."

"And clean up," said the guard. "We'll have your weapons for tonight, and inspect your cart. Then you're welcome to rest with us and travel tomorrow."

8

Lars heard Centurion Varro outside the cave, ransacking their camp and muttering to himself. But he could do nothing about him now. He had lost the fight before it started, played for the fool he was. As much as he hated Varro, he had to agree that he got what he deserved.

But it was not death.

No, Lars could not be killed by mortal men. Of this, he was certain, as he had proved it over and again since the bloody fight at Zama more than a decade ago.

His iron grip crushed down on the blood flowing from his leg. He felt his heart racing and his sight dimming. Had Varro really been a god in disguise? For it seemed certain that he might die beside his brother, Bellus. The hot rush of lifeblood between his fingers meant he had been cut deep. But his foe had aimed for his crotch and had missed. If the blade traveled even a thumb's length higher it would have cut a fatal wound.

But as he gritted his teeth in silent pain, he realized he still had a chance at life. The blood was not jetting, meaning an incomplete cut of the artery. It was why he collapsed to the ground and stopped moving. He did not want to finish what Varro had started by enlarging the wound with violent movements. To tie off the leg meant releasing his grip on the artery. The sudden loss of blood might cause him to faint, and then he would die. He needed someone to help him.

No one would come. He heard Varro outside cooing to the horse. He was going to escape and leave him to bleed to death in the cave. That heartless bastard couldn't even do a proper job of killing a man.

Bellus's voluminous robes had plenty of cloth for bandages. The trick was in pulling it free in time. As he heard the cart rolling away outside, he allowed himself to breathe heavier. He stared through his hazy vision at his brother. Both from the deepening shadows and his blood loss, he could barely discern him. His robes were now gray in the darkness, no longer the immaculate and brilliant cream color that so suited him.

Lars kept one hand clamped to his wound and then reached for the hem of his outer robe. He pulled hard at it, but it would not come free. More blood flowed between his fingers, and he realized trying to play it safe would kill him. He had to take the chance.

Using both hands, he was able to yank away the cloth. Blood pumped from his inner thigh and he swooned. It seemed the world shrunk to a pinpoint and his own breathing was a raspy echo in his ears. But his sheer will prevailed. He twisted up the robe then looped it around his leg, using the full force of his prodigious might to bind the tourniquet just above the deepest part of the cut.

Then strength fled him, and he soon found his head flopping back against the hard stone of the cave floor. He looked up in a red so deep it seemed black. He fell unconscious.

It was a cold and black place where he just existed. Moments from his life floated into his mind, shattered memories, half-spoken words, feelings. But mostly he was aware only of coldness.

Then a sting and a slap and hard words in a language that he first struggled to understand. But then he felt hot fingers against his neck.

"There is a pulse there, master. He lives."

"But of course he does."

The second voice was warm and familiar, full of deep wisdom. A friend, perhaps. Lars opened his eyes and struggled to see. But all he saw was a horrible orange glow of fire hovering overhead. He felt the heat pricking his skin.

"Easy, friend. We have found you in time."

Another hand patted his shoulder.

"We will take you from this place of death, Djebel. I am sorry we did not come sooner."

Djebel. This was his name, Mountain. Yes, Djebel was his name to the tribesman. And now they had come at Bellus's arrangement. Only too late as the voice admitted.

His lids fell shut once more for he could not endure holding them open. But hands clasped his body all around and lifted him onto something that felt like a blanket over hard rocks. As they settled him, his leg burned with agony. But he did not express it.

"Careful!" the familiar voice said. "His wound is deep. Move him to the fire where it may be studied."

Men grunted and groaned as Lars felt himself lift from the ground. He swayed in the litter as they moved him from where he had fallen. Fitting through the crack required them to drag him along the floor. Every jolt and bump made him wish for death. But he held back the pain, keeping his eyes closed and mouth clamped shut.

The fresh air bathed his exposed skin. His wounded leg felt the coldness more keenly than the rest of his body. But soon he was set beside a crackling fire that made all the flesh on his right side feel taut with heat.

"Can you save him?" The familiar voice came from over Lars's head. Another man who knelt much closer sighed.

"This cannot be sewn back easily, master. There is only one way."

A heavy silence filled the space. Lars understood the horror of the so-called other way but did not flinch. He must live. If he died, how could he have revenge?

Now the familiar voice was by his ear, speaking in a whisper.

"You cannot die, Djebel. Your gods have granted you proof against mortal weapons. So it seems they have entrusted me, a simple tribesman, to ensure their will is carried out. But to save you, that cut must be sealed with fire. Then you must not become infected and regain your strength. But this is for your gods to do. Tonight, I do my part."

Lars flicked his eyes open if only to see the man who spoke. But he was too close and the light of the fire overwhelmed his vision.

Men pulled away from him, mumbling among themselves. Lars hung in a strange space where time did not seem to matter. They could have delayed hours or mere heartbeats. Soon he felt hands pressing all over his body, while men sat on both his legs.

"Open your mouth," said the familiar voice as warm fingers pressed his jaw. "And bite on this. There will be great pain. But it will stop all bleeding."

Lars obeyed and took the hard leather between his teeth.

No one warned him. He felt the blazing heat nearing his thigh a moment before the searing iron struck.

He arched his back and felt pain he could never imagine. Even the sword blow to his head had been nothing in comparison. This was a brilliant light of pain that wracked his body, setting every nerve into a frenzy. Men pressed him down, and he bit on the leather as he groaned.

The scent of his burning flesh sickened him. Yet the man

searing his wound seemed to be progressing with deliberation, pressing the hot iron in a thoughtful pattern along the length of the seam Varro had opened in his thigh.

"It is done."

Someone spoke those words, and again Lars retreated back to that place of darkness where no thought or sound penetrated.

He awakened in a tent. He was naked but for a cloth covering his waist. The sun was a bright ball in the dirty cloth tent over him. After a few moments, he realized the droning noise was his own voice. He had been babbling.

Someone ran out of the tent, calling excitedly into the distance.

Lars's face ran with sweat and he felt his arms trembling as he tried to wipe is brow with the back of his wrist. The tent was large enough for several men to stand with in. Besides the pile of sheets he lay upon, there was a stool, and a low table with clay basins and jugs. He could not see over his head, but felt that there was nothing there. Unlit clay lamps hung from the tent poles.

"Djebel!" The familiar voice called from the tent entrance, where his feet pointed. "You are awake. You have lived!"

"I am alive."

His own voice sounded strange, like another person speaking.

"But of course you are. For I have saved your life."

The man entered and grabbed the short stool to bring it by Lars's head. He was a slender man, dressed in a dark gray tunic of the Massylii tribesmen. But his head cover was bright blue. It framed a regal face, creased with age, and pocked with the hard life of a desert chief. His black eyes gleamed with joy and his smile was yellow and full.

"Ajan."

"You speak my name! Yes, Djebel, I came to find my riches stolen and our prized hostage vanished. Instead, Bellus left us only blood and sorrow."

"I need meat." Lars felt the weakness through his body and knew meat would rebuild his strength faster than anything.

Ajan clapped his hands together with a gentle puff.

"Yes, you will be fed meat, Djebel. I will see that you recover. The healers say your leg wound will be fine. It remains to see if you can walk yet.'"

"I can walk."

Again Ajan clapped his hands and leaned back with a laugh.

"Well, I pray it is so. I am happy to see you survive. For now, the great Djebel owes me his life. What a boon to have you back with my people. Who can stand against us now? The tribe will be as it should have been, now that you are bound to me as a son to his father. So, heal quickly, my son. There will be much to do in my service."

"I will serve you."

"Excellent!" Ajan leaned on his knees and lowered his head. "I am sorry for your brother. You have slept too long and so we have buried him. We did it with honor, for Bellus was a great friend to me."

"I will have revenge. The Centurion escaped. I will tear him to pieces. First his fingers, then his hands, then his arms."

Ajan raised his palm to stop him.

"In time, Djebel. If mighty Ba'al permits, you shall see revenge one day. But until that time, you must focus on healing. Then, when you stand again, you must swear before the tribe your loyalty to me as your savior. These things must happen before you tear the hands and arms from your foes."

Lars stared into Ajan's black eyes. Bellus had trusted him enough, but Lars always suspected him of hiding darker secrets from them. Yet it did not matter what Ajan said. Nothing would prevent Lars from finding Varro again and destroying him.

"I will serve," he repeated.

The smile on Ajan's face deepened, and he left Lars to his

silent suffering. For now, he had both a life-threatening cut and severe burns to endure. But he would endure and survive.

For Lars could not be killed by a mortal man. Many had tried and none succeeded. His father had once beat him with a shovel in a drunken rage and left him in a field to die. But he stood up and walked home. He had been less than ten years old at the time and had not grown to his full size. His mother and grandmother both fainted at seeing his condition. But he stood and endured.

However, the greatest test and ultimate proof of the gods's gift of immunity to death by mortal weapons came at Zama.

His tremendous size and strength and what others called courage in battle had earned him the rank of Centurion. He led the Sixth Principes under Scipio's legion. His men hated him, and he hated them. But they were happy to stand behind him in battle, for no enemy could stand before him.

None until that day at Zama. It was after the battle had been won when a Carthaginian who had been playing dead sprang up from the pile of bodies concealing him. He had a long and heavy sword, unlike anything Lars had seen before. He heaved it overhead, and being of a similar size and strength to Lars, the Carthaginian easily slammed the blade down through Lars's helmet and cracked open his skull.

That pain had been less than what he felt in his leg today. Yet he collapsed senseless only to later awaken staring at the bright sun. Later the velites came to pull his body out of the wreckage of the battlefield and bring him to where the dead were to be buried. He grabbed one of their arms, making the young man shriek with fright. They then took him to an aid station for the wounded and set him beneath a wide awning to protect the injured from the sun.

The medics hissed through their teeth at him, each one shaking his head in disgust. Each proclaimed he would die before sunset, or if he lived would be of no use to anyone. The medics would grant him a swift and painless death, as they did for all hopeless wounded. They finished the work the enemy could not. But then Lars and the other fatally wounded were left alone for what must have been hours.

When someone returned, it was one of the triarii centurions. Lars could not remember his name, but he will never forget the arrogance and evil in his eyes. He arrived with a dozen tribesmen all garbed in gray tunics and with their faces hidden from the sun.

"I will care for all of these men." One of the natives spoke Latin, and he stood close to Lars as he surveyed the lines of injured. "For surely you will let them die. But I have skilled healers who can do more than your people."

The Centurion laughed. "I don't fucking think so. But if you pay the price, I don't care what you do with them. They're all as good as dead. You want to buy dead men? I say you're a fool. But I'll take a fool's silver."

At that moment, Lars understood he was being sold into slavery. If he were to live, he would become property. If he died, then a tribesman lost his investment. But it could not have been much, for the tribesman offered only a pouch to the centurion, who accepted it after inspecting the contents.

"Many will live," the tribesman said. "And many will die. But you have saved some of your friends today. You should rejoice."

"I sold citizens into slavery," the centurion said. "And damned my soul for a pouch of silver. But it's more than I'll get for all I've been through."

He looked down at Lars, then seemed to dismiss him as already gone, and looked out over the others.

"Better to be alive as a slave than dead."

Never were more evil words spoken by one so ignorant. For in the days to come, Lars would learn what suffering truly meant for those who did survive their wounds.

But he was taken by the tribesmen and during that night as

they reviewed their investments the man who had bought the dozen or so wounded Romans paused to examine Lars's head.

"I will make a bargain with you. If you do not die, and you can walk to me, then you may live among us as a free man. For you must surely die, and if you do not then you must have no wits left to you. But if you live, walk, and speak, then it is a miracle that I must honor. For it is the work of gods, yours or mine or both."

And so it was after many months that Lars lived, walked, and spoke, and his master and soon-to-be dearest friend honored him. It was another year before he regained his strength, and well into the third year before he proved to all the value of his strength and size in combat once again.

Nor had his wits been reduced. For he learned the tribesmen's speech and their customs. His mind had not diminished, yet his abilities to speak had. The head wound left him with a slur and trouble seeing anything in the distance. He could not put complex thoughts into speech. Always angry, he was prone to senseless rages more than ever. He appeared to all as a raging idiot thanks to this and his size.

For years he lived and raided with the tribe, learning the land and earning his fame. He grew to hate Rome for its corruption and treatment of its citizens. After all his service, he had been sold as a slave by his own people but the gods favored him. Not so his companions, who were sold off for a profit to lead bitter and short lives in terrible conditions. Such was the Roman way and he detested it.

When he had enough money, he paid a man to write and deliver a letter to his youngest brother, Bellus. He asked Bellus to join him before he became old enough for military service. It was the same year Lars's savior died, and Ajan came into leadership of the tribe through suspicious circumstances. Yet Lars left when Bellus arrived and the two reached an agreement with Ajan to provide slaves and information on potential caravans to raid. They in turn shared the profits. It was a good life.

Until Centurion Varro destroyed his world.

So he would survive once more. He would stand, walk, and speak.

And he would tear Centurion Varro into bloody pieces.

9

Varro immediately appreciated the military value of Cirta as he and the merchant caravan approached it. The city might have lacked the grandeur of Pella or Athens — and no city could compare to Rome — but it projected a sense of might that he felt even at this hazy distance. It stood high upon a massive block of yellow rock that was surrounded on all sides by deep gorges. His traveling companions noted that a river looped around much of it and that it was only approachable from the southwest, across a bridge constructed atop a natural rock archway. As the caravan drew closer, he could see heavy walls encompassing it.

"Has anyone ever attempted to capture this place?" Even as his feet were sore and his face gritty with road dust, Varro's curiosity at this stronghold won over. The guard trudging beside him shifted his spear from one should to another.

"You don't know your history? Scipio captured it."

Varro's face heated even as his eyes widened in astonishment. He thought of the brute force that must have been required.

"I was only a boy then. I can't imagine the bloodshed to get across that bridge and then over those walls on such a small frontage. Did he scale up from the gorges, then?"

The guard snorted and laughed. He had a dusting of gray in his brown hair that hinted he might have been around for the battle of nearly a decade ago.

"Not at all. He captured King Syphax on the battlefield and took him in chains to the city gates. Easy as pissing down a hill. The fool tried to ride out in front of his routed men, and lost his kingdom in the bid."

Varro nodded and smiled sheepishly. He should study recent history more carefully, especially if his new role in Servus Capax would take him over the whole world.

The guard gave him a sidelong look.

"You had a fight on your way in? You've got a lump on your head that looks painful. You should find someone to take care of it when we get into the city."

"I am to present myself to King Masinissa. Is there a bath where I can clean up before I do?"

"The king wants to see you?" The guard searched him with a frown. "I guess road travel makes all men look like beggars. Yes, there are Roman-style baths you'll appreciate. Cirta is one of the most civilized places in Numidia, though I can't say I've traveled far in it. I prefer this route to the others we take. But we go where the trade is, I suppose."

They fell into silence as the caravan rolled on toward Cirta. Along the way, Varro passed strange plants and cacti. Even though he had spent years in Greece, he never felt as distant from home as he did now. Seeing these fern-like plants and the violent thorns of the cacti lining the road reinforced the strangeness of the place. He was truly at the other end of the world, where a great desert swallowed up everything to the south. He was as poor a student of geography as he was of history. But looking into the dry, rocky hills on the horizon he saw no other signs of life and could not imagine people living amid stone and sand. In Greece, there was always a village or temple along even the loneliest paths. But here there would only be scrubby trees, cacti, and whatever animals could eke a living from such an arid place.

By late morning they had looped south to the main gates, letting Varro appreciate the rock of Cirta from different vantages. They crossed the deep gorge on a stone bridge over natural arches and into the city itself. After Russicada, he was better prepared for the sights and smells of the capital. For all its aloof remoteness atop a massive plug of rock, the city teemed with people. Native costumes of every shade of color flashed in the lights between the shadows of square buildings lining narrow roads. Hawkers plied their wares, their drinks, or their promises. They prattled in their native language at Varro as he followed the caravan into the city. His confused smiles did not rebuff their attempts, but as the caravan passed so did their attentions.

They arrived in an open square where trees and flowers were artfully arranged among columns and benches. Varro felt most at ease here, instinctively responding to the Roman sensibilities of the place. But in his final duty to the caravan masters, he stood guard while slaves and workers unloaded their goods. When this was completed, he parted ways with smiles and an invitation to travel with them again. He got reliable directions to the palace, which stood at the highest point in the center of the city. He also paid the caravan master to borrow a guard who could interpret Latin for him, just to ensure he could get his request noted by the palace authorities.

He treated his guard to the local bathhouse, where they both cleaned up from the road and relaxed. In their idle conversations, Varro learned the man had been serving his current caravan masters for years and that he enjoyed the free life. He in turn tried to pry out Varro's business in the palace, but as merchant caravans' number one trade good was rumor he declined to say.

At the palace, he made his request known through the guard, paid him his silver before parting ways, and then waited while the palace guards stared at him as if he were a strange beast captured from a distant land.

In the end, he was instructed to return the next day. Having horrific memories of being kidnapped by Bellus and Lars, he was quick to ask this Latin-speaking guard where he could stay for the night. He would not be so easily fooled this time.

When at last he went before King Masinissa the next day, he decided to show up in his full gear in order to impress the king. So he trudged through hot streets in a chain shirt that rapidly drew sweat to his brow. It flowed from under his helmet so that by the time he was in the audience hall, he could not stop blinking from the sweat leaking into his eyes.

The vaulted hall with its high ceiling and high windows did nothing to relieve the heat. Birds chirped merrily in the vertical windows while Varro awaited the arrival of the king. How could any living thing sound so happy in this unbearable heat? Yet their calls echoed through the chamber where guards stood at attention. They were more sensibly dressed in tunics and carried heavy round shields with long spears and no helmets. Varro might look like a master of war to some, but he suspected from the stolen glances he received that he looked like a foreign fool.

At last, the king arrived with attendants, slaves, guards, and old men who must be advisers. To Varro, they all appeared like exact copies of one another, all with hooked noses, dark hair, flashing eyes, and grim lines on their rugged faces.

But King Masinissa stood out from his entourage in both presence and appearance.

He was not as old as Varro had expected, carrying only faint grain in short wavy hair encircled by a crown of golden leaves. He had a pointed beard and sharp cheeks and his broad chest projected a virile heroism, as if he were prepared to tear away his toga and leap into battle at any moment.

Everyone in the chamber went to their knees before him. But Varro carried the pride of Rome on his back. He had dwelled on this moment all the prior night and decided he would not bend so easily. He remained standing.

As Masinissa approached the large white chair set out for him amid screens depicting ancient heroes and battles, he paused to stare at Varro. Rather than frown or shout, his face lit up with impish delight and he suddenly seemed ten years younger.

"A man with a spine. This is welcomed." His Latin carried a mild accent but was otherwise perfect. "But I am king and you are not. Kneel, young man, and feel no shame in it. It is merely respect for one above your station and your achievement."

Varro lowered his head to hide his blush, which spread warmth under his eyes, then knelt. King Masinissa was a great ally of Rome and his cavalry had been a key to Hannibal's ultimate defeat a decade ago. He considered this display of respect for that contribution rather than his kingship. It was a foolish moment, he realized, but one that held great importance to him.

When he was invited to rise, Masinissa had sat on his chair and his guards, servants, and advisors spread in a semicircle around him. A charming, young slave girl offered him a silver cup, which he took without a second look. As he drew a long sip, he studied Varro over the rim of it. Again he felt like an animal on display, but this time more like an animal to be butchered or fattened.

Taking Flamininus's advice, Varro would not speak unless addressed. Given he had already soured half of the king's entourage with his reluctance to kneel, he did not need to dig himself any deeper.

"Bring me his letter," he said in Latin, extending his hand out but never looking from Varro. A wry smile remained on his lips, and he seemed to relish the proceedings.

All Varro's weapons had of course been retained by the palace guards. But to his surprise, when the slave trotted forward with the wooden tube containing his letter from Flamininus he also carried his pugio, which had been discreetly given a new sheath.

Masinissa accepted the items. He first examined the pugio, flipping it around and running his thumb over the pommel where the silver inlay showed the owl's head. He set it on his chair beside his leg, then looked to the tube.

"You were bored along the way and decided to have some reading material?"

The king leaned the broken seal toward him and raised one brow in irritation.

"Sir, I am sorry. I was robbed and briefly detained upon arriving in Russicada. The thieves opened the tube and looked at the letter. One left his dirty fingerprints over it. I replaced it and did not read it."

"Briefly detained?" Masinissa's eyes flickered with playful light. "You choose your words well. My servants report you have an injury to your head. Was that due to this brief detainment?"

"Yes, sir." The top of his head began to itch at the mention of the wound.

"I am not your commanding officer. Call me King or Lord."

"Yes, Lord."

Masinissa extracted the papyrus and held it back as if to focus on it. In response, a slave brought a lit lamp closer to illuminate it. Faint letters showed through the papyrus in the resulting orb of light where the lamp shined. The king's brows flicked up as his eyes followed the lines of writing. He then rolled the papyrus back into the tube and handed it to the servant with the lamp.

"I believe you did not read it, or else you would not have come here so readily." Masinissa smiled. "Between this letter from

Proconsul Flamininius and the other endorsements I've heard about you, I admit to being surprised to find you so young."

"I feel the same about you, lord."

Masinissa blinked and gave a quizzical smile. "You do? Well, thank you for telling me, Centurion Marcus Varro. Now, learn not to interrupt me again. It seems a lesson in etiquette must be my first task with you."

Again the heat rose on Varro's cheeks. Here he was as a Roman citizen sent to the king of sand-dwelling barbarians, but he proved to be the uncultured fool.

"Everyone go," Masinssa said, waving his hands to shoo his entourage. "Baku, you remain."

Some of the older men whispered protests, but Masinissa's frown was enough to chase them from the chamber. The servants gathered everything but the silver cup and Varro's pugio, then left with the others. Varro stood in awkward silence while he waited for the king to address him again.

The man called Baku was of an age with Masinissa, or perhaps slightly older. He wore a cream-colored tunic, and stood like a man ready to accept any challenge. His hair was bushy and unkempt, forming a dark halo around his head, which titled back as he regarded Varro.

"You should never be without this." King Masinissa held Varro's pugio forward as the last person exited and shut the door at the far side of the room. "Take it."

"I was told to surrender all weapons." He accepted the pugio from Masinissa, who remained seated but now stretched his arms over the sides of the chair. Baku stepped to his right side, standing just behind his king, and keeping his arms folded as if in challenge.

"Is it a weapon," Masinissa asked as Varro stepped back. "Or a sign of your affiliations?"

"I believe it is both, lord. I have already killed two men with it."

Masinissa smiled while Baku's head leaned even further back.

"The robbers who detained you, I expect."

"I trusted the wrong people, lord. It will not happen again."

"I expect not." Masinissa looked to his silver cup, then drew it into his hand and swirled the contents. "In my presence, you may surrender that blade to my guards. Otherwise, you must keep it at hand always."

"My King, he is too young. Send him back to Rome." The one called Baku had a rough and deep voice that carried the room even at normal volume, perfect for a Centurion Varro thought.

"Nonsense." Masinissa paused to sip from his cup before waving off Baku's concern. "I was only fourteen years old when I dealt the great Scipio Africanus defeat. A man's age is not the only measure of is ability."

"My King, you are forever above normal men. Do not demean yourself by comparing with this one."

Masinissa laughed, but Varro's irritation flared. Baku could have easily voiced his doubts in their native language but he had chosen to let the insult be known.

"I would not have been sent to King Masinissa if I had no worth," Varro said. "And shouldn't it be your King's choice as to who he accepts or rejects into his service?"

Masinissa clapped his hands and laughed while Baku's frown deepened.

"My advice is valued here, Roman. It is my responsibility to share it with my king so that he may decide if it is beneficial."

Masinissa twisted in his chair so that he could see both Baku and Varro, the smile brightening as he listened.

"But you were certain to speak so that I would be offended. I have not come so far and suffered so much to be insulted without cause."

"A thin skin," Baku said. "It is easily burned by the sun and bleeds from the slightest cut. It is a dangerous trait in these lands."

"Are you threatening me?"

"Enough," Masinissa said, standing and chuckling. "Enough testing the man, Baku. He is right. Proconsul Flamininus would not have sent a fool to spy on me. He endorses the man, and his scars and character speak enough for him."

Varro's eyes widened at the accusation. Flamininus did expect him to report on the king, but he did not consider that his most important duty.

"Lord, I was sent to learn from you and serve you as I am able. I'm a poor spy."

"Not if you carry that dagger," Baku said.

"Peace now," Masinissa said, gently extending his strong arm to his advisor. "Baku was only having a bit of sport with you, Centurion Varro, as am I. Please, you cannot imagine how little chance I have for this sort of game. I know you will report back to Rome on what you see here. That is just common sense. Now, I have read your letter and understand how you can help me, while I help you. I honestly do not understand all that Capax Servus stands for, other than the advancement of Rome and her allies by all expedient means. But even if you were trying to spy, you would not be in any position to report much of use."

The king returned to his seat and Baku unfolded his arms, offering Varro a patronizing smile when his king turned away.

"My orders were to serve you," Varro said. "So I accept whatever you command."

Baku's smile widened and Varro felt a tightness in his chest at that look. Whatever they had planned was not going to be good for him, he realized.

"You will enjoy this," Masinissa said. "I am giving you command of a scratch force of about fifty men, That is close to your normal span of command as a centurion. You will maintain a border post with Carthage, and conduct raids and reconnaissance on my former allies. That is your formal mission."

He paused and smiled again.

"But a secondary mission is to search for and root out any resistance to my kingship. I have made changes to strengthen Numidia and bring our kingdom onto the world stage. This includes bringing the Massylii and the Masaesyli together. That can be a history lesson for a later time. More importantly, I have been enforcing a different way of agriculture upon my people. This blending of tribes, changes to their nomadic ways, and other so-called grievances sometimes produce pockets of revolt, particularly where you are going. So you will watch for these, and end them before they begin."

Varro nodded. "I understand, lord. What is the condition of the outpost? Is it abandoned or just needing reinforcements?"

Baku's smile widened into a grin as Masinissa looked aside and rubbed his nose.

"There is no outpost. You will be taking fifty men out to the border and constructing one yourself."

Varro blinked.

"Sir, I mean, Lord. I have no experience with constructing outposts. I'm fine with a marching camp, but that's it."

"And so you will be learning," Masinissa said brightly. "And learning fast. For I have arranged your force and you will set out at dawn tomorrow."

"Tomorrow?" Varro stepped back. "Lord, I have two more men joining me. They missed the transport and should be right behind me."

"Excellent," Masinissa said. "More hands are a welcomed help. But you leave tomorrow and your friends may follow when they arrive. But you must hurry. I've already delayed my plans for you too long."

Varro wanted to protest and explain that he'd have enough worries trying to command fifty men who were not trained legionaries never mind establishing a defensible outpost. While

Falco and Curio didn't have any more experience, he could at least use their help with training.

"Lord, do these men at least speak Latin?"

Baku laughed, folding his arms again. Masinissa's smile faltered.

"They do not. They are a scratch force, as I said. They're not regular soldiers."

"Or soldiers at all," Baku said under his breath.

"But do not fear," Masinissa said brightly. "You will have Baku to help with translating your commands, and I'm sure he'll bring you some reliable men. Now, you will be shown a place to rest, though you will not get much of that. Baku will introduce you to the men and then get you outfitted for the challenges of the border. There will be many, but I trust such a well-respected man like you, so full of youthful energy, will prevail against all the difficulties ahead. In fact, that is my command. Tell me truthfully, Centurion Varro, aren't you excited for this?"

"Of course, Lord."

Yet even as he smiled he felt a burning ember drop into his guts. No road was ever as clear as promised, and how much worse could it be if King Masinissa already promised troubles?

10

Mountains. Endless chains of mountains, ridges, cliffs, gorges, deadfalls, and every imaginable hazard that a country of rock could offer surrounded Varro. Based on Bellus's idle threats, Varro had expected to trek out into vast, sandy wastes where the sun scorched men to death by noon. Baku had told him such places existed and he could one day take him there. But it was far to the south and far from civilization. And there were more mountains in between. Varro declined the offer.

He sat in his command tent, which was nothing grander than yellowed hides sewn together and rough poles battered into uneven and rocky ground. His small stool was a comfort, for sitting on rugs over sharp stones was a torment to him. In the mountains, he was relieved of the terrible heat he experienced in Cirta, which Baku said was unusual even in the summer. He blamed Varro's arrival for bringing the heat as a sign of Ba'al's displeasure at Roman interference. Varro could not tell if he was joking. In fact, most of his men brought heavy robes into the mountains and Varro was glad to have the cloak he wore in Greece stowed among his belongings. By winter he was promised cold unlike anything he ever experienced.

The desk he sat at was a table only wide enough to slip his legs beneath. He had placed a yellow rock on one end to keep anything that could roll from sliding off the uneven surface, which was mainly his writing stylus. Somehow Baku and the so-called wisest of his men had selected this place as most suited for them and their horses to establish an outpost. The location had easy access to water via a strong mountain stream and was surrounded by high cliffs. It seemed unapproachable except by two paths. The mountains had enough trees and bushes for firewood and forage, as well as access to the foothills where horses could graze. So Varro could not expect to find much better himself, and fortunately no one expected him to.

He lifted the bronze stylus from where it rested against the rock. Outside the tent he heard men laughing and conversing. Varro closed his eyes and pinched the bridge of his nose. If he went outside he would no doubt find a score of infractions and lapses in basic protocols that he would need to correct. Baku, despite being King Masinissa's "right hand," was never much help in keeping the outpost at any sort of military standard. It all fell to Varro.

He unstoppered the clay pot of carbon ink and smoothed out the vellum before him. He had found papyrus too expensive in Cirta, at least for the limited time he had to shop. But he had a stack of hide vellum that would serve. He intended to record as much as possible about what he did here. Of course, he would maintain standard reports on combat strength and supplies. It was a foolish exercise, as only he and Baku could read these. But maybe when Falco and Curio arrived to find his dead body they might want to know if he had died of starvation from mismanaged logistics or else from his own men. Varro thought either possibility likely.

He dipped the stylus into the pot, then set his pen beneath the lines he wrote the day before.

I have been referring to these criminals and misfits as men in my prior entries. That has been an expedient to save writing space. But since settling this camp a week ago, I have come to realize that King Masinissa has given me a third task that he did not verbalize. That is, to make something out of nothing. These so-called men are indeed males, and so I may call them as such. But they are not men, as in the disciplined and skilled soldier I have served with for six years in Greece. The fifty-three males under my alleged command have no discipline and no skill, other than their ability to consume alcohol. In that they are unmatched. But to do as I have been commanded is an impossibility. This rabble might well raid the homes of the elderly and infirm, but I believe the first Carthaginian regular to stand up to them will route my entire force.

Baku was honest in his assessment, at least. Some of these men chose to follow me versus having their hands cut off for thievery. I've noted many of the men have been branded on their cheeks or hands. Despite all the scum I've been assigned, Baku has gathered ten respectable soldiers to join us. These men are at least understanding of discipline and the need for a command structure. Without them, I fear for my life from the very men I command. For every order is met with a deathly glare. Had I not learned from Centurion Drusus to return the same tenfold, then by now my corpse must be thrown into one of the many ravines surrounding the camp. Doubtless, it soon will, for the men are testing me daily and I fear I will have to show them I mean to be their commander either out of respect or fear. But there are far more of them than me, and I wonder if Baku and his picked men would stand with a Roman against their own. I doubt they would.

Falco and Curio are still missing. I dread they have run afoul of the scoundrels in Russicada. I so desperately need their companionship and their aid. Falco stands taller than the biggest brute in my command. They would respect that more than my imitative glare. Yet I am alone on this mountain range. I keep my pugio strapped to my hip always. I fear the first time I draw it on this mission will be against my own side.

His fingers cramped and he had come to the end of the page. He cleaned the stylus with an ink-stained cloth and set it aside. The vellum went into the stack he kept in his lockbox with all his coins. Masinissa had provided more silver to help establish the outpost, but it had hardly been enough to buy draft animals and transports. The vellum landed with a soft thump, and Varro clicked the lock shut again.

Outside of his tent, the camp was full of activity. The man on guard at his door rested on his oblong shield, hardly a posture of alertness but better than prior days when Varro had emerged to find his guard asleep.

"Stand up straighter, and look like you're alert."

The words meant nothing to the man, but Varro guided the man's weight off the shield and then pressed his shoulders back so his chest projected out. He held the posture as Varro examined him. He did not have a brand; so maybe he was just some poor farmer trying his best to fulfill his king's orders. Varro could have patience with those types.

Baku had to be nearby, but his equally grand tent — if anything in this mountain camp could be called so — seemed empty. The flap was opened and no guard stood before it. Varro saw him as the Centurion and himself as the military Tribune of this miniature camp. But as an officer, Baku was something of a failure.

He eventually found him at the edge of the camp looking down one of the long approaches. Two other men conversed with him to either side. Their arms were folded and fingers stroking their sharp beards. Varro cleared his throat at his arrival. The three of them looked at Varro and smiled.

"Salute me," he shouted. "How many times do I have to remind you?"

Baku sighed while the other two looked quizzically at him. He made his salute and the others did as well.

"I've had crisper salutes from rotting bog moss."

The insult seemed to exceed Baku's linguistic capacity, but he reacted to the sour note with a scowl.

"Waving hands at each other will not bring defeat to the king's enemies."

"I agree. But discipline will. Of all people, Baku, you should understand this. You fought alongside your king. Did your cavalry just ride off on their own, prancing around and carrying on with whatever caught their attention? No, you delivered victory at Zama because your cavalry fought as a disciplined unit."

"But they did not waste time with hand-waving and marching in circles."

Baku folded his arms and mumbled something under his breath that made his two companions smirk. Varro knew the proper response would be to strip Baku back to the ranks, flog him for insubordination, then rain shit on him for a month. But Varro needed allies and he was the only one from here to Rome.

"We will march in a circle every day, Baku. Until the men scream for mercy and then we'll march again. You know as well as I do that sitting idle up here will just turn us into nothing more than bandits. We will train because our enemies will train, and we will be stronger than them. So, if saluting is too much strain for your weak arms, then I'll let them rest for now. But I will not have you unable to out-march and out-last our foes. That is what your king wants me to do with these men. It is his order."

Baku nodded like a man impatient to speak his own mind, which he did not delay the moment Varro paused to draw a breath.

"I understand what our king wants," Baku said. "But these men are not soldiers."

"They are now. Once camp and supply lines are secured we

will begin raiding the Carthaginian borders, and patrolling for native troublemakers in the area."

Baku's face darkened and he again muttered something in his native language.

"Centurion Varro, King Masinissa wants you to do those things, but not waste your energy trying to turn criminals and vagrants into a disciplined fighting force. He already has his cavalry, a jewel in the world's military powers. He does not need fifty men whose only advantage is in their disposability. If you try to fashion them into Roman soldiers you'll have a revolt right here in your camp."

Varro bit back his anger, looking to the other two men who began to drift away from him and Baku. These were his best men, and if he made enemies of them then Baku's prediction would come true.

"I don't understand why I was sent here," Varro said more evenly. "If not to bring the benefits of Roman-style military structure, then what else?"

"But you are not here as part of the military, are you?" Baku waved generally at his waist. "That knife of yours marks you as part of some secret cult. You were sent for their purposes. I don't know what was written on your letter to the king, but you do. That should tell you why you are here."

"I never read that letter," Varro said, trying to keep his voice even. Yet the other two men were now stepping even further back, and he felt he was not doing a good enough job disguising his anger.

"But it was opened before you arrived." Baku shrugged. "In any case, you are trying to make too many changes too fast. King Masinissa did not give us a deadline. We are to remain out here until recalled. So go slow, Centurion. And leave out strange customs such as salutes and inspections. These men come from a different world where such things are meaningless, and most are simply here to escape punishment."

"Or are here as punishment," Varro said. He drew a deep breath and chose to move onto something else. "Now, what were the three of you looking at?"

Baku's frown shifted to a smile and he turned to face the winding, boulder-strewn path leading down from the camp.

"We have to clear the way for our horses to come and go with ease. If we are to be swift raiders, we must have the means to vanish safely back to our hidden camp. Not to mention, the horses have to go down daily for watering, grazing, and exercise. It seems clearing this path might be good work for the men, Centurion Varro."

"I thought you liked how hard it was to navigate for enemies?"

"With luck, enemies will not be following us back here. The Carthaginians can't bring a large force against us in our territory anyway. If the local tribes remain at peace with us, then we have even less to fear."

Varro nodded. "It is a good idea. Detail however many men you think are needed for that task. Also, I want mobile barriers constructed so that if we do need to defend this path, we have a way to delay and slow enemies."

Baku inclined his head. "Those are fine orders, Centurion. I will make it so."

"Also, I watched the men practicing with their slings yesterday. They are about as accurate as my grandmother, and she has been dead for fifty years. See to it they improve. There are plenty of stones around for daily practice. If we do delay the enemies on barriers, I want to be able to break as many of their heads before they reach our camp."

Again Baku agreed and Varro felt the tightness in his chest relax. He left him with the two other men who had nearly retreated down the slope.

He would never make infantrymen out of tribal warriors. He understood this as well as Baku. But he did not know what else he could do. The Legion was the entirety of his experience.

To make matters worse, half of his men owned horses and expected to act like cavalry. Masinissa had promised more horses for the others once Varro had demonstrated success. Varro knew nothing about cavalry tactics and could barely ride at a canter. He had managed to sit a borrowed horse for the journey out here, but he could not imagine riding one to battle.

As he crossed back through the camp, he passed lines of the small, rugged horses standing in the shade of the rock cliffs. Most had their heads bent to crop the vegetation that struggled to grow from cracks in the stony ground. Their short and bushy tails flicked lazily. The scent of their dung was more intense here, and Varro rushed through the area.

He would have to improve as well, he thought. He might criticize the men for being poor shots and undisciplined soldiers. But he would lose any respect from them if he could not at least keep up on horseback. It seemed all of these tribesmen prided themselves on riding and imagined they were brothers to the great Numidian cavalrymen who played so dramatic a role in the victory at Zama a decade earlier. Cirta was surrounded by vast grassland plains perfect for growing this kind of force. But he was now in the mountains and had twenty-five horses to look after.

He returned to his tent and began his first report to King Masinissa. He would send a rider with his letter detailing conditions in the camp, where they had established it, and anything else of note. He expected to send a weekly report to start, as the king had not specified any expectations. In fact, it seemed that Masinissa was happy to make Baku his representative and send them all off into the mountains with a vague hope of doing something useful.

After another hour of scratching out his report on vellum, he decided he would ask Baku for help with riding after the afternoon march. The men could use the time to rest, rather than practice slinging or drilling with spears. He had worked with Baku to divide up men into three units with a leader that functioned like an Optio. They system worked only half the time, but he held out hope.

Distant shouting echoed from outside, the heated voices of argument. He set the letter aside to dry, and stood up to see what was happening. But the shouts rapidly grew in volume and were shortly outside his tent. His guard at least tried to stop the men before they burst inside.

Varro's hand instinctively reached for his pugio. His gladius hung from the post within reach, but he expected an immediate brawl.

Four men crashed into the tent with his hapless guard trailing behind. They were all the same dark-skinned, pocked-faced angry men to Varro. With their head covers shadowing their features, he hardly knew one from the other. The lead man was unique for his startling blue eyes and the brightness of his teeth, which were bared in rage.

The shouting split Varro's ears as two of the four men jabbed fingers at each other in postures of accusation. The other two were more focused on curbing the violent aspects of their respective sides. Nothing they said made sense, for Varro could not understand the native language. The useful phrases he had learned notwithstanding, even if he were a master of their tongue he doubted he could tease out anything from their shouting over each other. Anger flushed their faces and their hands rose in balled fists at each other.

"Settle down," Varro ordered. "Do any of you speak Latin?"

But the men continued to shout and threaten violence, neither side listening to the other and both restrained by their friends.

Varro drew a deep breath and summoned his battlefield voice.

"Silence! Stand at attention or I'll flog the four of you!"

A centurion's orders needed to be heard over the chaos of battle, and Varro had trained to fill his lungs to bursting before unleashing a shout. In the confines of his tent, the explosive command silenced the four men and the guard and set them all on their back feet.

He again repeated the command for attention with full force. All of his men had learned this command and Varro's vicious bark brought them up stock-straight. He had to conceal his smile at their reaction and continue to glare at them.

"You do not burst into the commanding officer's tent babbling like madmen. If you cannot understand this with words, I will beat it into your heads. One way or the other, you'll learn order."

The five men stood dumbfounded. But one of the more adventurous began to mutter his complaints, drawing a growl from his enemy and reigniting the argument. Varro extinguished it with a repeated command for silence, then blasted Baku's name into his guard's face. The man understood and raced out to find Varro's lone interpreter.

While he waited, he stood with arms folded and glared at the men standing silently at attention. The two belligerents did shift their eyes to each other, but Varro threatened to backhand them every time they tried. Baku arrived just as Varro's hand began to itch.

"I could hear your scream from the other end of the camp," he said, smiling as he entered.

His presence immediately dissolved Varro's grip on the men. They again renewed arguments and accusations, now addressing Baku.

"Address me or I will strip the skin off your backs!"

Throat now raw, Varro once more commanded the tent. No one here had a shout to match his.

Baku unraveled the situation after a series of questions. Every time the men raised their voices, he shouted them down. Varro sat behind his desk while the proceedings carried on. Eventually Baku nodded and explained what had happened.

"One accuses the other of theft. His dagger is missing and he thinks the other one has it. But he claims innocence."

"That's it?" Varro knew his face must have dropped, for Baku raised his brow and the two accusers began shouting again. "Silence!"

The shouting stopped and Varro pinched the bridge of his nose.

"All this for a missing dagger? Why is that one so certain the other stole it?"

Baku gave a short sigh. "The two of them have been enemies from a long time back. He has no proof."

"So a false accusation?"

"We could search the belongings of the other man," Baku said. "But they've already done so. These two are witnesses. The dagger wasn't with him."

"Alright," Varro said. "So he came here to press me to charge the man with no evidence."

"I don't know why they came to you, to be honest." Baku shrugged. "I guess you're the leader and so have to handle justice."

"They are correct," Varro said. He stood from the desk and went to his rack of armor and other gear set in the corner. "Please give me a moment to get prepared. Assemble all the men in the area I've designated as the parade ground. I will hand out justice."

He did not look to Baku, but to the nine-tailed scourge with lead balls attached that rested on the floor beside his trunk.

This would test his men, but demonstrate he meant to command by respect or fear and no longer cared which.

11

"So he found the dagger?"

Varro stood outside his tent as the sun reached the zenith of the cloud-studded sky, glaring at Baku who stood with two frowning men. These were not the accused and accuser, but those who had restrained them. The two troublemakers were now confined to their tents with guards posted.

"That is what he says." Baku rubbed the back of his neck. "It was a misunderstanding, and he asks you to forget everything."

He had lost count of how often he had bit his lip today in frustration. He stared at his second in command. Baku's headcover could hardly contain the halo of his frizzy hair. His eyes were lined with dark circles, hinting that he felt more stress than he let on. But in his dark, watery eyes Varro saw a hint of challenge. It was nothing overt, but a challenge one fighting man recognizes in another.

The three so-called Optiones, all from Baku's picked men, had gathered their squads to the center parade ground. This was nothing more than a flat stretch of dirt-covered rock where he could address all fifty men. To either side were the lines of hide tents where men slept three or four to each one.

"And what do you think, Baku? Do you believe I am going to forget everything and hide in my tent the rest of the day?"

Baku gave a wry smile. "You have done much screaming in the last week. But I've not seen much else from you. I thought Roman Centurions had less patience than this."

"My patience is done." Varro pointed to the center of the parade ground. "Why are the stake and manacles not in place?"

"Because we don't have manacles," Baku said. He held up both hands before Varro could scream. "We have strong rope. And the stake is being set. I had to send men to gather the wood."

In perfect timing, two men arrived with a roughly hewn post and began hammering it into the hard ground while the gathered men watched.

"Bring both of the troublemakers to the parade ground and keep them under guard. Time for justice."

Baku inclined his head and then commanded the two men with him, while Varro went into his tent. The inside was cool and smelled faintly of bitter ink, which he had left unstoppered on his desk. He took his chain shirt off the rack and got into his war gear. The helmet felt heavy and reassuring on his head. He had not worn it since arriving and never felt right without it. He did not have any feathers or plume attached, but such touches were unnecessary when no one else wore the distinctive helmet.

Back outside the mumbling crowd fell silent at Varro's appearance. The two men, one with blazing blue eyes who looked as pale as Baku's robes and the other with a rage-reddened face who seemed resigned to what was coming. Blue-Eyes had been the accuser, and no doubt was bewildered at his treatment.

While Varro carried his gladius and pugio at his side, every eye fell to the scourge in his right hand. He stood before them, running the leather tails through his other hand as he looked into the shadowed faces of his men. Their head covers ran the gamut of light to dark tones of either gray or blue. All fifty-three of them gathered together made an impressive sight. For once, they were silent and only the sound of horses snorting in the shady distance by the cliffs broke up the quiet.

Varro pointed to the two men, then spoke to Baku who stood with his head tilted back and eyes hooded.

"Have them tied to the post and stripped to their waists, and translate for me."

Baku turned on his heel to order the spearmen guards to drag them to the post. Blue-Eyes protested while the other went without issue. As they were bound and stripped, Varro drew a deep breath to address his men.

"Discipline is the core of all army life. You obey and execute orders without hesitation or question. You maintain yourself and your gear at all times. You act with respect and alacrity to your officers' commands. If you do not, then you face the harshest discipline."

Blue-Eyes was shouting protests behind him, and Varro paused to let Baku's translation catch up.

"These two men are charged with the following: insubordination; failure to respect the chain of command; fighting in camp; falsely accusing a fellow soldier of theft; and failure to maintain one's gear in good order."

Baku glanced at Varro as he translated the charges. The men shifted uneasily, as all of them had broken one of those rules during the last week. When Baku finished, he pointed to the accused.

"I will remind you that I have the full authority of King Masinissa to organize and lead as I see fit. I enforce strict discipline and do not tolerate the kind of time-wasting antics I had to endure this morning. I have been too lenient in these early days of assembling this unit. That leniency ends today. Each of these men will receive ten lashes by my hand. If they survive, they will be granted one day or rest and are expected to return to full duty."

Baku raised his brow after finishing the translation. But Varro ignored him and faced the two men now stripped to their waists.

There had been a time when flogging a man nearly caused Varro to vomit. He thought of Placus, who had been lashed for less than these men. Later he became Varro's most trusted soldier right up to his unfortunate death. He doubted these two would turn out like Placus.

"Baku, please count the strokes for me."

He first lashed the quieter man, letting his vociferous companion develop more dread for his turn under the scourge. The first three stripes drew blood but the tribesman did not scream. The others behind Varro groaned and hissed, but the strokes continued until all ten were delivered.

Sweat rolled down Varro's brow, as he spared no effort. In fact, he poured his rage of the last week into the hapless man. His back was split open in at least five deep cuts. The scourge dangled bits of flesh from the lead balls.

"Take him to his tent, and have someone treat him," Varro said. Without any medical staff, he was not sure who would look after the wounded. Given the men were all criminals of some sort, they probably had no skills. If any one of them, Varro included, took a wound they they would have to look to their gods to save them.

Two men dragged the bleeding, gasping man away as Blue-Eyes struggled against his bonds. He was pleading now, doubtless carping on about his innocence. But Varro shook his head.

"You'll learn not to use me as a tool to make trouble for your enemies. Baku, count the lashes again, please."

Blue-Eyes collapsed into shrieking at the first lash. Varro lashed him harder for his screaming so that his own arm and shoulder ached when he was done. Blue-Eyes cried like a baby and bled as if he had been sawed open rather than lashed. In fact, the blood pooled beneath him.

"Gods, was his flesh made of cloth?" Varro looked to Baku, who narrowed his eyes at the bleeding man.

"That is too much blood," he said. "He should not bleed like this."

"Well, is there anyone who can help him?"

Baku shrugged. "Ba'al alone. We're not a Roman military unit, Centurion Varro. We've no medical orderlies and doctors."

Blue-Eyes hung from his bindings, blood pouring in deep red streams to drizzle into the hard earth.

"Get him down and back to his tent," Varro said. "I'll see what I can do for him if there's no one else."

"It would not do to take care of the man you just flogged," Baku said. "I have some experience. Let me handle it."

So Blue-Eyes left sagging between two men who dragged him away. Varro remained with his bloodied scourge before the assembled men, who had all turned pale. With a nod to Baku, he addressed them again.

"That's enough sport for one day. Everyone prepare for an afternoon march, which I will lead. And let me remind you of the rules in camp. Do not fight, drink, or gamble. Do not misplace or fail to maintain your gear. Do not sleep on duty. Do not disobey a direct order. The punishment for these infractions will be flogging and in severe cases, execution. Also, as is standard practice in the Roman army, anyone retreating from the enemy without a direct order to disengage or who has to be disciplined three times for any infraction will be subjected to death by beating. Remember these rules."

"Centurion Varro, the timing of this is wrong."

"Translate every word," he said, squaring his shoulders to the gathered men.

As the translation completed he watched every face shift from pale shock to a dark resentment. Slowly fifty heads shifted to him, and Varro wondered if he might be overrun and torn to bits by a mob of former criminals. But they simply glared at him, hating his existence but not daring enough to challenge him outright.

"Return here with full packs," he ordered. "And we begin the march immediately."

As the men broke up, many looking angrily over their shoulders, Varro ignored their unvoiced curses and pulled Baku aside.

"We'll leave a small contingent of your men to guard the camp. But otherwise, I want everyone to run off their hard feelings. Nothing like a good march up a mountainside to work out frustrations."

Baku put his hand to the back of his neck and laughed.

"You did not make friends today, though that was not your intention. I think you should double the guards at your tent for the next few days."

"That will not be necessary," Varro said. "I will not show any fear to the men under my command. If anything, they should be on guard for me. I'm serious about what I said. I've been too soft on them. They must be broken and reformed. It is not something I am good at doing, but I must learn or else I think all of us are going to die in camp before we even get to see an enemy."

Baku gave his characteristic shrug then jammed his finger beneath his head cover to scratch his temple. "As you say, Centurion."

As promised, Varro led the men on a five-mile march in full pack down and up the mountain paths. As former criminals and societal misfits, and even as King Masinissa's soldiers, none of them fared well. He had been working them up to greater levels of endurance, but with only a week of experience, today's march proved overwhelming.

Men fell out, and Varro did not have other centurions to help shout the fallen back into line. So he left them where they collapsed and promised to pick them up on the return. He expected this to lead to more men falling out. Yet there was a stubborn sense of pride and competition between them. Each seemed to watch the man at his side, and neither seemed willing to be the first to fall out. Inevitably one would and others would follow. But at the peak of the mountain, at least the peak as far as any trail Varro could find, he let them rest and counted off close to thirty men. He had left a dozen in the camp including the two flogged troublemakers.

So he offered encouragement as men complained about their feet. Only Baku seemed able to keep pace with Varro. But he noted the halo of his frizzy hair had deflated under his head cover. Sweat streaked down his face even in the cool mountain air.

The march down was easier, at least for Varro. He was still fresh from military service and undiminished in his capabilities. Yet for his men, their mouths hung open as they panted. They swept up the men who had surrendered to fatigue. In a normal situation, Varro would bawl them out. For now, he would assign them the hardest labors as punishment.

By mid-afternoon they stumbled back into camp, and the men began to chatter excitedly. Varro shouted them into silence. "Not a sound until you are dismissed!"

The command needed no translation. They were learning enough of his meaning just from his tone. Once they were lined up in the parade ground, Varro walked the lines and nodded to those who had completed the march. To those who fell out, he scowled but left them alone for now.

At last, he dismissed the men for a rest but promised more drills with slings in the afternoon. The lack of protest did not speak to his growing authority but to the exhaustion of the men.

"Baku, how are your feet?"

His second pulled up short as if irritated. He seemed to be escaping with the others until Varro called him out.

"Aching, along with my back and legs."

"Glad to hear it," Varro said with a bright smile. "It'll be something when you see these men go from recruits to proper soldiers. For now, go check on those flogged miscreants, and then I want riding lessons."

Baku's mouth hung open and his eyes sagged, but he nodded and wiped sweat from his brow.

Varro returned to his tent to await Baku, chuckling as he did. He could hardly believe how far he had come. By all the gods, he was turning into Centurion Drusus himself. Out of sight of the others, he removed his helmet then sat on his stool and worked stones from between the hobnails of his soles. A few were missing and would need to be replaced. He had a limited supply and wondered how he would get more.

"It is not good," Baku said as he ducked into the tent. "Menac is a hard one. But Darri is still bleeding. His bed was covered in blood."

Varro did not know their names, but he guessed Darri was the blue-eyed accuser who had bled too much. He put his foot down and then flung the stones from his soles out of the opened tent flap.

"That is not good. We need someone with medical skills. Is there no one among all of these men?"

"There is me," Baku said. He let the flap fall behind him, cutting the yellow light in half. "There are a few others. None of them are doctors, Centurion. You have to stop thinking this is the Roman army. If a man gets hurt, he is on his own. You should've known this before you flogged them so hard."

"I knew it," Varro said, clapping the dust from his hands. He worried for this man Darri, but he did not want to seem weak. "And so does everyone else. So hopefully they will think twice before doing something to get flogged."

Baku hissed gently through his teeth and again scratched

under the headband clenched around his sweat-flattened hair. "They do not think that way. You have been moving too fast with them."

"Not fast enough," Varro said, then stood. "Now, teach me some basic riding skills that I will need to at least reach the battlefield in one piece. I'll fight on foot if I can."

"If you ride to battle on a horse, you're better to stay mounted than not."

"Then teach me what I need to do. Because we're not going to sit idle for much longer. The men need to know there are enemies to fight. Otherwise, they'll not go another week with these drills and marches."

"You intend to strike at the Carthaginians now?" Baku's hand paused in mid-scratch.

"A short and easy raid to build confidence and show them why they need to train."

"But they're not ready. It could be months before they are." Baku withdrew his finger from beneath his headcover, and seemed stunned with Varro's conclusions. "Some of them might be killed."

"That will happen in a battle." Varro picked up his helmet from the table. "So maybe knowing a fight is coming will inspire them to be prepared. Speaking of which, I want that training."

So he and Baku left the camp and took horses along with a half dozen lookouts down to the foothills where the land allowed the horses more freedom.

Baku's lessons were hard and Varro fell from the horse three times.

"Learning how to fall will save your life," Baku said each time. "And learning how to jump away is just as important. More important than fighting. Your mount could be shot out from under you before the battle starts."

He did not complain, even if his shoulders and hips ached

from the jarring falls. His head still rocked with each impact, a remnant of Lars and Bellus's ambush. The scouts clearly joked behind his back, but as long as he could not understand their words he would let it pass. Besides, he felt it good for them to see their leader trying to learn new skills just as they were.

Baku kept him working hard, rotating horses so that they never tired. It was not until Varro noted the sun going down that he realized he had missed the slinging drills.

"You did this on purpose," Varro said from atop his short mount.

"I do as you order, Centurion." Baku smiled and bowed his head. He stood holding his mount, letting it relax while Varro drilled. "You did not order me to stop."

"A technicality." But Varro smiled and patted the neck of his mount. "But it was time well spent. I feel like I really learned something, and I think this horse likes me."

So they turned back to camp and as they traveled the final distance up the slope, he heard a strange wailing echoing off the walls of the cliffs rising on both sides of the trail.

"Those are our men," Varro said. "What are they shouting about?"

But Baku did not answer. Instead, he and the scouts gritted their teeth and kicked their mounts up to the best speed they could manage on the rocky path. Varro followed behind.

Everyone had emptied from their tents and gathered on the parade ground. The flogging post had been torn down and some men were kicking it. Some shook their fists at the sky with gnashed teeth.

There was no order here. Whatever tenuous discipline Varro had built dissolved into chaos. The crowd flashed through the shaft of setting sunlight reaching between mountain walls. They seemed to waver like barley stalks in the wind as they howled.

"What is happening?" Varro asked as he joined Baku and the scouts.

He thrust his fingers under his headband and scratched.

"Darri has died," he said. "And they are blaming you, Centurion Varro."

12

The mob that Varro formerly considered his command churned in a vague, directionless mass of gray and blue head covers. The sun rapidly vanished behind the cliffs, as if hiding itself from the rage about to be unleashed. Every face was red with anger, teeth bared and lines pulled taut. Fists rose to the sky and wails echoed off the surrounding stone walls.

"Was Darri a well-loved man?"

Varro sat on his horse, which to its credit did not shy at the chaos so close. Baku stared ahead in silence while the six scouts slumped on their horses. Unlike their brothers, they hadn't the time to work themselves into a frenzy.

He had seen this before, years ago with the Punic War veterans rose up against what they considered broken promises from their leaders. The veterans had never reached this level of discontent, but there were those among them trying to stir up revolt. Varro's situation was already out of control, and likely due to a few who manipulated the whole.

"Baku, snap out of it. Get these six scouts on our side before they go over to the madmen."

Baku did not respond and the scouts continued to stare in amazement as the crowd became more agitated. Someone hefted the toppled flogging post and sent in surfing along the top of the mob until someone again slammed it hatefully into their midst.

"Baku!"

"They're calling for your blood, Centurion."

"Get these scouts on my side," Varro said. "I'm going to stop this."

Now Baku twisted on his mount and faced Varro with wide eyes.

"You're finished, Centurion. We should ride to Cirta and leave them to their own plans."

"That would be failure." Varro kicked his horse forward, too hard so that it startled and nearly bolted. This resulted in drawing the attention of his men, who pointed at him as if at last finding their victim.

"Baku, support me here!"

Varro leaped down from his mount as he had just practiced. He at least slammed onto his two feet, the weight of his mail shirt driving against his shoulders. His gladius remained in the sheath, and he would not draw it against his own men unless forced.

The crowd surged the short distance across the parade ground. Varro stood with arms folded, planting himself like a new flogging post in the stony ground. It was an apt thought, and it brought a grim smile to his face.

The hatred of their curses was clear even if he did not understand the words. It seemed that a swirling mass of white, crazed eyes were headed straight for him. He could not pick out individuals, but he recognized some. His heart throbbed against his chest, but he did not flinch, waiting for them to close the final distance. They had not brought their weapons against him either, but their hands were outstretched like talons clacking before the killing swoop.

When they reached within spear's length, Varro set his hands to his hips and drew his deepest breath.

"Halt where you stand!"

He blasted the words so hard he felt as if his throat might have turned inside out from the force.

The leaders of the mob skidded to a stop, then rocked forward as those in the rear collided with them. It reminded Varro of a charge of recruit hastati, where they had not yet learned how to move in formation. They continued to press forward, though no longer running. Their endless steams of complaints and cursing did not end, so Varro drew yet another long breath.

"Silence! One more step and I'll have the lot of you marching all night long. Stand at attention!"

The order for attention was likely understood but ignored. Yet the mob halted and the shouting was reduced to a low hum of angry noise.

Varro remained with hands on his hips, hoping he looked unflappable. In reality, he was as frightened as if facing a Macedonian phalanx on his own and without a shield. He could almost feel the pikes slipping between his exposed ribs.

But the dark and hateful faces dropped away whenever he glared at them. The cursing came from the rear, where men hid behind others. Varro let them work out their anger as he stood as still as the post he imagined himself to be.

"Baku, where are your Optiones? They're supposed to be commanding this rabble."

He turned to find Baku and the six scouts had not moved. It shocked him, as he thought the mob might have stopped because they had lined up behind him. But instead, they seemed uncommitted, and Varro realized he might be far worse off than he thought. Baku was apparently loyal to King Masinissa, but what conversations had they held in private? Was he simply to drop Varro if he thought their mission would fail?

"Baku! Get up here and translate, or none of us will get any sleep tonight."

At last Baku's eyes shifted from the vacant stare across the mob of former soldiers to Varro. A dark anger shined there, but he did as asked. Confident that his orders would be followed, he turned to his men — if he could even still call them as such.

"What am I to do with you? I can't put fifty of you on charges. This is not the behavior I expect from my men. It is the action of undisciplined rabble. Is that what you are? You have come here in the name of your king. At least do yourselves that honor. You might have been criminals or unwanted men before. But now you are soldiers. You have become part of the glory that is the Numidian army. Can't you behave like it?"

Baku gave a halting translation, and Varro wondered if he was true to the words. But the men seemed properly shamed, as many looked aside or to their feet. But still, others cried out from the rear, bolder for being unseen.

"Your companion has died. There is nothing you can do to change this. Having been merely a week together, I suspect how much of your anger is at his death and how much at the hard work you've been tasked with."

Before Baku finished his translation the men renewed their angry growls of protest. He had to shout to finish the translation, and before Varro could demand their silence Baku shouted them down.

Still with his hands on his hips, Varro continued.

"I'm sorry to tell you, becoming a soldier is not an easy thing. Forget what you think you know about it. It's not all lounging in the shade of a guard house and yelling at beggars to clear the streets. You are fighting men, sent to keep peace in the land and harass your enemies. It takes discipline and hard training to do it. You hate me today. But when you face a wall of enemies intent on your death, you'll thank me. You'll know what to do because I taught you."

He let Baku catch up and studied their reactions. As expected, he seemed to touch no one. He could read nothing in their faces besides disgust and contempt. Shadows swallowed up the mob so that even if their expressions were softening he could not read them in the depth of their head covers. His mind raced for something to bring this to a swift end, while they were still listening. Whoever whipped up this mob might do it again, and Varro would not prevail a second time. He thought back to the Punic War veterans and how Consul Villius handled them.

"I know you would not be so upset without just cause." He tried to smile through the lie. He believed these men would riot for no better reason than the sun being up. "So when you speak so clearly and unanimously then I must listen. But not while you are in the heat of rage. I want you all to go back to your tents. It is sunset and time to post sentries for the night. But before you do, I want you to elect five men to represent your concerns. Send them to me at dawn and we will see what arrangements can be made. I will not yield on training. But neither will I be unreasonable. Now, you are dismissed."

Baku glanced at Varro while translating. This recommendation at last seemed to break through the mob's rage. He knew the longer he kept them at peace, the faster their anger would dissipate. But he also realized he could misspeak and restart the fire he had just put out. Now they saw a way to make their demands known that might preserve themselves in the process.

They might be rabble, but they were not fools. If they ousted Varro to become a bandit force, Masinissa would know exactly where they were and how to bring them to justice, which would be far worse than the punishments for their original crimes. It was better for them to die as soldiers than bandits, particularly if they had families that might benefit from their pay. He was not sure how the Numidian army functioned, but Romans paid a small sum to widows and their families.

As the men broke up into groups, Varro handed his mount off to one of the scouts, who looked at him as if seeing him for the first time. He then straightened his shoulders and headed for his tent, which had not been touched. The mob seemed to have taken all its aggression out on the flogging post, which was now splintered and broken on the ground. Baku followed him.

"You should double your guards tonight."

Varro laughed.

"Did you see any man who would stand in the way of a dagger for me?" He stopped at the tent flap and turned to Baku. "Tell me, is there even a single man here who would protect me if that mob decided to turn again?"

The question seemed to surprise Baku, as he leaned back with brows raised.

"Not every man was so bloodthirsty. Some of them are just poor men trying to make the best of their lots."

"And they stood with the mob," Varro said flatly. "Not even your picked men exerted any control. I wonder, Baku, if you would stand by and let me die? It seems you would. I don't blame you, of course. Why sacrifice yourself for someone so meaningless to you? I'm sure King Masinissa told you to ride back to him and abandon me if things looked bad here."

Baku's shock darkened to anger and he lowered his eyes at Varro.

"There was no such order. King Masinissa is a man of great honor." Then his shoulders relaxed and he stepped back. "You are new to me, Centurion. I do not know what kind of man you are. You charged in and started harassing the men with strange customs and work beyond their abilities, expecting them to behave like Roman citizens. Why would I die for such a foolish and inflexible man? But do not misunderstand me. Neither would

I betray such a man. I will see that you have trustworthy guards tonight. There must be someone foolish enough to think of murder tonight."

True to his word, Baku changed Varro's guards shortly after sunset. He heard the exchange as he scratched out his record of the day's events onto a vellum sheet. He did not go outside but finished his entry before extinguishing the lamp and retiring for the night. If anyone approached his tent that night, he slept soundly through it.

By dawn, five men appeared at his tent and he welcomed them inside. They glanced around as if entering a sacred space, their dark eyes glittering in the shadows of their head covers. He sat behind his small desk while the representatives stood. Baku was present to translate.

They started with predictable pleas for more lenient punishments and fewer restrictions. Varro did not give in and pointed out that to relax the standards now would dishonor Darri's death. It took some debate to get them to understand.

In the end, Varro agreed to a more progressive approach to their training. He would not relax the intensity but allow for more rest periods. He also did away with salutes but insisted men respect those placed in command above them. This seemed to satisfy their basic complaints. The men did not ask for much. They simply had not expected to be pushed to their limits when they began training.

They then asked to drink and gamble in the camp, and Varro flatly refused. When he pointed out more men would end up dead than happy for that change, he was surprised that the representatives laughed in agreement.

When the meeting ended, Varro had succeeded in keeping most of his structure intact and conceding little to the men. He was not a great negotiator. The tribesmen had little to bargain with if they did not intend to kill him.

When the representatives filed out, Baku lingered behind.

"The extra rest will do them good. I think you were right in everything else you insisted upon."

"Then you won't fight me on it? You'll see that the men you selected as junior officers will do their duties. I still have a mind to call them to account for yesterday's outrage."

"Do not stir that nest of bees again." Baku glanced out of the tent flap at the new morning sun. "They are already gathering at the parade ground to hear the outcome. Some men will still be angered."

"Of course," Varro said, standing from behind his desk. "But some men will never become soldiers. We'll shape who we can and the rest will be broken in the process. They'll be the first casualties of battle."

"Let's hope there will be none soon."

Varro gave a quick smile.

"We do not have to hope. We dictate the fights, don't we? So I want these men ready for their first raid into Carthaginian territory by the end of the month."

"You are joking of course," Baku continued to stare out the tent flap. "It'll take that long to get them to drill properly."

"It will take even longer if we don't show them the reason for it." Varro drew his pugio and held it carefully by the blade to display the pommel. "You remember I have a mission as well? I will be returning to Rome within the year, and I cannot return with nothing to show for it. One month, Baku, and then we begin in earnest. We'll start simple, and build up from there."

"That is too soon. You won't learn enough horsemanship in one month."

"I don't need to," Varro said. "I am an infantryman and horses are simply transportation. Believe me, I've seen how a true cavalryman rides and I've no will to learn to do it myself. It would take years of training. So, we will also begin scouting targets for the upcoming raid."

Baku sighed but nodded in agreement. "If we are to be successful, then we should befriend the local tribes. They will have to protect us from reprisals."

"What is the purpose of this mountain camp, then? We've no need to hide."

Stepping halfway out of the tent flap, he smiled back at Varro.

"They'll protect us from the scouts Carthage will send to find out who acted against them. We will need friends once the fighting begins."

"I don't disagree. See that it happens. Once targets are identified I want to accompany the scouting parties." Varro wagged the pommel of his pugio at Baku. "I couldn't have received this if I didn't know how to scout an enemy position."

In the weeks that followed from aborted revolt, Varro saw a change in both the men and Baku. At the same time, he realized this was not a regular unit of the Roman army. At best, his fifty men might rate as a reconnaissance force. In truth, they were just tribesmen who were better armed and taught better techniques than their nomadic brethren.

Scouts had turned up various targets of opportunity, with the best being a supply caravan to a border fort on the Carthaginian side. Any attack on the fort itself was sheer madness given the capabilities of his men. But Varro's mission was to lead harassing attacks that would draw Carthaginian attention to the border with Numidia, and into the prospect of breaking a treaty that would rekindle a war with Rome. A war they would lose badly given their hobbled conditions and Hannibal's voluntary exile from Carthage.

It was the night before they planned to set out to raid. Varro sat in a globe of orange lamp light. The thin ribbon of black smoke smelled foul and greasy to him. But it lit the vellum page where he scratched out his report.

I've kept these entries brief to preserve vellum. The man I sent to K.M. with my report did not return with the writing supplies I requested. No word of Falco or Curio returned with him either. I am worried sick, for they have certainly run into trouble. I keep thinking of the criminals Lars and Bellus. I don't think Falco would be as easily gulled as I was. But perhaps he and Curio encountered trouble at sea. My stomach churns just to imagine it. I would never know their fates and to think our last words were full of anger. My self-loathing for such foolishness is hardly punishment enough. How I have wished for them to join me. But now I would rejoice just to know they were alive and safe anywhere in the world.

Tomorrow I undertake my first raid of a regular supply train running to the border fort that guards the road to Simmithus and its marble quarries. The fort itself is beyond our capabilities, but it is vulnerable to disruptions. If we prick at it, the fort commander will have to take notice of us. Just being recognized by a superior enemy will be achievement enough for this small group.

Baku insists that he will determine tactics. I will lead overall and guide the footmen. We do not have a complete cavalry force, which is ill-suited to hiding in the mountains anyway. Shoveling horse droppings is what passes for latrine duty in this camp. In any case, I am both hopeful and fearful. Any kind of victory tomorrow will bolster spirits and confirm my training regimen to the men. Failure would be disastrous. But with a fast-moving force, we can vanish before help arrives. We have enough horses to double up riders during escape.

If only Falco and Curio were here. We might even dare the border fort! The Numidians have sacrifices to their gods prepared for tomorrow. I will offer one of the hares bought in this morning to Fortuna. We must taste victory or all I have worked toward will be undone.

13

The marching camp sat on the far side of a ridge out of sight from the main road. Varro did not have them dig ditches or set stakes, as much as he felt exposed for it. Instead, rows of tents and lines of rope horse pickets came together in a rough square and guards had rotated through the night to keep the camp safe. He did not want anything identifiably Roman left for the Carthaginians to discover. As it was, the night had passed without event. The border fort did not send out regular patrols in the region, at least during the time Varro had them observed. The local intelligence was that not even bandits dared to operate in view of a fort and the supply guards were all veteran soldiers. So there was no need for patrols.

In the morning when the two riders returned with reports of the merchant encampment on the move, Varro's time had finally arrived. The morning sun was bright and merciless, and much hotter than the mountain temperatures he had accustomed himself to. This bend in the road offered one good hiding spot, and if the escorts were of any value they would scout this position before their caravan approached. He set his best slingers and horsemen at the ready for the scouts appearance. That would be the signal to begin the attack.

He wore his heavy mail and crestless helmet, adjusting the chin strap as Baku approached. His eyes squeezed to slits against the bright sun.

"You worry for leaving signs of a Roman presence yet you outfit yourself like this." He waved his hand up and down. "You make no sense. You should dress like one of us and fight like one of us."

"Dress? Half of the men are practically naked. I don't fight with a javelin either," Varro said, then patted the gladius at his hip. "I plan to get my hands bloodied and this is the better weapon for it. Besides, I have in on the authority of my kidnappers that the locals like to buy Roman war gear and claim it as an old battle trophy. Maybe I'm just one of them, eh?"

"Your skin has tanned but not enough to pass as a Massylii. And you'll be shouting in Latin and fighting like a Roman." Baku shook his head. "I think any survivor will know who you are."

"I'm willing to give up my scutum and pila. To give up more you might as well ask me to go into battle naked and wielding a handful of flowers."

"But the for flowers you will fit in better."

Baku smirked. He let off his head cover and let his frizzy hair lift in the breeze. The head cover was supposed to be a liability in battle, risking getting caught in the warrior's face. But it seemed Baku's hair could do the same.

Varro chuckled at the jest and looked over the men preparing themselves. The cavalrymen wore either light tunics and sandals or nothing but a cloth over their waists. The infantrymen all wore tunics and carried round wood shields with their javelins. These shields were so small Varro doubted their effectiveness, but this was not going to be a formation battle. It was going to be swift destruction and looting, then a retreat. They did not need more armor for their task.

"It would be better if we were all mounted," Baku said. "Including you. We split our force this way."

"All the more important we begin reporting success to the king. Then we will be sent more horses." Varro turned back to the crest of the hill. "You've got the men watching for the caravan scouts? Take them out swiftly. I'll then take our men in on foot, and you'll be right behind me."

"The plan is sound," Baku said, yawning. "But like all plans it can go wrong."

"See that it doesn't or there will be no need for more horses from Cirta."

He admitted an anxiousness he had not felt in years. Though he hid it from his men, walking among them and nodding his approval no matter how they actually appeared. He realized he had not joined a significant battle since the siege of Argos two years ago. Being the height of his service, he had at that time become inured to the worst of pre-battle jitters. But now he felt like a recruit, and in essence he was. He did not understand the people or the enemies he faced. He had learned to fight Macedonians primarily, who fought in similar ways to his own. The Carthaginians of course would fight like civilized people, but he did not have the same understanding of them. They were famous for their tricks and traps, and nearly had conquered all of Rome were it not for Scipio.

"This isn't Hannibal," he muttered to himself as he left the camp to his pseudo-officers and mounted the slope to where Baku had relocated. He crouched against the rocky edge with five slingers with javelins set at their feet.

He crouched beside them and then looked down into the road. It was flat land rolling away to undulating grassland with scattered trees. They were perched on the south side of the road, not to

Varro's liking as they would be fighting into the sun but the best position they could reach ahead of the caravan. To his left, the squat, blue shape of the Carthaginian border fort was hardly bigger than a thumb on the horizon. The caravan was miles away from their help.

"The scouts haven't come," Baku said flatly. "And the caravan approaches."

Varro followed the gazes of Baku and the slingers. A brown cloud of dust blossomed into the sun on the eastern horizon. The caravan was just over it, still too far to hear.

"They might not be scouting far ahead," Varro said. "This is supposed to be a peaceful road. It will not change our plans. Once the caravan is passing below, I will lead the charge of footmen. Once they try to surround us, you lead the charge downhill. It should spoil their attack and devastate their numbers. From there, kill or drive off whoever remains. I want to carry back those supplies to our own camp. There has to be good wine in this delivery."

Varro imagined better eating than the tasteless vegetables and bits of fatty goat meat he had subsisted on for a month. Of course, he had not expected better, but wouldn't mind a change.

"And prisoners?" Baku asked. "We kill all of them, yes?"

"Kill only those who fight. If someone wants to run, let them. If we earn too vicious a reputation, we might find ourselves hunted too earnestly."

Baku frowned into the distance, watching the dust cloud. Varro had already answered this question the night before, leading him to believe his second-in-command was more bloodthirsty than his mild disposition suggested. He honestly feared making their band a priority target for the Carthaginian garrison too soon. But he also did not want to kill people only doing their jobs if he could avoid it. He was a soldier and not a barbarian.

He and Baku left the slingers to watch for the caravan scouts, while they assembled their men into two groups. Varro took twenty-five men with him further down the road to where he planned to launch the attack. He reasoned the front caravan might still travel forward when the back was caught. Anything he could do to stretch out their force would aid him.

Now the often boisterous and always undisciplined men fell quiet. Separated from their mounted companions, each one seemed to realize how vulnerable they were without the mass of horses to shield them. Varro saw their dark knuckles turn white as they gripped their javelins. Each had a dagger or sword at his hip, personal weapons of varied suitability for battle. He expected more than a few would bend or break in battle.

The limitations of speech rankled Varro. He must learn enough of their language to at least calm them and give them confidence. Lacking words, he looked as many in the eye as were willing to meet his and gave a slow, reassuring nod. A month of training was not enough, but Varro had seen men with less training step into the battle line. It had to be enough for today's task.

They hunkered against the sharp crest of the slope, now out of sight from the cavalry. Varro could hear the distant approach of the caravan, the clatter of wood and jingle of metal mixing with creaking wheels and snorting of horses. Still, the slingers had not signaled anything. The caravan scouts had either missed them or were never dispatched. This ensured the caravan was unprepared, but it seemed slipshod for a veteran force.

Now voices reached them, nothing that made sense to Varro or his men. The Carthaginians had their own speech, which from this distance sounded like the casual talk of men who expected no danger.

His own footmen instinctively huddled to him. Despite their drills and their bluster, they were frightened. It seemed strange that men who were presumably sent to him for criminal and violent acts would seem so frightened when a fight was in the offering. He held his finger to his lips in the universal sign for silence. They had practiced hand signals so he could command them in battle, and he held his palm out low to indicate they should hold in place.

He got on his belly and removed his helmet, then shimmied up the ridge to see the caravan's progress.

His heart flipped when he realized how close they were. Long lines of heavy, mule-drawn carts were flanked by men in beige tunics with shields on their arms and spears parked at their shoulders. They walked in time with the caravan wagons, just as Varro had traveled to Cirta. He swore one of them, a young man with a thin beard, looked right at him. He scuttled back with a curse, far enough down the rocks that he could replace his helmet.

Small stones stuck in his mail links, but some tumbled out to clack against the hard ground as he raised his hand in the gesture for them to follow. The mass of them picked up off the ground, keeping low and clutching their javelins, and joined him behind the edge.

Though no one understood, habit compelled him to speak in a whisper.

"This what you've trained for. Stay together and don't leave the group. We've got surprise with us. We'll hold down the guards until the horses arrive. You'll do fine. I believe in you."

"Thank you, sir."

Varro nearly fell flat to the ground. He twisted aside to see one of the men staring at him intently. Over the last month, he had spent more time training with the horsemen than the infantry and knew them better. This was a mistake, he realized. For he knew so little of the footmen that he did not realize one of them understood Latin.

"You understand me?"

The man's expression did not change, but he gave a short nod. "Some of it."

"Well stay close to me," he said, then turned back to the ridge. "You can help with translating if I need it."

The sounds of the caravan continued to stretch past their position. Varro crawled again to the ridge, once more removing his helmet and peering over.

This was the tail end, where the dust clouds blinded the guards and fouled their moods. This was the moment of the attack. The moment he had built toward for an entire month.

He looked over his shoulder and used hand signals to beckon them forward. Twenty-five lean warriors stood up to a crouch.

Varro lumbered to his feet, and drew his gladius. He pointed it toward the caravan, a spark of the morning sun running down its white edge to leap off its point at the enemy below.

"Down with Carthage!"

He staggered up the short rise to the edge and looked down in the swirling dust clouds as men trod along with cloths tied over their mouths. His battle cry was lost in the crunch and thud of their passing.

But the shouts of twenty-five Massylii warriors — no longer rabble in Varro's mind — broke over the ridge, drawing the attention of the trudging guards.

Varro raced down, screaming with sword raised. It felt strange to carry no shield. He had practiced with the smaller ones, but he could not find the technique. Going without would in fact be less dangerous to him than if he fumbled with something unfamiliar.

The slope was not too steep on this side, and his hobnailed sandals glided over the rocks and scree as he careened for the first guard he saw. The guard had foolishly set his spear on the wagon he walked beside and now reached for it as Varro closed.

With a quick thrust through the ribs, Varro claimed the first casualty of the assault. The guard had no armor other than a shield he forgot to bring to bear. He crashed against the wagon, slid with it as it rolled forward, and then vanished into the brown haze along the road.

The other Massylii warriors joined him, shrieking their war cries and swooping in with them. Whatever trepidations had stalked them now seemed to vanish. They were a whirling flash of snarls and eyes bright with battle madness. The caravan guards shouted and raised their shields, caught by surprise by the onslaught.

A horn blared nearby. Varro stepped over the body at his feet and reached the end of the wagon where he found a guard now with a lowered spear and shield to his front. Yellow dust swirled around him like ethereal armor.

Varro's shield arm felt too light, and an urge to punch and step swept through him. But without anything on his arm, he simply had to react faster to get inside the spear's range.

The guard understood it as well and slashed in an arc that prevented him from moving forward. Fortunately, one of his men joined him and used his shield to move in.

It was the distraction Varro needed. Splitting his attention between two advancing men, the guard chose incorrectly and struck for the shielded man to Varro's left. He leaped into that gap, slashing low beneath the guard's man shield. He felt the gladius fight the resistance of muscle and bone, but he tore through it. The guard screamed and toppled with the back of his knee cut open. When he collapsed, the Massylii warrior drove his javelin into his belly.

The initial wave of confusion had passed. With his immediate threats dispatched, Varro looked to the others. His rescuer continued to stab the guard on the grounds, javelin rising and falling. Beyond him, the caravan seemed to be grinding to a stop as his footmen swarmed two wagons.

"Free the goods!" But his shout was wasted since only Baku

and one other warrior knew what he meant. Earlier he had instructed the men to topple and destroy as much of the delivery as possible. While the Massylii were clambering onto the wagons, they used them as fighting platforms rather than hacking at the bindings and coverings that protected the deliveries.

"Get down from there," he shouted, gesturing them off the wagons. "You're making yourselves targets!"

His shouts got the attention of his men. But they smiled and shouted in victory to him. His translator was nowhere he could see in the moments he had available. All around the wagons, the guards had been killed in the fierce surprise attack. But there was the entire length of the caravan ahead of them and more than enough guards to see them all killed.

Pulling at the legs of the men atop the wagons, who all stood poised with their javelins ready to cast at the first targets, Varro managed to get a few to the ground with him.

"Form up on me!" He shouted the command and raised his balled fist to signal the order. Of his twenty-five men, only a dozen or so compiled. The rest seemed to have moved on to other targets emerging from the billowing dust.

Baku had to rescue them now. He had planned to deliver a shock attack, draw the counterattack to his mass of warriors, and then have Baku shatter the gathered guards from the rear.

But with his men scattering, the caravan guards would not concentrate as Varro had hoped.

The first line of caravan guards arrived out of the dust. He counted at least fifteen with possibly others filling the rear of their block. They were not ranked up, but close enough for mutual support. To Varro's surprise, they wore heavy chain shirts of thickly padded vests in addition to their spears and shields.

"Remember your training," he said. "Where is my translator? Baku?"

But the guards now closed in, their smiles grim and eyes flashing.

"Hold!" Varro shouted, raising his open palm to signal his men. The dozen of them pulled closer together, but Varro sensed it was more the action of scared men seeking comfort than the discipline of drilled troops.

He wanted the guards close enough to cast javelins, and then they would close with dagger and swords. Hopefully, Baku would arrive shortly thereafter and relieve them.

But when the first guards fully emerged from the rolling yellow dust, Varro heard more in the rear of his small band flee. The guards saw this as well and it galvanized them, raising their spears and letting go war cries to charge forward.

The remainder of the rear melted away from Varro and the men at his side looked between him and the enemy. Varro gritted his teeth and stood firm.

"You fucking cowards! We only have to hold for Baku. Get back here!"

But more men fled until Varro realized he would be the fool to remain.

Yet in the same moment, the guards passed beside the wagon in front of them piled high with barrels stacked under a tarp. Massylii appeared standing over these then kicked them free onto the oncoming rush of enemy.

The heavy barrels rolled onto the guards, and the Massylii on the wagon leaped down into their midst, shouting mad battle cries.

Varro added his own and looked to the three men still standing with him.

"Kill them all!" Then he charged in.

The barrels shattered and sprayed dark wine like a premonition of bloodshed. The charge had been totally disrupted. Barrels rolled men off their feet and set others crashing into the man in front of them. The Massylii fell upon them with daggers, their naked torsos shining with sweat as they danced among the confusion.

Reaching the front where blood and wine mixed together, Varro stabbed a man scrambling to regain his footing. He pressed in with the remnants of his men at his sides. They swept through shattered barrels, splashed through puddles of wine, and killed whoever they found.

Those who had not been caught in the trap offered some resistance, but the Massylii ambushers had every advantage and killed or routed them.

With a quick glance at the slain, he saw only one Massylii among the score of dead and dying.

He looked up to the wagon, where the man who had spoke Latin now stood with one naked leg on the rail and poised as if he had defeated Hannibal himself.

"Great work! There'll be a reward for you back at camp!"

The man leaned back and laughed.

Varro saw the rest of the caravan stretched out ahead. Baku's horsemen had engaged the front, rather than reach the back. Relief from him would never have come in time, Varro realized. But without engaging the heavy guard at the front of the caravan he would have been overrun. The cavalry swooped around and through the wagons, sewing chaos and death. Now he realized getting everyone on horseback had to be a priority. They steered their beasts with expertise, using their knees while keeping their hands free.

He saw Baku among them, circling what must be the caravan captain and his guards. His sword rose and fell as his mount leaped in and out of the combat.

It seemed the rear guard had been destroyed or else moved forward to deal with the greater threat of the horsemen. To his disbelief, it seemed they would capture the entire caravan when they had only intended to snip off the end of it.

The Massylii footmen had ended their attacks, panting and out of breath. While their savagery had saved Varro this time, he knew they would need to learn discipline to pace themselves. If he could gather together enough to charge the rear of the caravan guards, they would be broken in an instant.

He looked back up at the man on the wagon. Now he had selected a cask from among the wagon goods, cracked it open, and hoisted it overhead. His wiry muscles bulged as he steadied it over his opened mouth to let the wine drizzle out.

"Gather the others," he said. "We need to help Baku."

The Massylii tipped the cask back to stop the flow of wine but still held it overhead.

"You don't remember my name, Centurion Varro?"

The questions caught Varro off guard, and he felt a sting of embarrassment for not knowing.

"I will know it better after today."

The man laughed again. "You will."

Still holding the cask overhead, he twisted to reveal his naked back.

It was crossed with ten furrows of scabs and pink flesh.

"I am Merac," he said, turning around, keeping the cask overhead. "And you will regret lashing me!"

Merac hurled the cask down. Realizing the intention too late, Varro threw his hands up to block it. But the heavy weight of it stuck his head. The cask cracked open, soaking him in vinegary wine. His helmet spared him injury, but the force staggered him.

He stepped on a corpse and slipped to crash onto his back.

Merac's shouting in his native language echoed through Varro's head, and as he stared dazed at the blue morning sky dark shapes gathered at the edge of his vision.

14

A sword hacked down, slamming across Varro's chest. The mail shirt crunched under the impact, pressing into his muscles and driving the wind from his lungs. But rather than cut the links, the blade chipped and shattered. A shard of bronze landed under his eye. The Massylii footman hovering over him shouted in frustration.

Varro shook shard from his face, cursing and shoving off from the puddle of blood and wine under him. He butted his head into his attacker's causing him to stumble aside as Varro leaped up from prone. Even with the heavy weight of his chain shirt, the sheer terror of being downed in a fight fed him strength.

Five men surrounded him, as Merac stood laughing atop the wagon and pointing at the man holding his head. He stuttered out something in his native language. Varro thought he heard the word for sword, but wasn't sure. Instead, he faced the tightening ring of others converging on him.

His own sword had fallen from his grip and sat in a red puddle. A sandaled foot stepped on it, and Varro met the confident smirk of the man who stood on it.

"Glad I never wasted time learning your names." He drew his pugio, which was perfect for the close work ahead. Only he had attackers on every side and had to trust his mail to turn the blades of his foes while he evened his chances. It would only take one lucky stab to end him.

"You're nothing but shit," Merac said. "Is that the right word? Shit? Yes, I think that it is and that is you. Like shit, we wipe you off our feet with disgust."

Merac pointed with his own sword and the five men lunged at once.

"With a grunt Varro skipped aside from one blade, only to find another slip across his chest. The man at his back stabbed, not wise enough to cut his exposed hamstrings, and the point of his sword broke links in his mail, but he twisted aside to avoid a deeper cut.

His own pugio popped the throat of the man to his right. A clean, effortless thrust and the foe went down whistling from a bloody gap in his neck. He punched out with his left, his arm strengthened from years of hoisting a body-length shield. His forearm knocked aside the sword thrust at his face.

Then horses thundered across his rear, sending his enemies screaming and flailing away.

Varro did not hesitate.

The way up the cart lay open and Merac paused in astonishment. His finger extended at the men riding past him as if he had expected their cooperation. Varro took one stride over the puddles and bodies underfoot and landed on the cart runners. Then he grabbed the rail and hauled himself into the bed with Merac.

The half-naked Merac, wine stains glistening on his chest, brought his sword up in some strange attempt to parry a blow Varro had not even taken. The lack of discipline was so astounding that Varro nearly missed his chance.

"Too bad you speak my language," he said. Stepping into the

thrust, his pugio plunged under Merac's extended arm and into his ribs. "Yet you don't seem to understand me."

Hot blood sprayed over Varro's hand and he withdrew the blade with a thick popping noise. Merac's eyes were wild with hatred as he collapsed onto his knees, both hands clasped over the puncture wound in his side. His grunting voice wavered between a scream and a sob as he struggled against inevitable death.

"You are a fool. We are free men, the people will not—"

Varro cut his neck with a swift strike, ending his self-important death speech. He did not even spare a second look but stepped past Merac to the end of the cart. He heard him thump to the wagon bed.

Baku and his riders chased off the last of the traitors, who ran back up the slope or down the road. Every man went his own way, disorganized and chaotic to the last. Looking toward the front of the caravan, Varro's eyes brightened with amazement.

They had killed all the guards willing to fight and sent the rest into flight across the grassland. Many headed for the scrubby trees on the northern horizon.

He laughed, blinking blood and sweat out of his eyes. He had captured the entire caravan and all the supplies.

"Centurion Varro, we have won the day!" Baku was at eye level with him, sitting atop his horse.

"The cavalry are loyal?"

"Of course! They have horses, and therefore something to lose." Baku waved a dismissive hand at Merac's corpse. "I wondered about that lot."

"Thanks for mentioning it."

"I saved your life, Centurion. You are indebted to me."

"For now, I'll command you. But I won't forget." Varro turned back to Merac's corpse, strangely wondering if he had killed him. He lay face down in a spreading pool of his blood that shimmered with the morning sun. "We've got spoils to seize. I want everything of use loaded up into carts and the rest destroyed. The fort will send a column after us once word reaches them. How long do you estimate we have?"

Baku stroked the neck of his horse, staring out across the twirling dust of battle and men cheering their victory. His frizzy hair lifted in the wind as he stared.

"An hour before the column is sent out. After that, I'm not sure how soon before they reach this spot. If they march like Romans, then half an hour after."

"Garrison soldiers won't be in that fighting condition, even on the border." Varro rubbed his hands together. "We've got to act fast and get away with what we can."

One of the cavalrymen had dismounted and retrieved Varro's gladius from the mixture of gore and wine. He wicked the blade before offering it up to him.

Varro accepted the gladius with a nod, then without conscious thought, he used the Massylii phrase for thanks that he had heard so often in the camp. It came unbidden, startling both him and the cavalryman. Even though it must have been poorly pronounced, the cavalryman smiled brightly and gushed out a dozen more words that Varro did not understand.

Baku chuckled. "He's glad that you are learning to speak like a man, meaning for yourself and not through others. You know I've told you a hundred times, Centurion. You should learn the language of the men you lead rather than horsemanship. You ride now about as good as you will get in the time you have. But you'd be better off learning our speech. What will you do if King Masinissa recalls me?"

Varro smiled at the cavalryman, who remounted his horse with practiced ease. He knew he would never slip onto a horse's back like he did — and that was just a common man. How much better must the formally trained cavalry ride?

"You've got orders," Varro said. "I will learn how to call the men undisciplined fools later. Now let's hurry."

They culled as much food and wine as they could, which seemed to be a large portion of the delivery. Varro imagined a fort of fat and lazy Carthaginians. For he hadn't seen supplies like this even when marching with full legions across Macedonia. But beyond that were the spearheads and javelins his men needed. They found tools and materials for repairs. Lumber and nails for construction. And more valuable than gold was salt. It was only a few barrels, but Varro wanted it all.

They also captured the merchant's strong boxes, but lacked any keys. These could be broken open in camp, but Varro knew he was taking it more to deny the Carthaginians than as spoils for the men. They were more focused on barter than using money, and they seemed to express wealth in the quality of their horses rather than sacks of coins.

At last, they had stocked wagons and regrouped the small horses to draw the carts. The rest they destroyed, hacking up what could not burn or be spilled into the ground.

"If this all gets back to camp you will be a great hero," Baku said. "We can live many long months with this stock."

Varro had lost half of his men, the majority from the footmen who had followed him into battle. Slain horses were replaced from the caravan. The rest they let go, as they would not have the ability to feed extra horses. There was only enough feed with the caravan for their own needs. Rather than kill them, they sent them packing. While Varro thought it a poor decision, returning valuable horses to the enemy, the Massylii could not kill riderless horses. They had too much respect for them.

So their heavily laden caravan trundled off the road along the rocky and uneven ground. Varro guessed they would have to transport the goods up into the hills themselves, and later barter off the wagons to locals. The camp was too secluded to reach by cart and would not have room for them in any case.

But his idle worries were swept aside by late morning as a lookout at the rear of their column shouted a warning.

"They were faster than expected," Baku said. Both he and Varro rode in the front, enjoying the breezy morning that swished the grass that hid rocks and ruts that invariably found his wagon wheels.

He twisted on his horse to see a column of heavy dust twirling into the air. It was thick like a black tail of an angry lion snapping in the wind.

"That's too much dust for a marching column," Varro said.

Baku's agreement came as a deep growl.

And Varro's heart sank.

"It's a mounted force. You didn't say they had cavalry in the fort."

Baku shrugged. "I thought you would know that. How else can they patrol the border roads?"

Looking back over three heavily laden wagons, Varro grimaced.

"How far to the Numidian border?"

Baku now squinted into the distance, cocked his head, then asked one of the other horsemen a question in their native language. His answer sounded hesitant.

"We can make it," Baku said with a firm nod.

"He didn't sound confident. Are you sure?"

"Then learn to ask on your own if you want to know. I said we can make it."

Varro looked back again. The black column of dust moved with the speed of Mercury. It now seemed twice as large.

Clearing his throat, Baku leaned closer. "I didn't say we can make it at this pace, Centurion."

Varro raised his fist and shouted for attention. The horsemen had spread out around the wagons in a rough wedge, with their own acting as drivers for the pack animals. Their covered heads swiveled from looking back at their pursuers to him.

"Ride for the border at full speed!"

Baku translated his order and the men shouted in answer.

The horsemen raced past Varro, abandoning the carts.

"Apollo's Teeth! What the fuck are they doing?"

Even Baku seemed about to urge his horse on. He pulled up with a frown.

"We're riding at full speed for the border."

"Get them back here! We need to defend the wagons."

Baku glanced back at the men urging the horses drawing the wagons and sucked his breath.

"Do you want me to stay with you, Centurion?"

The question drew his ire, but then he realized there was wisdom in it. The Carthaginians would ride for the wagons first, looking to recapture their stolen goods. It was a chance for the main force to escape while Varro and the three unlucky wagon drivers had to fend for themselves.

Varro shook his head. "You make sure there is discipline in that camp. When I get back with these carts, me and drivers are going to have first choices of anything good."

Baku gave a wry smile. "I guess you were not wrong to learn riding after all. Good luck! Show me how good a Capax Servus Centurion is."

He had not heard that name in months and had nearly forgotten it was his entire cause for being here. It was also the cause of Falco and Curio being lost. He suspected he might soon learn where they had vanished to. For if the fort cavalry reached him, he would no doubt be forced into a fight he could not win while outnumbered three to one. Perhaps he would meet his friends in the Elysian Fields.

Baku snapped this rope reins and raced ahead with the others.

The drivers let out a collective wail, but Varro turned his horse to face them. Sizing up the distance and the speed of their pursuers, he knew no matter what direction they traveled they would be overtaken as long as they hauled those wagons.

"We're just buying time for the others," he said. "We'll lead them on a short chase, cut the wagons, then ride for the border."

The carts had now caught up to him and the three men looked to him as if they had all been stabbed in the back. He also realized they couldn't understand him, and Baku had been right. He needed to learn the language and swore he would after this day. For now, he circled his horse around and waved the men on to follow.

They caught as much speed as the weight of the wagons and the terrain allowed. Varro felt as if they fled in slow motion, like men trying to run through an incoming tide. The horses worked hard, and he belatedly realized his plan would exhaust the animals and leave them stranded for their pursuers.

He swore at the brilliant blue of the sky above. He was learning alright, but too late.

Still, the men drove their horses and the carts shook and rattled over the uneven ground as they headed for the road they had followed in. It would lead back to the border, though there was no border fort to oversee it as the Carthaginians had. He wondered how much safety crossing it would offer.

Now he heard the distant echoes of the shouting pursuers. His horse, fortunately, knew better than he did and needed little guidance to avoid ruts and stones. But Varro held the rope reins so tight his hands ached. The road lay ahead across a stretch of grassland. Trees waved behind it, solitary and lonely stands and purple mountains were a ragged stripe far behind the trees.

When the carts lurched onto the flat, and dusty road, Varro could feel their speed increase.

One of his men shouted, and looking back Varro saw a dozen

horsemen now close enough to mark their faces under their tight-fitting bronze helmets. They had wicker shields on one arm and long cavalry swords flapping at their sides.

"Alright, let's cut the wagons here."

Being without the burden, Varro had ridden ahead of the drivers. He pulled his horse up short, then stroked its neck. Sweat slipped under his palm and he felt its sides heaving against his legs. Holding up his hands, he stopped the three carts following him. Their horses fared far worse and seemed completely spent.

"Cut the wagons," he said, making a chopping motion at them. Then he gestured for them to mount their horses and pointed west. "Ride for the camp. Ride until the horses die."

The drivers understood and slipped off their carts to unhitch the wagons. They might have initially been unwilling to give up so many spoils, but they counted their lives better than a wagon full of provisions.

Behind them, the Carthaginians had also gained the road. Their horses would be tired as well, but not as badly as Varro's. It seemed the entire column had come after them, and let Baku and the others slip away. He wished he had been making a sacrifice for men more worthy of it. Yet they had just saved him from betrayal.

After each driver unhitched his horse, he remounted and urged it ahead. Varro waited patiently until the last man freed his mount, then joined him in escaping toward the west.

He did not know the limits of a horse and how to get the best of it. This one had been his since he first began training. Baku had told him its name, but he forgot it now. He wished he remembered, just to be able to whisper encouragement to it. The Massylii seemed to be able to speak to their horses and encourage them to greater speeds.

"Come on, boy. Run a little further then you can rest."

The open road was easier footing but the exhaustion of their mounts canceled that advantage. The thundering of their pursuers broke over his shoulders and he dared not look behind. He heard their laughter as they closed.

Varro realized he was not going to make it, and neither were the drivers. They had demonstrated great loyalty in remaining with the wagons. In his heart, he knew they were likely motivated more by greed than better intentions. But it did remain that they had sacrificed for the benefit of the whole.

He was their leader, and he knew what must be done.

"Ease up, boy." Varro ceased urging his horse, then pulled gently on the rope reins to slow the pace. "Your run is over. Soon, you'll rest and drink. I'm sorry you got stuck with me for a rider."

The horse stumbled to a halt, while the three riders continued on ahead. One of them glanced around, then slowed his horse's gallop. He called out, and the other two slowed. Now all three slowed to a trot as they stared questioningly at Varro.

He waved them on. All three stared at him for long moments, then urged their mounts forward again.

He turned his horse now to face the Carthaginians. The majority of the riders swarmed around wagons. Four more rode toward Varro. When they saw he had stopped, they also slowed their tired mounts. Their scowls and dust-caked faces were clear across the distance.

"Well, let's really find out how good a Capax Servus Centurion is." Varro drew his gladius, the wrong weapon for horseback fighting, and waited.

15

Lars roared with anger and fury, shoving away the two tribesmen who tried to steady him. Even after wasting away for a month while his leg healed, he was still stronger than anyone in the tribe. The two flew aside, staggering to catch themselves against the tent poles.

Yet the moment their support left him, Lars wavered and collapsed back onto his stool. Sweat rolled down his forehead, stinging his eyes. He patted his bald head, feeling the cratered scar there and reminding himself that he had overcome worse wounds.

"Djebel, you must go slowly. Build the strength of your legs with patience."

Bezza, the healer who had ruined his leg with his so-called medical attention, leaned against the tent pole where he had stopped his fall. His young assistant helped him. Bezza's white hair hung in front of his watery eyes, and he swiped it away with a gnarled hand.

"I will walk," Lars said. "I have rested too long. I need more meat."

Bezza sighed and waved away Lar's complaints.

"You have eaten all the meat there is. Master Ajan wants you to fully recover. It is his command. But if you rush, your leg will become injured again."

"I don't care."

Lars ground his teeth together, staring past Bezza and his assistant to the brilliance outside. As was the way of the Massylii tribes, at least until the new King came to power, they wandered wide swathes of countryside. Lars had not been far from Russicada since leaving the tribe. He did not know exactly where they were now. But he had to get back to Russicada and Cirta as soon as he could.

Centurion Varro was there, waiting to face revenge for Bellus's death.

Dreams of ripping Centurion Varro into bloody bits had sustained him. These were not abstract thoughts for Lars. His mind no longer worked that way. These were true visions of what he planned.

He would entertain feverish dreams as he lay on his bed recovering, encouraging his mind to conceive every detail of Varro's death. In each dream, he relished pulling apart his face. His thick fingers sank into those staring-mad eyes of Centurion Varro, and he crushed them into jelly. The bloody remnants of these leaked down his cheeks as he screamed. Lars then pulled his jaws apart, snapping bone and tearing flesh so that his chin hung like a gory helmet strap. Then he tore both ears off the way a man might rip a patch from his tunic and finally chewed his nose from the bones of his face.

Hours and hours from days and weeks were passed in vividly envisioned dismemberments of Centurion Varro. By now, Lars had shredded his flesh so many times that the actual moment might disappoint him.

But that day would come. If he had to sail back to Rome to find that scum, he would. And he would break every bone, twist every joint, and pull every piece of him apart. Then he would carve out his heart and eat it. That was the meat he desired above all, the only kind that could end his hunger.

"Djebel? Are you alright?"

His eyes wandered back to Bezza and his assistant. Both stared at him with furrowed brows and both stepped back when his eyes met theirs.

"You took my leg. Now make me walk again."

"I saved your life!" Bezza's expression shifted to insult. "You would not be able to dream of killing this Roman were it not for me. Oh, yes, Djebel. I know what you were just thinking. It is the only time both of your eyes focus. You lust for revenge. In time! Master Ajan will grant your wish if he can."

"He cannot stop me."

Bezza shook his head in frustration and mumbled curses.

"Enough for today. You have exerted yourself. I will send your medicine. And yes, do not remind me. I will get you meat."

He remained seated, watching the old healer and his boy hurry from his presence. They did not like him, he knew. No one liked him, in truth, except for his dear brother Bellus. Now there would never be anyone to like him again. He put one hand over his bad eye, feeling it turn of its own accord, another scar from a head wound that should have killed him.

He pulled back his tunic to look at the horrible seam of burn scars where Varro had slashed him and Bezza had healed him. Though the flesh still hurt, he shifted his hand from his eye to his inner thigh. That cut should have killed him. Varro thought it had. But he had not died, because he could not die from any enemy's weapon. Nor would he allow himself to be weakened by this injury.

His strength had returned after losing so much blood. But the muscles of his leg needed to rebuild strength and the skin there still burned with the same fury as the night Bezza had cauterized it. The pain was good. It would drive him to find Varro.

With no responsibilities other than to rest and recover, Lars lay back down on his bed. The wood frame creaked. It was a small thing, barely enough to contain him, and meant to be broken down for travel. He expected one day it would collapse beneath him.

After an hour during which he bobbed through sleep and wakefulness, he heard a rustling at the tent flap. His vision remained fuzzy and dim, even as golden light spilled inside with the person who entered. It was not the weak, sliding footstep of Bezza or the light step of his assistant. Neither was it Ajan's heavy stomp. Whoever approached came upon him with a hesitant and fearful gait.

He raised his head and found two men inside his tent, one who he did not recognize remained at the tent flap. The other had entered halfway and paused when Lars lifted his head. He wore a light blue tunic and his head cover framed a rugged face of high cheekbones and a hooked nose. His eyes widened.

"Djebel, I am glad you are awake."

"I am."

The man smiled now, nodding to the lookout by the flap. Lars was not worried if they intended violence. He could kill both while lying down if necessary.

"Do you recognize me?" The man grabbed the same stool the healer used when assessing Lars's leg, and drew it to the side of his bed. He leaned forward to display his face. The smile was crooked and insincere, like every smile Lars had ever seen.

"No."

The man sighed and put his hand to his chest as if hurt. "I am Tanan! But I was a boy when you were last among us. Now I am a man. Has my face changed so much?"

"Yes."

Tanan's smile dropped at the single-word answer, seeming to leave him searching for something to follow it.

"Ah, well, then you do remember me. At least my name. And if you do not, no matter my friend. Yes, you shall name me a friend before long. For you and I, Djebel, have much to discuss. But it must be a private and quick discussion. Chief Ajan does not leave your tent unguarded for long.

"Why? I am in no danger."

"That is what you believe," Tanan said, his smile returning. "And there is truth to it. Ajan does not want you harmed, but healed. So do we all. But to what purpose? Ajan has claimed your life boon. Your strength is legendary, Djebel, as is your proof against weapons."

"Look at me," Lars said, lying still on his bed. "I'm not dead. But I'm not living."

"Ah, now that is true. But it is a temporary situation, if you listen to me that is. If you are to swear yourself to Ajan and serve him, then you will never live as you wish."

Lars stared harder at this Tanan. He tried to recall him, but memories were slippery since his head injury. It seemed he might have been a nephew to the former chief, the one before Ajan who had saved Lar's life. Tanan had a similar nose and mannerisms.

Though Lars appeared to all as an idiot, he knew he was not. It enraged him when others considered him as such, and if this Tanan thought he could play him for a fool, then he would practice the dismemberment of Varro on him.

"I will serve Ajan. He saved my life. I could not have revenge if I died."

"I am so sorry about your brother," Tanan said, shaking his head. "It is right to want revenge for him. He was a good partner to our people, keeping us rich with trade and slaves."

"I helped, too."

"Of course, Djebel. You are the great strength of the tribe.

When you stand again, you will ride as you once did and your mighty sword will reap the heads of those who oppose us. And we will once more become the greatest tribe of all. But not under Ajan's leadership."

"You don't like him?"

"I like him very much," Tanan said. His dark eyes glittered as he leaned closer, dropping his voice. "But I don't trust him. He is a supporter of King Masinissa. Our king, who was once a great hero, now wants to settle us, teach us how to grow crops and make us farmers. He wants us to become Carthaginians, or worse, Romans! No offense to you, Djebel, of course."

"I hate Rome."

"As do we all." Tanan spread his hands as if to encompass the entire tribe. "But Ajan has agreements with the King, and they have negotiated peace among the tribes. Masinissa has divided up our lands, limiting where we may roam. And Ajan has agreed to this."

"I do not care about your land. I will kill Centurion Varro. That is what I will do. Land is your problem."

Tanan's smile widened and he leaned forward to place his hand on Lar's forearm. It was cold and damp.

"You will never kill Centurion Varro, Djebel. That is your dream but not Ajan's. Besides, the King is allied to Rome, and so those allied to the king are likewise aligned. How would it be if you, a sworn servant of Ajan, killed a Roman right in the shadow of Masinissa's palace? No, it will never be allowed."

"I don't care." Lars shoved the hand from his arm. "I will find him and kill him."

"Djebel, you are strong and you are blessed by all the gods to suffer no man's weapon. But there are limits to what you achieve alone. Right now, you have no allies. Has Ajan come to you with news of Centurion Varro?"

Lars shifted his head to stare at Tanan. He did not answer but felt a deep rage building in himself. Yet somehow it could not fill his arms with power. He wanted to throttle this fool and end his tiresome speech.

"I thought not." Now Tanan leaned back and nodded again to the man at the tent flap, waving him over.

He had been peering out of the seam, leaving a bright stripe of light on his gaunt face. But now he scurried to join Tanan's side. He knelt on the ground beside him, lacking any place to sit. Lars thought of a trained dog.

"This is Djebel. He would like to hear your story."

"Master Djebel, it is an honor to meet you. A Roman who can speak for himself!"

Lars's vision focused and he curled his lip. The man shuffled back, again like a dog fearing the stick.

"Just tell him the facts," Tanan said. He put his hand on the man's back to steady him.

"Of course, well, I know where Centurion Varro is. I served with him until just a week ago. Now I've found a new home here, thanks to Tanan." He offered an ingratiating smile. But Lars growled and the man immediately resumed, stuttering his apology. "King Masinissa has given him fifty men to lead against Carthage and against our own people. Can you believe it? Setting a Roman on your own? Many of us would not serve. He was a cruel bastard, and a fool as well. He knew nothing of us, and cared nothing for us. He cannot even ride a horse properly. We were to raid a caravan over the Carthage border. But most of us planned to leave him before then. So we did, just when the raid began. We left him to die."

Lars let out a roar that made both his visitors jump. Yet he could not find the strength to lurch from his bed and grab the scrawny fool who had stolen his revenge.

"Only I may kill him! I'll tear you to bits!"

Tanan stood now, hushing him with palms out.

"Djebel, please! We have not told you all yet. If we are discovered now, you will never have the Centurion. He is still alive. Do not fear. Now settle down."

The scrawny man had paled at Lars's outburst and hid behind Tanan as if anyone could protect him if Lars chose to kill him.

"Varro defeated the caravan guard with some men who would betray their own for scraps of praise," he said. "I saw him leading three wagons back to camp. So he must be there now."

Lars fell back onto his bed, his mind racing with thoughts of mutilating Varro. He was so close now, he could taste the blood in his mouth. Then he realized he had bit his own tongue in his rage.

"Djebel, Ajan knows this and has known for a week. But you've not been told, because Ajan does not want you distracted and does not want to anger the King. But I have no such cares, and neither does most of the tribe. We do not see the benefits Ajan and his brothers see. It is time to change leadership. Before you join with Ajan, you have a chance to gain your life back. If you swear loyalty to him, even if you were to kill him no one would allow you into the tribe as such a dishonorable man. But before you formally swear your service is another matter."

Tanan paused and returned to his stool. He folded his arms and whispered again.

"I see you are enraged. Yet don't you wonder why your strength fails? I see how you struggle, like a man in chains only your hands are unbound."

"I am strong." Yet Lars flexed his fists to find his grip weak and trembling.

"Not as strong at the great Djebel should be." Tanan slipped his hand into his tunic as he spoke, then withdrew a small gourd. "That is because Bezza feeds you a brew to calm you. It weakens you and clouds your mind. You will go willingly to Ajan and he will keep feeding you this so-called medicine. You will never be as strong as you should. Just strong enough that Ajan can use you to intimidate those who oppose him. And there are more every day."

"What are you holding?" Lars had a hundred different questions, but they crashed around his head. A feeling of dread overcame him, but he could not express why. Was that an effect of Bezza's poison?

Tanan held out the gourd.

"This will dispel the poison in your blood. It will make you clear again, and give you the strength to defy Ajan."

"Give it to me."

Yet Tanan withdrew his hand, stuffing the gourd back into his tunic.

"Do we have an agreement, Djebel? You help me replace Ajan as chief, and I will give you the highest place of honor in the tribe."

"I want to kill Centurion Varro."

"It seems our purposes are again joined. For as I have learned, this Varro has captured a large bit of wealth from the Carthaginians, and the land where he makes his camp is where our allies live. So I will bring you to him, and together we will profit. You get the centurion, and I bring wealth to the tribe and join allies to us. It is important to the tribe that I do this soon after claiming leadership. With you to fight by my side, there can only be victory."

"I will serve you. I have not sworn to Ajan yet. Give me that gourd."

"Be warned," Tanan said. "Once you drink from it, you will soon be flooded with mad rage. It will fight with Bezza's poison and so you will be out of control. Drink it just before you go to Ajan. Then use your strength to reclaim your life."

"I want to eat meat every day."

"All the meat of the plains shall be yours." Tanan extended the gourd and Lars accepted.

They helped him stand and steadied him. Tanan offered him

his own dagger, but he needed none. Lars tottered to the door, his leg trembling and weak. But he pulled the stopper from the gourd and threw it aside.

Outside, a dozen men stood guard and looked side-eyed at him.

"Halfway to Ajan's tent, drink the potion." Tanan gave him a gentle shove forward. "Restore us to glory, Djebel."

Every step was easier than the last. When he finished with Ajan he would tear Bezza to shreds. As the chief's tent filled his view, he saw a man standing outside it. A guard. Lars's eyes now focused, and he quaffed the liquid from the gourd. It was bitter and burned like fire running down his throat.

But by the time he reached the guard, his vision had fogged to red mist. His mind and heart raced as if he were running for his life and sweat poured down his face.

Yet he was full of strength. The guard looked up to him and his expression showed fear in the moment Lars grabbed him by the neck. He jammed the guard's head under his arm and then snapped the neck.

Bursting into Ajan's tent, he found him with his wife and two slaves.

Later he would only have the faintest memories of what happened to the wife and slaves. But for Ajan, he recalled it vividly. He did to him as he would do to Varro.

He crushed his eyes to jelly and pulled both arms from their sockets so they hung limp at his sides. Then he broke each finger, biting them off when they would not twist free. Ajan screamed, but no one came to his aid. Outside, Lars remembered the sounds of fighting.

When all was done, a thing that had been Ajan lay at his feet. It had bloody holes for eyes, ears, and a nose. The jaw had been shattered and ripped open and the hair of his head torn back to reveal his skull.

Ajan's body was twisted as no human shape should ever be. One hand was a bloody stump. Both legs bent at different angles, like a ghoulish geometric pattern.

Lars heaved over this ruin. The wife and slaves were dead too, twisted necks all. But he had no time or desire to tear them to bits. Instead, he would find Bezza and take his time in shredding the old man. His great rage had caused him to go too fast with Ajan, spoiling his enjoyment.

So he stalked out of the tent, trailing blood and scraps of skin, in search of Bezza and dreaming of his plans for Centurion Varro.

16

Varro waited atop his panting horse, watching the four Carthaginian riders for signs of their plan. They spread out, two to each side. Armed with a gladius, he knew he'd have no chance against even one of them with their longer cavalry swords. Four were impossible for one unskilled rider. But he was buying time for the three wagon drivers to escape. He did not intend to fight to the end or to fight at all.

The four men held their swords out to the side as if each would ride past and slice off one of his limbs. He did not doubt they could do it. Their faces were hard and glowering. They wore light tunics overlaid with leather vests for protection. Bronze greaves shined on their legs. They were well-equipped soldiers and not at all the fat and lazy border guards he expected. In fact, as they closed, he realized he had only thought of them that way to ease his own fears of rousing them to action. These were trained and drilled men, outmatching Varro's rabble.

They shouted in what must be the Carthaginian language. Varro had known one Carthaginian in his entire life, the slave Yasha who cared for him when he was a child. But she never taught him the language or ever had cause to speak it. The cavalrymen's words did not sound like Massylii speech. Yet clearly they wanted him to surrender.

Varro raised his gladius.

"You ask me to surrender? A Roman soldier never retreats unless ordered, and only then with reluctance. I'm afraid you'll have to fight me."

The four men sat back on their mounts, clearly surprised to be addressed in the distinctive sounds of Latin. But they did not understand and simply glanced to each other as if confirming their plans. Their pace had not slowed either. One man pulled ahead of the others. He had light brown hair that blended into the same colored dust that coated him from his hard chase over the plains.

He extended his hand to Varro's sword, clearly indicating he should drop it.

Varro looked behind, and his drivers must have ridden off the road for he glimpsed nothing but the tan strip of it winding into the rolling grasses. A short rise masked a bend where they could have also vanished.

With a sigh, he understood he had bought enough time for his men. There was nothing more for him to do now other than endure the humiliation and likely torture that awaited him at the fort. If the fort commander was wise, he would get what information he could from Varro before sending him back to Rome. Carthage was in no condition to use this as a pretext for renewed war. Their defeat had been so complete ten years ago that they were still reeling from it.

But then Varro could not depend on the fort commander being wise.

"Very well," he said with forced confidence. "You've captured me. I surrender my sword."

It was one thing to accept surrender, but quite another to

simply drop his sword into the road as they clearly wanted. That would be too humiliating and unbefitting of his rank. Instead, he turned it around to extend the grip to his captors. The leader frowned and shook his head, but said nothing. The other three studied him with bemused expressions, looking at his Roman helmet and searching down to the small horse he sat. It must have made for a foolish look.

Three of the four halted their winded mounts while the leader drew close enough to Varro to take his sword. He wore a tired and chiding expression, like a father who had warned his son one too many times of the consequences of disobedience. His fingers brushed the grip and he inhaled to speak.

Then three Massylii warriors burst over the small crest to the side of the road. The sound of their pounding hooves and their high-pitched shouts shattered the moment.

Varro snatched his gladius back, spun it easily in his palm, and then rammed it into the cheek of his bewildered captor. He fell back, screaming as he covered his face.

With the same motion, Varro cut down to drive the sword into the neck of the Carthaginian's mount.

The road exploded into chaos.

The Carthaginian horse screamed and bolted, and frightened Varro's horse at the same time. He could not control the animal as it turned to flee into the grassy plain.

But the Massylii had converged on the others, swooping in with javelin and sword, guiding their mounts with their knees. In moments, the three other Carthaginians had been driven off their mounts. They collapsed to the road screaming and thrashing against wounds or dead before they fell.

Varro tried everything to calm his horse, but it charged the wrong way no matter how he tried to guide it. He thrust his bloodied gladius into its sheath and grabbed the reins with both hands.

"Curse this animal!" He shouted back toward the road. "Someone help me!"

His three men rode hard for him as his horse raced for the trees ahead. The wild gallop of his frightened mount rocked his joints, sending bolts of pain through his knees and hips as he held on for his life. But his men overtook him, shouting Massylii words that sounded familiar but still unintelligible to him.

As they galloped in unison, one of the men grabbed the reins from Varro.

Then to his shock, Varro found the man shift horses onto his. He shoved back to make space, and almost instantly the frightened beast seemed to come to its senses. The other horse, unfortunately, dropped out of the tight pack.

Behind them, the Carthaginians at the wagons had remounted their horses after having dismounted to inspect their goods. They had behaved as if considering Varro's capture a foregone conclusion. It was a lucky break, as now their scramble cost time that left them far behind.

Varro let his rider guide the horse back toward the road. But they cut a long loop to lose their pursuers. He clamped his legs down on the horse's flanks and hugged the torso of the man who had essentially saved him. The Massylii whooped and laughed, and drove their horses relentlessly. They understood their mounts like no others in the world, encouraging them to fly over the ground well past their willingness to do so.

The Carthaginians did not have this same rapport. Their mounts had slowed and several had dropped out. By the time they had reached the road again, the last of the fort cavalry surrendered the chase. As much as Varro was certain their riders thirsted for blood, their mounts had reached their limits.

So had Varro's as well, for the moment the Massylii decided they had shaken pursuit they stopped their horses. They dismounted to the side of the road, celebrating their victory. They looked eagerly to Varro for his approval, and he could not contain his gratefulness.

"You men save my life, twice in one day." He clasped arms with each man, a foreign gesture to them but one they understood. "You three are the best of my men, and I'll find a way to reward it. I promise you."

They let the horses rest and graze, all while keeping a watch down the road. Though the rises obscured the view, still no dust rose above them. Varro was shocked to see his abandoned horse come trotting around a bend to rejoin them, but the others did not seem surprised. He greeted it with some joy since he had been practicing with it for over a month with it. So once the horses had time enough to recover, they walked them the remaining distance to the border. From there, they traveled into the foothills and up into their mountain camp.

Varro was glad to see it but dismayed no one challenged him on the road up. The barriers they had constructed had all been set aside and not replaced. It was a mixed feeling, as he desperately wanted to throw himself onto his sleeping roll but also wanted the camp defenses up at all times.

Their return was met with cheers. Varro did not know what to expect, given the extent of their losses. No one seemed to care that the wagons had been lost. The men swarmed them and began to chant something in their own language. The three who had remained with Varro were singled out for praise by their companions. Varro himself remained to the side of the celebration, glad to at last be in the shadowy, rocky place he called home.

Baku had joined Varro after celebrating with the survivors. "They act as if they have defeated all of Carthage."

"I am certain at least one Carthaginian was killed," Varro said, folding his arms as he watched the excited group share their war stories. They had clustered in the parade ground, reminding Varro of the larger group that had gathered there over a month ago seeking his death.

"Many of them carried back spoils," Baku said. "To men who own so little, it is as if they are as rich as kings now."

"No one cares about the wagons." It was not a question, and Varro felt his face warm at knowing he had ultimately failed to do anything other than irritate the Carthaginians.

"You did not say the wagons were important." Baku shoved his finger beneath his head cover and scratched along his hairline. "The enemy are dead, and they are not. Plus they have stolen weapons or other trinkets taken from the battlefield. So they have riches as well. They were tested today and succeeded. Do not downplay their victory."

"I surely won't. But look at how many remain. Any more such victories and we are done for."

"We won't have a revolt again," Baku said, folding his arms to match Varro. "You killed Menac and scattered his followers."

"You should have warned me about him. You let me go off with a group of traitors to what might have been my death. If you hadn't come to my rescue, I'd believe you were in league with them."

Baku's face wrinkled in disgust. "You don't think I have more honor than that? I had one eye on the objective and one eye on you at all times."

"It is your duty as my second in command to advise me of all threats, especially internal ones." Varro narrowed his eyes at Baku. "I'm grateful for what you did, but that does not mean I will go easy on you."

Baku's frown rose to delight. "Of course not, Centurion Varro. I would have it no other way. This is your operation to fail. But since you demand my complete honesty, let me advise you that there would have been no revolt if you did not make martyrs by flogging two men. Merac was just a street thug until you made him the voice of an aggrieved mob. Darri was a smooth liar, too, and had many friends in camp. And you flogged him to death. Let this be a lesson, Centurion. Roman ways are good for Romans, but not for all. Especially when there is but one Roman among fifty others."

The heat on Varro's face increased, but he did not deny anything Baku said. Instead, he nodded toward the celebrating group.

"Twenty-five men remain?"

"Twenty-three," Baku corrected. "Two rode off with the traitors. That surprised me. But no serious wounds and no casualties but for the deserters."

"If I find any of them, I will flog them to death."

Baku gave a deep nod. "Only if the others hand them over while they are still alive. They will have their own justice for deserters."

"What can we do with half our numbers?" Varro unfolded his arms and at last removed his helmet, grateful for the cool mountain air to run through his hair.

"We always had half our numbers," Baku said. "Those who fled were a drain on resources and nothing more. We can do all that we have planned."

Varro bit his lip and scanned the remaining men.

"We're a fully mounted force now."

"With the exception of the force commander." Baku grinned. "But you are much better than when you started. You will need a different weapon to fight from horseback."

"And you will teach me the language."

"I will."

They stood in companionable silence as they observed men showing off what they had swiped from the fallen. Others reenacted their battles for their fellows, who shook their heads in denial of what must have been exaggerated tales. Someone started a cooking fire and it seemed that the men had decided to eat together and turn the night into some sort of feast. With their rations and meager trade with locals, Varro wondered what they would feast on.

"I will be in my tent," Varro said. "We will still need guards detailed for tonight. They can celebrate, but not at the expense of discipline. If they complain, remind them discipline is what brought them victory today."

Baku grabbed Varro's shoulder as he turned aside.

"Celebrate with them, Centurion. You waste a chance to bond with these men."

"I cannot speak to them," Varro said with a shrug. "What kind of bonding will I make?"

Clucking his tongue, Baku turned Varro toward the group.

"You're a veteran soldier. You might not feel you dared much today, but these men did. Just eating with them and sharing the relief that you are alive will be enough to bring you closer."

"It's not what officers do."

"This is not Rome," Baku said. "You are not here to turn us into Romans. You are here to learn new things. Learn the way of the Massylii. Do not forget that we fought alongside your greatest general to bring down his greatest foe. There is something for you to learn here, and it can start tonight with a shared meal and shared cup."

Varro did join the celebration, and at first the men deferred to his rank. But as the night fell, he forgot about sentries and found that despite having no common words with his men, he had a common language. It was the language of the soldier, the shared dangers and shared pains of a life lived at the edge of death. By the time he did return to his tent that night, he and his men had finally communicated with each other without a translator.

In the days that followed, Varro found leading them much easier. They were more willing to drill and carry out assigned duties. They began to show pride in their camp. The barriers were reset on the approaches. He did not need to harangue Baku to set a watch schedule. Things were changing.

But there were still not enough men in the force. They could not absorb casualties with so few numbers, limiting what they could achieve. One wrong choice of battle and they would be wiped out. So Varro thought to write back to King Masinissa but hesitated to report his loss. Baku suggested that he could raise men from the local tribes.

"There a plenty of young men looking for adventure," he said. "I will bring them and their horses to our camp."

Three weeks after the first raid on Carthage marked his second month living in a mountain camp. He sat at his desk on one early evening with a small cup of wine as a weekly luxury he granted himself. Out of his lockbox, he drew from his dwindling supply of vellum and ink. He still had space to write beneath his last entry of several days before. Smoothing the vellum and then dipping his bronze stylus into the carbon ink pot, he began to scratch his thoughts out beside the warm glow of his desk lamp.

A mere two months, but it seems a year since I first left civilization to become a mountain brigand. What else am I to call myself? I try to bring as much of my military training to this task as I can. The men accept most of it, but in the end, we are just disciplined brigands. Baku reminded me a few weeks ago that I am not here to make them Romans. Why did I ever think I could? It is for me to learn to think like them. Consul Flamininus had told me as much, yet I chose to act otherwise. Having accepted my actual mission, I believe I am in a better place to succeed here. Whatever I am to learn must be for a purpose I cannot see yet. But whatever it may be, I intend to excel in it and all else that I do.

I am learning the language and horseback riding and doing surprisingly well at both. I can now make basic orders and requests. As for riding, Roman cavalrymen would mock me, for the Massylii don't even use saddles. But I am growing in closeness to my horse, whom I have renamed Thunder. Not an original name, but I've no creativity for such things. Falco would be better at it.

Where are they? How strange is fate? For they missed my ship by mere minutes and now are at least two months behind me. I think of them constantly, and sometimes I hear either Falco or Curio speaking nearby. But it is merely the wind that blows constantly through the gaps in the rock walls surrounding the camp. Is it truly their speech, carried to me by the gods so that I do not lose hope for their survival? That is an arrogant thought. The gods do not care for what worries me. By now I would be satisfied simply to know they are dead. Not knowing anything at all is far worse.

The page runs out before me. Baku has recruited an astounding 15 men along with their horses from local tribes. They seem excited for battle, and more so after speaking to my so-called veterans. One skirmish makes a veteran! This place is so different. I will plan a new raid while their spirits are high.

And I will watch the horizon for Falco and Curio. They cannot be dead. They must not be. But if not, where are they?

17

Varro stood over the circle of his men scratching landmarks into the gritty dust of the floor in his tent. Baku squatted with the two scouts and his three picked men, who were quasi-officers in this loose organization of Varro's. Sticks scratched out landmarks and etched new ones in their place. He tried to follow the conversation, but he found it hard to understand when the words were spoken over each other and not clearly to him. He understood more of their language now but was nowhere near proficiency.

"They are certain it is better to raid to the south," Baku said, retracting his drawing stick and staring at the map in the dirt. "The north brings us too close to the heart of Carthaginian territory. And there are people there some of the men would not want to hurt."

"They don't want to hurt Carthaginians?" Varro kept his arms folded tightly as he tried to see what everyone stared at.

"Before there were borders, the Massylii wandered all throughout these lands. So the people to the north are more like kin to the tribes represented in our group. Less so for the people to the south. Those people are more like the Carthaginians you are thinking of."

Varro glanced out the tent flap to the morning sun. His guard stood at attention outside, casting a shadow across his view. Men drilled with swords and shields in the parade ground, while the best sword fighters watched and instructed.

"How many tribes do we have in our ranks?" Varro asked. "Was that part of the cause for revolt during the first raid?"

Baku shook his head, his uncovered, frizzy hair wobbling as if it might slide off his scalp.

"We had so many different tribes that none were dominant because King Masinissa pulled from a wide pool. But since my recruiting, we have more of one tribe than any other."

"And that won't be an issue?"

Baku sighed then stood up.

"We should respect their wishes and raid the south. I know it bothers you to have the men dictate the plans. The Roman army wouldn't do that. I understand. But these are real issues for these people. You would not lead a raid into the lands near Rome, would you?"

Varro smiled thinly. "You've no idea of Roman history, do you? Well, in any case, north or south makes no difference to me if there are no tactical differences to consider."

"A southern raid should be easier, and it will disturb the Carthaginians just as much. There are plenty of farms in open country to destroy." Baku extended his hand toward the map. "And there is plenty of space between those farms and the border fort. Now that we know they have cavalry, we will keep out of their range."

"And the scouts have reported nothing back from the fort?"

"For the time they observed it, it seemed routine has continued as it ever has. No increased patrols or other signs that they noticed we killed their caravan drivers and led their cavalry on a chase."

Varro rubbed his chin and recalled the surprised expression of the Carthaginian he had killed to evade capture.

"It doesn't seem right. We gave them a good bite, enough to draw blood. There should be a response from them."

Baku stared blankly at him, and Varro had learned the expression well enough to know he had nothing more to add. His so-called scouts were not professionals or even experienced in their roles. Varro had insisted that the men sent to observe the fort were loyal enough to return with a report and diligent enough to not just want time off from routine duties. Baku had guaranteed them, ending any further questioning.

"Then it will be a quick raid," Varro said. "We drive off the farmers, burn their crops, and generally terrorize the countryside. While we don't want to be caught, we do want the Carthaginians to know we have stung them once more. So we'll be sure to let the farmers know who we are."

"Just not where we are," Baku said, raising his brow in concern.

"I know you believe anyone who can't ride as if he were born on horseback is a fool, but I am not so stupid. Our location is of course a secret. They will know we come from Numidia. Once they get serious enough about dealing with us, they'll send scouts of their own to locate our camp, even if they can't send a force over the border to deal with us."

"They might try," Baku said. "A small and swift force would work. They could deny it ever happening if Rome became aware of the breach in their treaty."

"A small force could reach us," Varro conceded. "But we will destroy them, and double their pain. I intend for us to be a never-ending bleed on the Carthage border until we are given new orders. We will hurt but not hurt so bad that they must deal with us. We just cannot be caught, and I'm relying on our fast horses in that regard."

"They have the same horses," Baku said.

"But not the same riders."

Both of them laughed and agreed on the final shape of the raid. They would set out this day, encamp, then begin razing the countryside at dawn. As they broke up to each prepare for the days ahead, Baku delayed at the tent flap, his expression suddenly pensive.

"I sent my own report back with the last one you sent to King Masinissa." He scratched beneath his frizzy hair, his dark skin barely showing a blush. "I did not tell you at the time, thinking you would be angry."

"And now you think I am not angry?"

"You are always angry. I thought that was the first duty of any centurion. I mention it now because I expect our messenger will return soon. I asked for more supplies and more men."

Varro bit his lip. "I did not mention my failures in the caravan raid. I will look deceitful if you send a report back describing it."

"You didn't lie about anything," Baku said with an easy smile. "You just did not reveal everything. I have known the King for decades, and I am confident in his response. He knows the challenges he has handed you. Besides, he did not ask you to send him reports. You took that upon yourself."

"Well, the reports will soon dry up. I was hoping to capture some vellum out of that caravan raid. What else did you tell him? Why are you bringing this up now?"

Baku looked to his feet. "We've been living shoulder to shoulder for months. I have come to realize when you are distracted. You are worried for your friends. You think you do not talk about them or that you hide your fears. But their names are ever on your lips and you have the eyes of a man searching for something he believes he'll never find yet hopes he will anyway. I asked the King about them, and if he could do something to learn their whereabouts. Do not keep looking for your friends. Be with our men instead."

"I am so easy to read?" Varro turned to fiddle with the writing kit on his desk.

"You are a fine soldier, but a terrible actor."

"Then I shall never be elected to the Senate." Varro turned back with a smile. "Thank you for asking King Masinissa's aid. I fear something has happened to them on the journey."

"Maybe they never followed at all? You've said they were only at the docks when you last saw them."

Varro shook his head. "They had decided to join me. Their bags were packed. They are not the type to quit just because they missed a ship. In any case, I will try not to let my distractions show."

"The men won't notice. It's only me." Baku ducked out of the tent, leaving Varro to stare at his desk a while longer before he began preparations.

That morning they rode out of their mountain camp. Varro left a guard of five men, who would only be effective against locals who might want to have a look around while the main force was gone. He had little interaction with the local tribe since Baku insisted that a Roman face would win no friends among them.

The feel of this raid was already different from the last. For one, his raiders were all mounted, including himself. He was armed with a longsword to fight from horseback. But he kept gladius and pugio strapped to his harness if he should end up on his feet. Of everything he had practiced, falling and dismounting were his best moves. Fighting from horseback felt more like wild hacking to him than proper combat.

The difference this time came from the men. They were more unified and more confident. In fact, it worried him that none showed any fear. Of course, they intended to be the terrorizers of innocent farmers and not face any real opposition.

As for the innocents Varro was about to victimize, he felt a strange mixture of regret and indifference. He had already broken his vow a hundred times over, and as much as he joked about meeting his friends in the Elysian Fields he was certain he would be cast into the gloom of Hades. Still, he knew what a farmer's life entailed. Even if not a single person was hurt in this raid, if he burned the crops and destroyed the farmhouses then the farmers were as good as dead. Some might survive on the generosity of others. But most would go hungry and eventually starve. Even if they ate, their income source would be shattered until the next season. So much suffering and their only crime was being born into a country that Rome hated.

But he had his orders. He never enjoyed it, but he had participated in razing farms while in Greece. It was a common ploy because it worked. If his orders were to rile the Carthaginians then burning their farms was even better than burning their forts.

They encamped in rolling hills where they could hide but keep watch on the cardinal directions. They set up picket lines and threw down tents in neat rows. That was as much discipline as he could get from them. They were not going to trench a marching camp ditch and hammer down spikes. They didn't even have entrenching tools like a legionary would carry.

They awoke before dawn, whispering to each other in excited and eager voices. Varro reiterated that the main targets were the crops and property but not the people. They would not take prisoners and only fight those who resisted. If someone fled, they were to be allowed to escape. The men balked at showing mercy, but Varro explained that the disorganized pursuit of enemies often led to bad ends for the pursuers. He also said Carthage would suffer more if they had a displaced and angry population to contend with. The argument seemed to assuage any fears that they were showing weakness by letting innocents escape.

The first farms were taken completely by surprise. They swooped through the fields, their mad charge driving off anyone foolish enough to try to stand their ground. At one farm, one man stood before his house and shot arrows uselessly before a rider took his head in one pass.

From there, they paused to loot these pathetic wood and stone homes. Varro watched from horseback as they carried out chickens and egg baskets, neither of which would ever make it back to camp. They hauled out every bit of worthless junk while others brought torches into the fields and then to the dwellings. Livestock were killed or driven off. They had no way to take the spoils for their own. This was a purely destructive raid to weaken the local border. They did not yet need to steal supplies from their enemies.

So the process repeated at the next set of farms. By the third set, smoke smudging the horizon behind them betrayed their presence. The farmers had wisely escaped with as much of their valuables as they could carry. Still, they moved with speed and often overtook farmers fleeing to the next settlements. They scattered before the horse but some were killed either accidentally or through the overzealousness of Varro's raiders.

By the afternoon, they had gone deep into Carthaginian territory and had sewn as much wanton destruction as Varro could stomach for one day.

"We've gone deeper than we should have," he said to Baku as the men set fire to the latest grain fields. "It's as if the Carthaginians don't care for their borders."

Baku shoved his finger beneath his head cover to scratch as he looked along the horizon.

"They have unwisely expected peace from Numidia. But I think your Roman masters want to bring more of Carthage's soldiers to the border. The more soldiers on the border, the greater the chances they will make a mistake that will give Rome the excuse to finish their hated foes."

Heavy clouds of gray smoke rolled past them. Orange flames licked up from the grain fields while the farmhouses creaked and snapped as fire consumed their timbers. The scent of ash had stained Varro's nostrils such that he believed he'd smell it for weeks to come.

"But there is hope for Carthage yet." Baku angled his horse aside to reveal what he saw. "It is hard to see through our own smoke, but there is dust on the northern horizon."

Varro leaned forward and squinted.

"You've quite good eyes for an old man. We better start our retreat. The bees are finally roused from the hive."

Baku gave him a sidelong look. "You are in a finer mood than I expected. And I'm not old yet, but I plan to be one day."

Varro shouted his orders and those Baku had selected to be officers gathered in their men. Some still had sacks of live chickens on their small horses and others were laden with packs bulging with stolen goods. Soot darkened their head covers from blue to deep gray, but also heightened their gleeful smiles.

They rode at a strong pace, retracing their path toward the border. They did not race, as they needed to preserve their horses's strength and the enemy did not have a good read on their location. The smoke of the burning fields and houses would mask their own dust from being spotted. It also masked the enemy's dust behind them. It did not matter as Varro expected to reach the border before late noon.

He was correct in the estimate. For as the sun lengthened their shadows and turned the yellow rocks to orange he saw the hill ranges that marked the Numidian border.

And he found a mass of Carthaginian cavalry waiting in ambush.

They charged out of the setting sun, the direction of Varro's travel, racing down gentle slopes that had masked them from early detections. At the sound of pounding hoofbeats on the hard earth, he felt the sting of shame for not scouting ahead. He cursed himself as the first of the enemy burst into their loose formation.

A high note sounded from a Carthaginian horn as they shouted for revenge. Varro fumbled with his longsword, finding it impossible to draw under pressure despite his constant practice. In the end, Baku shouted the orders.

The long blade finally rang from the scabbard, sparking with the afternoon sunlight. It came none too soon, as a Carthaginian sword swiped for his head.

He guided Thunder with his knees and the horse lurched aside in time to let Varro parry the strike. The rider continued past him.

"Protect the Centurion!"

He heard Baku shout this, in the Massylii language no less, and realized that he would be the prime target being dressed in mail and greaves along with his shining bronze helmet.

"Fight clear," Varro shouted back. "Ride for camp if you can."

But the Carthaginian charge had done its work. In one swoop they had broken his formation, leaving pockets of his raiders encircled and cut off from mutual support.

Despite begin mounted, Varro discovered he could see less of the battle. He had too much to manage between his horse and his own men drawing to him. He dared not look away or else steer his horse into a collision. Baku shored up his left.

"I'll keep them off your side. Just cut a way out."

"Easy to say!"

Behind the last rider came another. Rather than try to kill Varro in one blow like his predecessor, he used momentum and better maneuvering to attempt to unhorse him. Thunder screamed at the closeness of the enemy and shoved left into Baku's horse. But it was the right move, denying the Carthaginian his moment.

For all that he disliked the chopping of a cavalry sword, Varro's strong infantry-trained arm found it easy to wield. He hacked as if cutting wood, and he slashed down into his enemy's leg. He saw and felt the bone beneath the flesh he carved off. The rider bellowed in horror as his horse veered away.

Totally the Carthaginians might have had thirty cavalry. Varro could not count them, but it seemed they held a slight numerical advantage. His men appeared bogged down compared with the sweeping run of the Carthaginians.

Thunder whinnied and fought his direction, but Varro had learned the importance of controlling his mount after his last fiasco. With Baku on the left, it narrowed Varro's choices to something more manageable for his skills.

"They're gathering for another pass," Varro shouted. "Now is our time."

Baku shouted an order that seemed to be what Varro had just said. He picked out enough words to know what it meant.

Indeed, the Carthaginian tactic seemed to be hit-and-run. They planned to whittle Varro's raiders down with each pass. But they must not have had experience with Numidian riders. As they regrouped, Varro led his men forward into the opening.

His heart lifted, knowing his men had the speed advantage. They would escape.

Urging Thunder to a gallop, he pointed his bloodied longsword toward the hills of Numidia.

Then Baku screamed and plunged from his horse. Two Carthaginian horses stomped around his prone body, and one reared up as if to slam its hooves into his body.

Varro cried out, then turned Thunder back. He could not lose Baku now.

18

Horsemen raced past Varro, seeking escape from the regrouping Carthaginians. The men who had surrounded him charged for the safety of the hills, stripping him of their protection. It felt as if his shield had been pulled down.

He turned Thunder back toward the enemy.

Two Carthaginians circled Baku laying flat on his back. His horse bucked and jumped between them, eyes white and rolling with fear. It was all that had kept the enemies from finishing him. But one reared his horse as if to stomp on Baku while he was prone.

Varro urged Thunder forward and raised his sword.

The Carthaginian horse slammed its hooves down on Baku. His body bounced up and blood jetted from his mouth. Varro screamed in anger as he reached the enemy who was preparing his mount to strike again.

With a brutal slash, he buried his cavalry sword into the Carthaginian's neck. He had been so intent on Baku, he had not realized the danger. Now he sloughed to the side, and his horse read it as a command to veer away.

The sword ripped from Varro's grip, or else he would be pulled off Thunder's back.

The second Carthaginian gave him no quarter. His blade hacked across Varro's back, snapping links in his chain shirt but otherwise only bruising him from the force of the blow.

They circled around now over Baku's prone body. The main group of Carthaginians had reformed a good distance back and their commander bellowed orders. But the snarling man on horseback beside him demanded his full attention.

Drawing his gladius, Varro found it as light as kindling compared with the longsword. His mail had spared him the first blow. But the second required him to pull away. The Carthaginian had angled behind him, setting him at a terrible disadvantage. In a different situation, he could charge away into the open field ahead. But he would not leave Baku.

Calling on all he had learned, he guided Thunder around and counted on the sense of his mount to avoid stepping on Baku. Thunder whirled to face the Carthaginian, who had just taken a vicious swing that snapped behind Varro's shoulder before he turned out of range.

Now their horses were head to head and were more like fighting platforms than mounts. The Carthaginian had the advantage of skill and reach. But Varro read the fear in his eyes. He was trained but not a combat veteran.

That fear fed his confidence in overcoming the cavalryman. Training on horseback mattered little if he feared death. Varro feared nothing. Neither life nor death.

He growled as he drove his heels into Thunder's flanks. The horse bolted forward and the Carthaginian did likewise.

Varro ducked under the sword thrust and rammed his gladius into his enemy's ribs. It sunk to the depth of a man's thumb, enough to pierce organs and slump the rider over the neck of his mount. Due to the shallowness of the strike, Varro effortlessly retracted his sword. The gladius once more proved the superior weapon. The rider slid from his horse, which danced away from the bloodshed surrounding it.

But he had no time to gloat. The Carthaginians had regrouped and started a second charge.

Baku lay prone beside Thunder. Blood leaked from the corner of his mouth, but his eyes were closed as if he had fallen asleep.

Varro leaped from Thunder's back, landing hard beside Baku. He hovered over him as the shadows of mounted men reached ahead of their charge.

Hooves slammed the ground all around him. He threw himself over Baku, hoping the mail on his back and the helmet on his head would deflect the worst of the charge. Being on the ground for once was an advantage, as the cavalrymen did not carry spears and would have to lean far out of their saddles to reach him. He had seen Roman cavalry do just this scores of times. But today he huddled and let the danger pass. Sprayed dust and rocks pricked the exposed skin along his arms and the backs of his legs. The ground shook under him.

But no blow landed, and no one dismounted.

He raised his head and found that his own men had returned to the battle.

Now cavalrymen joined together in a circle of fast-stepping horses. Being at the center of it, the sound of clashing swords, screaming men, and clapping hooves deafened him. Dust thrown up from dueling fighters blinded him.

He pressed his fingers to Baku's neck and felt a pulse.

"Come on, old man. I'm settling my life debt to you."

Sheathing his gladius, he then slipped both arms under Baku's body. With a curse, he lifted him over Thunder's rear flank.

Swords clanged around his ears and men shrieked in horror and pain. A horse butted against him just after securing Baku, sending him stumbling forward. But he recovered and held Thunder's reins.

"Good horse," he said, patting Thunder's neck. "Now we're escaping this mess."

Varro imagined horse and rider were aligned in their goal of escape. He remounted Thunder as the horse sidestepped and protested the awkward process. He had never practiced mounting a horse with a casualty draped over its body. But he was again mounted and drew his gladius while taking up the reins.

Being at the center of the press, he could not find the edge of it. Nor could he determine the right direction. The sun had vanished into a brown haze as men and horses churned the earth. His head rang with the clamor of battle, and despite his dire circumstances, he found himself smiling. This was his element and what he was born to do.

So he turned to the first enemy he could find and ran his sword into his back.

Thunder moved with him, but was growing increasingly frightened by the blood and violence. He was not trained to fight close engagements and so naturally carried Varro out of the press.

When he saw the opening and realized Baku was still in place, he called out in what he hoped was his best pronunciation.

"Retreat! Get back to camp!"

The melee had left openings for some, while others were cut off. It was the worst feeling a commander could experience, leaving trapped men behind. But he had to salvage as many as he could. Varro led the escape.

Thunder sensed the break, and required no urging to flee the carnage. Varro wound one hand into the reins and pressed the other to stabilize Baku's body. Together they spearheaded the headlong flight from the battle.

The Massylii who made it away soon matched then outstripped him. Perhaps they did not weigh as much as he did in heavy armor. Their mounts were no different from Thunder, yet they flew across the ground leaving a wake of brown dust.

The Carthaginians pursued but once the Numidian hills were in view they dropped off. Yet Varro and his companions fled as far their mounts would carry them. Due to their own terror, this was farther than Varro had expected. But once their limits were reached, the horses slowed then stopped and the riders dismounted.

Immediately his quasi-officers came to tend Baku. They carefully lifted him from Thunder's back, which was foamy with sweat. Varro stood behind them, straining to see Baku's face. While the covered heads of the others obscured it, he heard Baku groan and then curse. He also deciphered a complaint that sounded like "he rides like the infantry."

"You are alive?" He asked in the Massylii language, turning the heads of his officers so that he now saw Baku's face.

It was ash-pale and haggard as if he had not slept in days. The blood at the corners of his mouth has crusted into this beard.

"For now."

The men tending Baku set him on level ground and began to peel back his tunic. Varro did not want to see the damage. So he stood back and looked to his men.

"I will check on the others." Whether they understood him, they did not respond. Instead, they hissed through their teeth and mumbled together over Baku.

Varro counted twenty-two remaining. He had lost about a dozen men, which considering the madness of the last hour seemed a small number. Of those remaining, half were wounded and half again were seriously wounded. These wounded lay on the ground, stanching their injuries with the hems of their tunics. Some men tried to offer what help they could. But no one was a trained doctor like those employed in the Roman legions.

Even the horses had been wounded. Many had long gashes on

their flanks and one collapsed. It was a horrific sight, for it landed on its breast with a heavy thud and let out a terrible sound Varro had never heard from a horse before. One of the men, probably its rider, took his long knife and cut its neck to speed its death.

A dozen heads turned away from the scene, including Varro's. For some reason, he could bear a disemboweled man better than witnessing a loyal horse die from its wounds. So he moved to the most injured man he could find and offered what aid he could. He was no medic but he had endured enough gore-soaked battlefields to know the basics. His experience ran more toward puncture wounds than the hideous slashes of cavalry swords. More than anything, the wounded needed stitches and no one carried such supplies. Worse still, he wondered who would know how to stitch a wound properly.

Yet he bound up what he could, then moved to the next until both of his hands were covered in blood. Even if he achieved little in actual medical aid, his attentions gave everyone hope. At last, he came to Baku again.

"Is he alive?"

One of his chosen men looked up from squatting beside Baku, his hand on his shoulder.

"Alive," he said. "But I cannot tell how bad." He then elaborated in more detail Varro could not yet understand. But from his hand motions and where he indicated on Baku's body he guessed all the wounds were internal.

For now, Baku remained with eyes closed and a gray blanket tossed across his body. Varro had seen men who had no outward sign of injuries die overnight. The medics would say they bled from the inside, which was nearly impossible to treat before it was too late. This was likely Baku's situation. Many men died from a single horse kick. He did not need to wonder what damage must have been done when a horse stomped both hooves into a body.

"Make a litter for him. I don't want him injured anymore on the way to camp."

He had to revert to Latin for this command, and already he felt Baku's absence. But between his gestures, tone, and common sense, eventually, men returned with sturdy branches from the lone trees spread throughout the area. They built liters for the severely wounded, chiefly Baku. Two others had taken huge cuts to their waists. Varro wondered how they ever sat upright, probably just out of plain fear. Now they could no longer and so had to lay flat.

The Massylii proved just as ingenious with using their horses to transport the wounded as they did in riding them. The liters were suspended between two horses, and the men tied down. Fortunately, there were no more, for they had used rope captured from one of the farms and it ran out. But they were no longer going to gallop, but keep a steady pace until reaching camp.

They walked beside their horses, conscious that even a slow pace was a strain on the animals that had been pushed hard throughout the day. Despite everyone's desire to reach their mountain camp, nightfall forced them to stop.

The high-spirited discipline of the morning was now as tenuous as a chipped sword. With the right pressure, it would shatter into uselessness. The men were exhausted, with many moaning over their wounds, and others aimlessly patting their tired horses. They had not planned a second night of camp, and so they carried no provisions other than what they might have stolen. They stopped where their strength finally could not meet the challenge of the terrain. They were heading into the hills, increasing the pitch of the slope and the rockiness of the ground. With a few hours more daylight, they could have made it. But in their current condition, they had no chance.

So camp was settled near a pathetic creek surrounded by a few dozen palm trees and attendant bushes. While the water was desperately needed, the area was indefensible. The trees masked much of the approach from the east. The creek was naturally in lower ground, flowing out of the steep hills miles away, and curtailed visibility. Varro grumbled but accepted it as an act of desperation.

Before settling for the night, he checked on Baku. He had one of his men with him at all times, and Varro approached as one tilted a wineskin into the corner of his mouth.

"He's awake?"

The man nodded while Baku sucked on the skin like a baby at a breast.

"You'll be alright," he said in Latin, squatting at his feet. "You're a tough old man."

Baku released the skin and tried to look up, then let his head flop down.

"I should have expected a trap. The Carthaginians are a crafty lot. And they're as cruel as Romans. They'd let us burn out their farms just to set a perfect snare."

"Well, it wasn't perfect. We escaped."

Baku gave a weak wheeze.

"We are shattered. These men are not fighting for anything other than freedom from prison. But after today, I think some will feel safer there. Set your watch well, Centurion. Tomorrow morning you might find fewer men than you started with."

He left Baku to sleep with his loyal attendant at his side. A tent would have been welcomed if only just to shield him from the silent accusations following him to the patch of thin grass he selected to sleep on. At least they were not calling for his death this time, he thought. But by tomorrow it might well become a reality.

Sleeping in a chain shirt was difficult, both for it pressing into his already sore back and against his chest as he tried to breathe.

But he had learned to do it. His helmet would be his pillow and he would sleep with one hand on his gladius.

Tomorrow he would awaken to find out who had abandoned him in the night. He did not set a watch, feeling it was utterly useless if those he placed would simply flee into the night. Yet his officers seemed to be making some attempt at convincing men to trade rest for a sense of safety. He did not interfere with them and did not learn the outcome.

One thing Varro had learned in the infantry was how to fall asleep in any circumstance and under any kind of stress. Enemy pikemen could be marching over his bedroll, and he would remain asleep if it was his designated rest period. Those who could not master this suffered all the years of their enlistment. So Varro set his helmet backward and braced it against a stone, then rested his head to stare into the star-brightened indigo above him.

And soon he was asleep.

He dreamed of the god Jupiter, who stood at the peak of Mount Olympus and hurled thunderbolts at Varro, cursing him for his failures and his arrogance. The bolts crashed all around him, sending clods of earth flying into the air along with himself. He spun helplessly as the god raged, casting bolt after bolt.

But then he realized the crash he heard was not from thunderbolts. Nor was he asleep any longer.

Horses raced through the camp. Men wailed as they were trampled or cut down.

Varro did not even know how he got to his feet, or how his helmet was strapped to his head, or gladius in hand. He was already screaming a war cry as the black shadow of a horse bolted right at him.

He evaded the horse, but in his confused state he struck too late and missed his target, punching into the air.

Fire leaped up in the grass and climbed into the palm trees. Who had set a fire? But he saw some of the riders carried flaming brands which they threw on anything that burned. Men and horses scattered everywhere.

Varro ran for Baku, shouting his name.

But he was already surrounded by horsemen who had penned him and others who squatted as captives with their hands on their heads.

The other attacking horsemen, Carthaginians by the silhouettes of their helmets, were riding down horses and those who fled.

Inexplicably, Varro seemed outside their notice.

"Centurion," a desperate voice shouted from behind. "Get on my horse!"

He could not see who beckoned him, but it seemed one side of the camp had not yet come under attack. Four others struggled to calm the horses next to him.

Swallowing a curse, he jumped onto the rear of the horse and his rider urged it forward. Three of the four others mounted, but one shouted out and fell from sight. Varro could not see why. His horse continued to run with the pack of them as they escaped into the night.

He looked back, watching palm trees crawling with fire that was already dying out. Beneath burning fronds and lit in lurid orange light, the Carthaginian cavalry destroyed whatever was left of his men.

Baku had been right, just not in how they would be finally shattered. The Carthaginians had seen to it themselves.

19

They rode through the darkness, somehow avoiding ruts and rocks that would throw a horse's footing. If Fortuna had granted any favors this night, sure footing was the best of them. For they outpaced any pursuit and left behind the mayhem at the creek encampment, where Baku and others were captured or worse. When at last they slowed the horses, a white line stained the eastern horizon and a cool wind scoured the hillside where they dismounted.

Varro and three others stared vacantly at each other, their eyes glittering with the coming dawn. The riderless horse had remained with them, now becoming Varro's mount. He thought sadly to Thunder's fate and hoped his horse was simply captured rather than cut down like so many others.

"Centurion?" The voice was hesitant and quiet. He spoke in his tribal language. "What do we do?"

Varro removed his helmet, pausing to regard it as if it belonged to another. He had no recollection of wearing it or drawing his sword. He had just found himself standing confused among even greater confusion.

"There is nothing to do," he said. "The others are either captured or dead."

The three appeared confused while they seemed to piece together his terrible pronunciation. He probably misspoke as well, further delaying their comprehension. But soon all three nodded solemnly.

"Then where do we go?"

"Back to camp," Varro said, turning to the western hills. Over those ridges was the safety of the camp and Numidian territory. "Any survivors will go there."

They rested in the morning twilight, finding more palm trees amid the increasingly rocky and desolate hills. As he rested, he heard an animal bolt through the tall grass to its hiding place. He envied that creature, for he would have liked nothing more than to join it in a small dark hole and wait for danger to pass. But he was still the commander of this force, even if it was now a force of three men. He had a responsibility to at least appear confident.

The three did not speak to each other, but likewise lay in the grass and stared into the brightening sky. When dawn finally broke, Varro felt his stomach rumbling and an intense thirst raking his throat. Their horses were likewise tormented and less tractable for it. They remounted to head for camp. Varro felt the loss of Baku and others like a weight on his back, and when he turned west an actual itch between his shoulders flared.

"We will have to free them," Varro said to the other three. "Baku and the rest. Before they are killed."

The three shared glances but did not reply. Maybe his poor speech was misunderstood or they simply dismissed the idea as impossible. If he could not attempt the outpost fortress with his original fifty-man force, he could not even attempt an open latrine with what he had available now.

But he held out hope for himself and the others. Baku and the rest would likely be interrogated and then executed as brigands. If

Baku could somehow make his connection to King Masinissa, then he might be spared for a ransom or outright release. But Varro wondered if the King would acknowledge Baku. If he did, he would be in some ways admitting to stirring trouble on the border. Varro was not certain he wanted to do that directly.

These thoughts occupied his mind as the gusty wind shoved them along the line of hills and through the passes that eventually led to their camp. Along the way, they celebrated meeting a handful of survivors. These were greeted warmly by his original three. The survivors were formal with Varro, and as more joined his ranks he began to wonder when the accusations would start. With eight now joined to him, the tribesmen were beginning to give him cool looks as they spoke softly to each other.

Varro returned a bitter smile. Before long he imagined they would be hanging him from a post to let the buzzards tear his flesh. It was a terrible feeling to mistrust your own men, but he could not truly blame them. A leader bears final responsibility for all outcomes, especially defeats.

They at last came to the path Baku had ordered cleared and where Varro had hoped to set up barriers against attack. To his surprise, those staked wooden barriers and crude plank blockades were in place.

He halted at the foot of the path leading up to camp.

"I don't recall having anyone put those barriers back into position."

Speaking in Latin, since he did not have the words to voice his worries, the man who saved him at least seemed to understand. He answered in his own language.

"Those were not there before, sir."

Varro saw a flash of a covered head pop up from behind the boards and then vanish.

"It's one of the five I left behind," he said. "They set up the barriers. Good men."

The realization seemed to ease the others, who sat higher on their mounts studying the signs of unexpected discipline. Varro had forgotten about them in his despair. Together with the eight survivors of the raid, he would have twelve men to lead back to Cirta in defeat. He planned to ride fast, in the hopes King Masinissa would do something to save Baku.

Varro called up to the sentries behind the barriers, trying to think of the correct way to phrase his command to move them aside to let them pass.

A half dozen covered heads popped up in answer. His companions raised their hands to wave.

But Varro saw the slings spinning overhead.

With a shout of warning, he leaped off his horse to land behind it for cover.

Two of his eight men did not fare as well. Stones struck their heads, shattering their skulls. The man next to Varro slid from his horse to spill his brains into the dust.

Stones crashed among them as thin voices hurled insults and curses along with the speeding stone bullets.

The horses took the worst of the hits, and Varro's mount reared up in pain.

"What the fuck are they doing?" He screamed the question, hugging the ground as more stones pelted around them. Two men were dead. All were unhorsed, and another rolled on the ground holding his broken shoulder.

During the pause to reload, he raised his head. There seemed to be even more people within the camp answering the slinger's call.

Somehow, his camp had been taken over.

More shots zipped down the slope, and one cracked loudly against the bone of a man outside of Varro's vision. He tried to look, but a stone banged off his helmet. The bronze clanked and compressed against his head, the leather liner absorbing what might have been lethal force.

"Pull back!"

The horses were running everywhere now, maddened by thirst, exhaustion, and more violence. The slingers were incredibly effective against them, having had a few days to prepare. While there were only five of them shooting, Varro's force was down to four men who were already fleeing. Two lay dead with a horse between them bucking and screaming from its wounds. Two others cried on the ground, clutching broken bones as more stones landed among them.

"The one drill they paid attention to had to be slinging." He muttered to himself as he scrabbled back down the slope to hide behind a low rock and a patch of dead weeds. Only one of his men remained crouched behind a similar rock to his left, and the others ran after their horses.

Varro's arm tingled, yearning for his scutum shield. If he had five legionaries with the same shield, he could march up the path and destroy the slingers.

His final, loyal man cowered behind an orange rock, holding this cheek to it like it was his lover. The slingers knew their range well and did not waste their shots. Varro had trained them for it, after all. They returned to hide behind the barriers.

"There are only five of them," Varro said to his last man. "I'm good for four if you'll take the other one."

He spoke Latin, just words to calm his rage and make him appear confident. Finally, the Massylii tribesman looked at him with brown irises lost in the white pools of his eyes. He had a brand mark on his forehead, an obvious criminal of some sort. He just blinked.

"Where are our fathers? Our husbands?"

At first, Varro was not certain he understood, but the branded man blinked in surprise along with him. They dared to peer over the rocks, finding a barrel-shaped woman standing defiantly among the barriers. Her skin was dark and her hair stained as gray as her tunic, which was immodest at best. Varro had not met Massylii women before and despite everything was shocked to see her bare legs.

"What do they want?" He asked his branded companion, but he just repeated what the woman said.

The woman, growing in anger, began to shout curses Varro could not understand. She was like a child having a tantrum, kicking up dust with her bare feet and picking up rocks to hurl down the slope. She eventually began to sob, then retreated behind the barriers.

"What's this about?" Varro asked.

But the final man had made his decision. He shook his head at Varro, stood in a low crouch, then fled after the others. The slope tumbled down to wide fields where Varro had learned to ride with Baku. This man and the others would vanish into its grassy folds and never be seen again.

He set his helmet on the rock and pressed against it.

"Varro, you fool, you're the only one left. How could you make such a mess of this?"

Curling back from cover, knowing he was beyond the effective range of the slingers, he staggered up under the weight of his chain shirt.

The slingers still tried to reach him, but their shots fell short. They had drilled but were far from experts. Their opening volley had the advantage of a prepared ambush. Their latest shots pinged off the ground or crashed through dried grasses. Varro drew his gladius and pointed it up the slope.

"All gods have a special torment for traitors. I'll send you to yours. I swear it!"

But the slingers mocked him, making sounds that they must have believed mimicked Latin speech.

Regardless of his dramatic display, he could achieve nothing.

He was one man hovering at the far range of deadly slingshots and unknown numbers. He hadn't felt this small since he was a child crawling at his mother's feet.

He thrust his sword back into the scabbard and followed his men while the slingers jeered at his retreat.

Halfway to the flatter fields, he pulled off his helmet to examine the dent. He thumbed away stone residue from where the shot had struck. The helmet had saved his life. With a crooked smile, he gave the slingers begrudging credit for their aim.

"Maybe I should've relied on slingers rather than cavalry."

But his bitter musings were cut short as he entered into the plains.

A column of mixed cavalry and infantry raced through the knee-high grasses of the plains. His heart slammed against the bottom of his throat and he began to wave with both arms.

"Baku, you bastard! What did you write in your message?"

King Masinissa had sent him reinforcements, and by their formation and stride, these were not rabble. They were soldiers, trained and disciplined soldiers. He sped down to meet the column, and his heart lightened.

Yet halfway to them, he realized this many men must have their own commander and one who would likely relieve him of command. The thought slowed his stride but did not stop him. After all, he had earned his demotion. He could only count on being a member of Servux Capax to keep King Masinissa from executing him for incompetence. But that did not mean the King would be prevented from making him want to take his own life.

Still, for the moment, he ran with shadowed joy in his heart. Relief was at hand, and at the precise moment needed. Baku had foreseen this outcome, and Varro could not be more grateful to him for it.

He began shouting as he approached, both hands up and waving so they did not mistake him for a threat. The cavalry was in the lead, with whoever commanded it at the head. He was flanked by several bodyguards, with a few wearing heavy chain shirts. Their horses were the same small but sturdy breeds of the Massylii tribesman.

Varro shouted in the local language as he drew near. The leader raised his hand to halt the march and regarded Varro with his sharply shadowed eyes. He sat his horse like a prince, and remained still as Varro crossed the final distance at last stumbling into the commander's presence.

"You are from King Masinissa? I am Centurion Marcus Varro." He paused trying to find the right words in the Massylii tongue. He swept his arm behind to indicate the steep mountains that contained his former camp. "They are all gone. Dead. Captured."

He had not learned how to say they had deserted. Wiping his hand over his mouth, he sought a way to express the idea.

"I speak your language, Centurion Varro." The man's voice was rich and deep and caught Varro's attention. "It is why the King has appointed me to this task."

"Thank the gods," Varro said. "Well, I'm all that's left who hasn't been killed or captured. The rest are traitors and have taken over the camp. They ambushed my survivors and killed half of them. The other half...."

Looking across the fields, he glimpsed dark shapes fleeing into the waving grass and gentle folds of the land.

The commander turned to follow his gaze, then nodded.

"Your camp has been overrun? Who led them, sir?"

Varro scratched his head and looked back at the mountains.

"I'm not sure they have a leader. There are women in the camp, asking after their sons and husbands." Then he paused and turned to squint up at the mounted commander. "You called me sir? You're not relieving me of command?"

The rider shook his head but frowned as if agreeing that he should.

"King Masinissa ordered us to report to you and Baku for instructions. There is more happening in this area than you seem aware of, sir." He searched over Varro's head toward his camp. "And this is only part of it."

But Varro lowered his head. "I am afraid Baku has become a prisoner of the Carthaginians."

The commander gasped. "What? When did this happen?"

"Only last night," Varro said, he then looked down at the long column of soldiers. "But now we might be able to do something about that."

"Sir, we should discuss the full scope of what has happened. But may I suggest we encamp first? We must plan our next moves carefully."

"I agree. Yes, please, give the orders. And what is your name?"

"I am Captain Isan and I bring you fifty cavalry and thirty infantry to quell the unrest in this area. Like I said, sir, we will work together to execute the King's orders."

"But Baku is in danger." Varro considered for a moment that Baku might be the only consideration and the other captives planned to betray him eventually. But they had not. "And the rest of my men are prisoners. They will be executed, I am certain. They must be freed, or at least we must delay their execution until we can enter discussions with the outpost commander."

Captain Isan nodded. "I agree, sir. But the King has asked me to remind you that one of your duties is to pacify uprisings in this area. Well, as I said, we should discuss further. But you've got a taste of these uprisings yourself. We must move as swiftly as our enemies do. Dealing with them must come first."

Varro considered reminding Isan that he was still in command. But he had nothing practical to enforce his authority. Nor would it avail him anything to argue a valid point. He had not paid any attention to pacification as no one had reported it as an issue.

Perhaps because the men doing the reporting sympathized with the rebels. So he nodded in agreement.

He glanced at the bodyguards surrounding him, hoping they did not also speak Latin and understand how quickly he ceded the argument. But their eyes were set further ahead, ranging into the mountains and surrounding fields while searching for threats.

All except two men in chain shirts who watched Varro intently. Their head covers cast shadows across their faces. But there was no shadow to hide who they were once Varro got a direct look at the two of them.

"You are not dead? You didn't perish at sea? Instead, you took riding lessons and started dressing like the locals?"

His body quivered with equal parts joy and confusion. Was he really seeing them or had his mind broken at last?

"It's good to see you, too," Falco said, pulling back his head cover. "I was wondering when you'd notice me. Curio is such a tiny shit, even on a horse he doesn't stand taller than my armpit."

"I'm taller than your armpit," Curio said, twisting on his horse and stroking its neck. Then he too pulled back his head cover. "We've wanted to join you, but the King kept us in Cirta."

"The King?" Varro's eyes fluttered as he considered what heard. "You were detained at Cirta?"

"Yes," Falco said. "And I've been teaching Curio to read all those reports you've been sending. I didn't know you were so good with the stylus. You should write histories or something."

"I'll think about that."

And he began to laugh.

20

Wind gusted against the side of the tent where Varro sat cross-legged on a worn-out rug. Falco and Curio sat opposite of him. Whenever the hide wall bulged in, it smothered Curio's left arm. Yet they had properly staked it against the wind of the plains, working together in silence as if they had not been separated for so long. Only now that the column had established a temporary camp did they have time to speak.

Varro could not think of what to say or ask. He wanted to hug both of them, yet they were more relaxed about their reunion. After all, they had been reading his reports and knew he was fine. It was he who went to sleep every night believing he had led his best friends to their deaths.

They each set a pugio down on the rug between them. A stylized owl head was inlaid in silver on all three, only Varro's now had the stains of hard use.

"I was wrong the way I handled everything," Varro said. "I thought I was doing the right thing and it turned out to be the total opposite."

"No argument from me," Falco said. "You did a shitty job explaining things."

"I don't think he actually explained anything," Curio said.

"True," Falco nodded then tilted his head at Varro. "One thing you'll never be is a recruiter for the organization."

"Organization? I thought it was called Servus Capax?" Light fell across Varro's shoulder from the open tent to frame Falco and Curio. They both looked at each other, and Falco smirked.

"I think we might know more than you now. We're not supposed to drop that name where it can be overheard. We're a secret, or don't you know?"

"I suppose. But living as a mountain brigand for the summer makes one forget about things like secret organizations and basic sanitation."

"Well, you've kept your face shaved," Falco said, leaning closer to examine him. "It couldn't have been all that bad."

"So what happened? How did you end up like this? I've been worried sick for the two of you. You were supposed to be right behind me."

"That captain of your ship made quite a stir," Curio said. "He had some powerful and angry enemies. They were threatening everyone at the dock. And they were looking at us like we had let you escape."

"Right," Falco said. "So we did some escaping of our own. Honestly, I had such a hangover I couldn't fight. Not that it would've been my first choice, but those friends of your captain's were looking for one."

"I suggested we go see Flamininus and just ask to join the organization." Curio folded his arms with a proud finality and nodded to the three pugiones arrayed between them. "And you see how that went."

"But that's what caused our first delay," Falco said, frowning. "It took a day to get an appointment with him. Some asshole secretary of his treated us like we were washed-up soldiers looking for a hand out. He never passed our names on."

"We had to catch him in the street," Curio said. "When he was heading out of his house, we got his attention."

"Consul Flamininus always said I could bring you both in. I can't imagine he would protest now."

"He's not Proconsul anymore," Falco corrected. "Now he's a simple senator, as he likes to say. But he'll be sponsoring us for the time. He was happy to learn we had changed our minds, and he passed us off to someone to give us orders."

"Which were for me to learn to read and write," Curio said. "And it's not easy."

"Sparta was easier than teaching him letters," Falco said, rolling his eyes. "But we all need to be able to read and write. So that cost us weeks just getting the basics down. All day with scrolls and a stylus. I swear, Varro, I became our old tutor. You remember him and those elephant ears of his?"

He nodded but pinched the bridge of his nose in frustration. "Maybe part of your practice could have been to send a letter to me and explain what happened. That would've been nice."

"Good idea," Falco said. "Next time I'll do that. Look, I expected to be packed off after you too. But we ended up filling vellum pages with letters. Flamininus insisted on progress before we did more. Curio can do some basic reading now."

"I still need to look at words before I can write them," he said, pantomiming himself bent over a desk and writing. "But it's not so hard if you concentrate on it all day."

"And you've been learning the local language," Falco said. "That's impressive."

"It's more like I've been learning to accept failure." Varro shrugged. "Anyway, it has been months. Why were you delayed at Cirta?"

"Because the King said you were to stand or fall on your own,"

Falco said. "And that he wanted us properly trained for long-term work under his command. So we've learned to chirp a bit in the local language. Not as good as you, though. You saw we learned how to sit on a horse and not fall off."

"The head covers were presents from our trainer," Curio said, beaming. "He said I was a natural."

"That's only because I think Curio likes horses more than women."

Curio and Falco shoved at each other while Varro looked on with a smirk. He was so pleased to see the two of them together and happier still that they were in the same mixed-up, ambiguous future as he was.

"Stand and fall on my own?" Varro said as the two settled down. "I suppose the both of you arriving means I've fallen in the king's eyes."

"When you it say it like that, it makes me feel like you'd rather not see us." Falco feigned injury, pressing his hands over his broad chest. "But I suppose so. We weren't shown your last letter, and only got word it was time for us to join you. No more prancing around on horseback and writing lessons for us. Time to get our swords bloodied."

"Well, you've missed plenty of opportunities already. But there'll be more."

"So we're going to fight Carthaginians like our fathers?" Curio's eyes lit up at the thought. "We won't have to hear it from the old timers that think we had it easy in Macedonia. Now we can say we fought Carthage too."

"If I get my way, we'll be bringing down a fort of them. They've got Baku and the rest of my men, as loose as that term is."

"So, you've heard our situation," Falco said. "And we know what you've reported back. But what's the real story? What are we getting into?"

"It seems like you could tell me better than I know myself."

Varro nodded toward the tent opening. "But I guess while we're waiting on Captain Isan I'll tell you the truth of things, starting with how I got myself kidnapped."

"You owe me three denarii," Falco said, extending his palm to Curio. He shoved it aside.

"I don't have any with me. You know that."

Varro raised his brows and Falco smirked.

"I made a bet that you got yourself into trouble without me being there to keep you straight. And so you have."

"Wait, you keep me straight? All my life you've been the problem. Starting from the day our mothers set us side by side in the grass."

"That's right. I can be your problem, but I won't let anyone else be. Anyway, Curio, you owe me and I won't forget it."

"Of course you won't, you cheap bastard."

Varro shook his head and chuckled. Then he described all that had happened to him since they parted at the docks. He detailed Bellus's trickery and how he managed to defeat him and his giant brother, Lars. He covered all his troubles with discipline and authority over the rabble assigned to his command, and how two floggings almost destroyed the camp. He ended with his most recent raid and the final dissolution of his command at the foot of his mountain camp.

"I hate to say it, but that camp was beginning to feel like home. Not to mention I have a lockbox of denarii up there that I'd hate to see squandered on these bastards. But they're more interested in chickens than coins, it seems."

They settled into silence. Both Falco and Curio had grown serious throughout his summary. As usual, Falco was the first to speak.

"Well, that was some bad business with Bellus and Lars. You can't even trust a fellow citizen anymore."

"That's true," Curio said. "The rebels even have a Roman with them, and he sounds like a match for that brute Lars."

Varro waved his hand dismissively. "Lars was a mountain of rage and stupidity. I killed him easily."

"Well to hear Isan's account of what the rebel Roman can do, you'd think he was a god and not a man." Falco sniffed. "But stories like that get overblown. We'll deal with him and whatever else we need to. You've got a real cavalry and infantry now. They've got, I don't know, a bunch of angry tribesmen with sharp sticks."

"It's not so simple."

Captain Isan's shadow darkened the tent entrance as he spoke. He crouched down and Varro made room for him on the small rug. All three of them quickly snatched their pugiones back into their sheaths. If Isan noticed, he merely groaned with the effort to squeeze into their tent.

"What is this rebellion?" Varro asked. "King Masinissa suggested there might be some discontent, but nothing large scale."

"There have been changes in the tribes, sir," Isan said as he adjusted to the tight space. "A rebel of some charisma has overthrown his chief and is spreading dissatisfaction with the King's policies to other tribes. His is a major tribe that held much power and territory in older days. They have squandered it due to bad leadership, but they blame King Masinissa."

"This tribe," Varro said. "We're currently in their territory I assume. It seems the desire to rebel was in them even before this. Baku mentioned many felt put upon to become farmers."

Isan nodded. "We have been a free-roaming people for generations. But now the King asks us to settle down and take up agriculture in the manner of the Carthaginians. Like many others, I see the value in this. The King wishes Numidia to become the breadbasket of the world. We have the land for it, but not the society to support it. If the people would change, then Numidia will rise in greatness. But many cling to old ways, and just as many are threatened by new ways."

"But this has been going on for a decade," Falco said. "Why rebel now?"

"A decade?" Isan laughed and shook his head. "It took years for the king to even bring his closest friends to his way of thought. And as for why now, well, the time is ripe. There is a great hero reborn among the Massylii. He is a Roman they call Djebel, which means Mountain. But he is the main power of this rebel tribe. They say he cannot die and that he tears his enemies apart with his bare hands."

"Sounds like exaggeration," Varro said. "I've seen big men before. Even the strongest cannot tear a man into pieces."

Isan shrugged. "Does it matter if it's true? The tribesmen believe it, and so with a clever schemer to incite them and a brute to encourage them, they rise up. Not with sharpened sticks, but with spears and swords and plains horses that ride as fast as our own."

"And so we must crush them before they convince other tribes to join," Varro said.

"That is King Masinissa's orders. The rebels move swiftly, and according to what we know they move this way. It is possible they may try to encourage tribes across the Carthaginian border to join them. I cannot understand why else they would travel here with such speed."

"Whatever their reason," Varro said. "If we can take back my camp, we'll have a fortified position from which to strike them. We picked this spot because we can reach the border and the plains easily. Perhaps that is why the rebels head here as well. They might have designs on using my camp."

"Whoever holds it now would likely join forces with the rebels," Isan said. "So we must retake the camp if only to deny it to the enemy."

Varro smiled and spread his hands. "You have my full agreement. I built those barriers, and so I know what to expect. If we could make a testudo formation I'd march up the road and destroy them. Unfortunately, they have slingers defending the approaches and they are good shots."

"There's three of us," Falco said. "I've got your scutum packed on my horse. I figured by now you'd need it."

"Three makes a good line, but it's not a testudo. They have others who could get into the surrounding cliffs and drop rocks on us. It is a highly defensible position with enough numbers, and it seems they have it."

"We've no time for fancy tactics," Isan said. "I am not sure who else is up there with your deserters, but we will have to storm the camp."

"The infantry at least have shields," Falco said. "They can take the barriers and the cavalry can ride into the camp."

Varro shrugged. "It's as good a plan as any. There is another approach, though. Not large enough for a column of men to traverse but good enough for a small scouting force. It will be watched, I'm sure. But we might be able to send men to create a distraction to the rear."

Isan agreed and had men in mind for the task. After a rest for the soldiers, who had been fast-marching all morning, they broke camp and headed for the mountains. Varro described the cleft in the high mountain walls where the task force could enter. Ten infantry were dispatched that way and the rest followed Varro to the foot of the main path into camp. The dead horse and bodies remained where they had fallen, and a flock of crows and buzzards shrieked to announce their arrival.

Varro wrinkled his nose in disgust. "They were former companions. They couldn't even retrieve their bodies?"

Isan looked down from his horse with a bitter smile. "There is no brotherhood among the men you were given to command, sir."

"They could've fooled me. They seemed pretty united in their disobedience."

He winced at these words, for not every man had been so bad and it was unfair to portray them as uniformly horrible. Yet he felt intense resentment toward all of them, even Baku to an extent. It all felt as if he were the butt of a cruel joke. For he could not see why King Masinissa would have handed him this so-called scratch force knowing they would not cooperate and likely fail in anything they attempted.

But he set aside his wondering and now looked to the barriers still in place. The camp seemed deathly quiet, but he knew they could not have all abandoned it so soon.

"Give them a chance to surrender," Varro said to Isan. "I would make the challenge myself but I'm not sure they would understand me."

"You speak well for one who has only just learned," Isan said. "Your friends are less talented."

Falco and Curio both curled their lips. They sat with Isan between them and Varro. Falco leaned back on his horse to roll his eyes at Varro.

Isan stepped his horse forward and shouted for attention. At first, no one answered, but when he repeated one of the slingers stood and attempted a shot that flew wide.

"Time for the infantry," Varro said. Having lost his horse, he was on foot and now had his scutum shield on his arm. "Falco, Curio, don't tell me you're going to ride into battle?"

"I'd feel safer on the ground," Falco said, already sliding from horseback.

"It might be fun," Curio said. "Right up until someone sticks me in the leg. I'd rather use the scutum."

Varro stood at the fore of the twenty remaining men. He did not need to explain the danger of the slingers. He had Curio and

Falco flank him to form a tight wall. It was not much, but no shot would break through.

"There are five of them and twenty of us," he said as best as he could in their tongue. Men on both sides nodded and raised their spears in answer.

Now lined up with his friends, he felt invincible. They fell in together and marched in lockstep. They hadn't even trained together in months, but they had lost none of their discipline. The rest of the infantry bulked up behind their massive shields.

Wordlessly they tramped past the corpses into shot range. It took only a moment for the first stones to crash against their shields.

"You trained these boys?" Falco spoke as if they were strolling a market lane rather than into battle. "They're good shots."

Stone after stone broke on their shields. They must have been reloading furiously. To their credit, they did not falter. Varro only knew their progress by peering through the gap between his shield and Falco's.

From the far end of the camp, he heard screaming and realized the task force had broken into the camp.

"Forward!" Varro's shout rebounded off the shields. He and the others remained in step to charge to the first barrier, drawing their swords in unison. The hum of the bronze weapons announced the end of the slingers.

They reached the first log and stake barrier, easily battering it aside to flow into the gap. The slingers had picked up spears and gnashed their teeth while stabbing out.

But three heavy Roman infantry was more than a match for five unarmored rabble. They trampled a man, and Curio stabbed down as they passed over him. The rest of them fled back into the safety of the camp.

The infantry now fanned out from behind them, sweeping aside the barriers leading into the base.

Varro looked up to where he knew men could be placed to drop rocks but found no one there.

He waved Isan forward, and the cavalry surged past them into the base. The pounding of their hooves and the whooping of their riders echoed through the camp.

Varro stood aside to let them pass, beaming a smile to Falco.

"Just like old times," he said.

Falco who had shoved down one of the sawhorse barriers, smiled back.

"It sure is." He pointed with his gladius opposite of the passing cavalry charge. "Because trouble is always right behind us."

Varro followed the line of his blade and saw a black smudge on the horizon. The rebels were coming.

21

Thirty Massylii had occupied Varro's camp, almost all of them women. Many had still chosen to fight, and their half-naked bodies lay sprawled out beside the weapons they had captured, blood pooling beneath them and black flies hovering above them. The rest had been rounded up in the center of the camp, on Varro's parade ground.

Isan's men were disappointed at the lack of a fight and had dismounted to chase down the surviving slingers and execute them on the spot. To Varro's relief, none of Isan's men attempted to molest the women captives. They sat cross-legged on the hard dirt of the parade area, red-faced and downcast eyes.

"The dust clouds thicken," Isan said. He had dismounted and now stood outside the ring of his warriors guarding the prisoners.

"How long before they arrive?"

Varro squinted at the cloud on the horizon. It was harder to see with darker clouds rolling in from the east, driven by the steady gusts that had begun that morning.

"Arrival versus attacking are two different things," Isan said. "They will probably be here in a few hours. But they will try to estimate our strength and defenses before attacking. They are full of fight, but not foolish."

Varro nodded. "Put head covers on these captives then tie them to the barriers. Let them know if they call out they will be killed. At the least, we will look stronger to them from a distance. At best, they will have to kill their own to reach us."

Isan's mouth tightened and he looked to the captives. "That is harsh punishment."

"Harsh punishment is spearing them where they kneel. At least by my way they might deter attack and save some lives."

"For a while," Isan said. "What of our supply situation here? I have food and feed enough for a few days. We did not expect to have to fend for longer, and certainly did not expect to feed captives."

Varro saw Falco and Curio crossing back across the camp. From their grim expressions, he did not anticipate good news.

"These captives are likely the ones who helped supply us. We were doing a nice trade with the locals, and they seemed supportive up to now. I don't know what changed."

Isan gave a short laugh. "You let Baku draw reinforcements from them, that's what changed. He probably pressed them into service and left the families without enough men. From what I've heard mumbled, that seems to be their whole cause to revolt."

"But Baku said they were excited to join us."

Isan laughed again. "Baku has learned to choose his words carefully after being around a royal court for so long. He is a good man, a good warrior, and an excellent talker. I would follow him anywhere. But you must look beyond what he says. He needed men fast, and so said and did whatever he must to get them. Now, we have angry mothers and wives tearing up your camp."

He turned back to the shabby crowd huddled behind spear-wielding guards. The majority were women of every age, with a few young boys and older men sprinkled among them. None of them were of the fighting age Baku would've selected. Of those men, they were either dead or captured, or else running back to their homes to find their families gone.

Varro let out a long sigh and his shoulders slumped.

"I can't use them as shields. That would be a shame I could never live with."

Isan nodded. "It was a good plan, but would have only justified the rebels and probably encourage them to greater zeal."

"Send them out of the camp immediately. I don't want them to report any of our preparations to the rebels."

While Isan gave the orders to his men, and the captives began to speak excitedly of their freedom, Falco and Curio arrived.

"The two of you don't look hopeful."

"Your cistern was dry," Falco said. "I mean, there's some water in it, but the men and horses are going to consume that before I'm done telling you that we have shit for supplies as well. I think your camp visitors decided to wreck everything they found."

"So no water and only the food and feed you carried here?" Varro looked back out to the cloud of dust and saw the glint of metal beneath it. "I don't suppose we have time to make a run for it."

"It would be a fight in the open," Falco said, frowning after Varro's gaze. "Trained cavalry against a bunch of rabble. Probably good odds for our victory."

"Hold on," Curio said. "What about that Mountain character, Dribble, or whatever his name is?"

"He's just one man," Varro said. He narrowed his eyes at the billowing clouds. "But the rebels seem to be numerous to make clouds like that. I've been learning how to judge enemy numbers by the dust they kick up in this land. It's not easy to sneak a march here."

"Well, you're right," Falco said. "Isan told us there are about two hundred combat effectives with them and many more family tagging along. It's a whole fucking tribe of these bastards, and they're all in some frenzy against Masinissa because of this blowhard leading them. So maybe their children will join the fight too."

"I don't want to kill children," Curio said.

"You will if they want to kill you," Falco countered.

"We would deny their numbers advantage by remaining here," Varro said. "Their horses would be useless after we get the barriers back in place. Those won't move aside so easily now that we have sufficient men to defend them. So they'll have to fight on foot, and I've learned the Massylii would rather use hit-and-run tactics than line up and battle it out."

"True," Falco said. "Sounds great right up until we die of thirst. Once they realize we are plugged up here, they can just wait us out."

Varro scanned the sky and felt the wind on his face. "It will rain. If not today then tomorrow. We have horse meat if it comes to that. I know the tribesmen would rather die than kill a horse. But I think Isan's men might be more practical."

"You make it sound like a merry little party," Falco said, folding his strong arms. The sun striking his wide brow cast his eyes into shadow. But Varro knew they were alight with mischief nonetheless.

"I thought you enjoyed a good fight," Varro said, smiling. "Besides we're going to meet Dribble and cut his balls off right in front of his band of worshipers. Once we do that, and maybe put a spear through the heart of their leader, we won't have to worry about their numbers."

Isan returned from the edge of the camp after having overseen the ejection of the prisoners. He had fresh blood splashed on his arms, and only as he reached them did one of his attending bodyguards give him a cloth to wipe up.

"I mounted the heads of the slingers on the front barriers," he said as joined them again. "Thankfully none of the captives were of any relationship. I left the bodies at the foot of the approach to rot."

"I knew I liked this fellow," Falco said under his breath.

Varro explained his plan and Isan agreed that an open fight might not go well as outnumbered as they were. He would send one messenger on horseback to Cirta with a request for a relief force.

"Even if we kill every last one of them, we will need a stronger presence in this area for years to come."

"We might need them to free Baku," Varro said, glancing to the east. There was only a high cliff wall there, but he saw through it to a distant border fort where his men were held captive. "I cannot imagine the Carthaginians will delay in dispensing justice. If we do not reach Baku soon, I think King Masinissa will be displeased, to say the least."

He then detailed his plans for defense, including sending men up into the cliff walls where he had previously prepared boulders and rocks to disrupt an attack up the path. He also wanted barriers erected at the spot where the task force entered.

"I'm afraid we gave up too much information with that unnecessary attack. Now the captives will report that approach to the rebels. They'll never get more than a dozen men through, but if they come with lit torches we could find the camp ablaze before we know it."

He and the rest looked to the billowing hide tents still in place. Their former occupants were long gone, and they had been ransacked by the tribe that had come after them. Due to the narrow layout of the camp, the tents were close enough that fire could spread easily from one to the next.

"We have a few hours before the fighting starts," Varro said. "Keep men on watch but have the others get what rest they can. Isan, you should take Baku's tent over there and see what he might have left behind. Falco, Curio, you will be sharing my tent. Let's go find out what they left of it."

None of the tents had been pulled up, but the interiors had been raided, either searching for signs of a loved one or just out of anger. Varro's desk had been overturned and the last of his ink and wine spilled into the dirt. Someone had defecated on his bed, filling the tent with a horrid stench and buzzing flies.

"Don't ask me to clean that out," Curio said. "This is your mess, sir."

His stool had been flipped over and someone had chopped at it with a blade. Lastly his lockbox had been shattered, likely by using his armor rack which lay broken beside it. The coins had spilled out, and unsurprisingly they remained untouched. Coin did not matter much to tribesmen. But his velum had been scattered on the floor and soaked with urine. The careful lettering was mostly ruined and all the sheets were stained.

"Someone took your place for a latrine," Falco said, holding his finger under his nose. "Maybe I'll go sleep with the horses. It'll probably smell better there."

"I don't think they enjoyed my writing as much as you did, either." He toed aside vellum sheets but found they clung together. "So much for keeping records of what I did."

"Look, I was just kidding about writing histories," Falco said, gently patting Varro's back. "There's not much to save here except the coins and some of your clothes. Rather than clean up, let's just move your things to another tent. Later we'll get a rebel prisoner to do it."

They left the tent to find a place to relocate. However, the camp was now overcrowded with eighty men and fifty horses plus baggage. Even the parade ground was now being covered by men setting up tents. Baku's tent was just as large as Varro's. The interior was largely untouched, with only a few items scattered. But he had already promised it to Captain Isan. So in the end they pitched a small tent in the corner of the camp. They could not move all of Varro's items over.

"We'll trust that Isan's men will be too busy to loot the coins from my tent."

Falco wrinkled his nose. "Maybe tribesmen don't care about money, but these are soldiers. You can be sure if they learn the coins are just sitting there, then there will be trouble."

"We'll handle that later. Let's get some rest."

It was like their days as recruit Hastati, or so it felt to Varro. They piled into a tent meant only for two men and slept shoulder to shoulder. Neither Falco nor Curio took any time to sleep, but Varro's mind planned the battle ahead. He might have stolen an hour's nap before he heard men shouting warnings.

All three of them were out of the tent and had dragged their shields and weapons with them before Captain Isan found them. He had gone to Varro's tent instead.

"The rebels are here," he said. "And they demand to speak to you."

"They called me by name?" Varro asked.

"They asked for the Roman," Isan said. "I'll go with you, sir."

At the top of the incline, he saw what felt like an endless stream of horses and men. Head covers of white, blue, gray, and green bobbed like flower petals on a pond.

"It just looks like a lot because they're jammed together." Falco covered his heavy brow with one hand to get a better look. "But I'll agree there's quite a few."

"The barriers are all set in place," he said. "I have all thirty infantry here to defend them."

"That feels thin," Curio said, peering out over the swell of enemies below.

"The barriers will make it impossible for them to get more than a few men to attack any one of them," Varro said. "We'll just have to wear them down."

"And not get worn down ourselves," Curio said in a smaller voice.

Varro passed between the interwoven barriers to come to a line of wooden stakes where he could see the group of men standing forward from the rabble.

"There he is," Isan said. "His name is Tanan and he leads the rebellion. Those are his brothers and other family members with him."

"If we had a ballista we could take them out in one shot," Falco said.

"But we don't. So let's hear what they have to say." Varro cupped his hand to his mouth and called out in Latin, "Come forward and I'll speak to you. I guarantee your safety while we speak."

The group of about eight men seemed confused and leaned into each other as if confirming their understanding. Then the one called Tanan leaned back in laughter. He wore a bright blue tunic and head cover that distinguished him from the others and had a long sword strapped to his hip.

Tanan and his group came forward and he spoke in his own language while Captain Isan translated.

"We have a simple demand. Put down your weapons and surrender the camp to us. We will only take the Romans as prisoners, and everyone else may go free."

"That is a lie," Isan said after translating. "They have killed everyone loyal to the King since they began their uprising."

"Well, then please embellish your translation of my reply accordingly." Varro pointed his gladius at Tanan as he addressed him. "It is you who should put down your weapons and surrender. Otherwise, I will see all of you dead, right down to your families. There will be no mercy if you do not submit to the rightful authority of King Masinissa."

Before Isan's translation finished Tanan's men were already

shaking their heads. He laughed once more, then drew his own sword to point back at Varro.

"Your head will decorate my camp tonight. You have chosen death for yourself and your men."

Tanan and his entourage returned to their lines as did Varro.

"We had planned for slingers to defend the path," he said as they wove between barriers and their grim-faced defenders. "But I don't expect you have any."

"The infantry carries javelins," he said. "Enough for two casts each."

"Then we must depend on sixty dead. Every cast must count."

"What about the rocks?" Falco asked, nodding up to the ledges. "That ought to do some damage."

"We'll wait for their main force to try their push. Once that trick is revealed, it will be easy enough to avoid a second time."

Normally Varro would try to rally his men before the fight, but his limited command of the language denied him the opportunity. Perhaps it was not a custom in the Numidian army, for Captain Isan just shouted orders and his men obeyed.

The cavalry mounted in the camp, in case they had to deal with a breakthrough. Varro expected cavalry to step into wherever the infantry failed. This seemed to rankle them as Isan translated the command, leaving them with disgusted frowns.

"Cavalrymen sure are alike everywhere," Falco said, staring after them. "Always better than the infantry in their minds."

"Well, we all know who wins the battles," Varro said. "The three of us have shields equal to any barrier I've managed to build. So we'll fight from the front and plug any gaps. There are a lot of enemies, but I wonder at their heart for a real fight. So far, they've been drunk on easy victories. Today, we'll teach them defeat."

Curio tapped his shield to the stony ground. "They won't get past me. I swear it."

Varro smiled and then looked up at the darkening sky. "And a storm would be welcomed now. Both for water and to keep the enemy off of us while our messenger gets back to Cirta. If it rains hard enough then water will flow down the path to wash them back."

"Easy as slaughtering lambs," Falco said. He clapped his sword to the side of his scutum. "Let's get in line."

Captain Isan stood with Varro behind a plank barrier. Varro stepped on a rock to see over the top. His bronze helmet might draw attention, but he did not think these Massylii had slings or other missile weapons. Their first line was comprised of footmen with small shields and spears held before them.

They marched up the slope and the Numidian infantry prepared to cast their javelins. Isan held his command until the enemy was committed enough that they could not flee back to safety before a second volley.

Varro felt the urge to give the command himself but knew to trust the Captain. At the moment he could not hold back, Isan gave an explosive shout.

White streaks sped down the slope as the enemy held up their small wicker shields. The front row collapsed into screams, and the rear ranks stumbled over them. A second volley followed and sewed devastation into the next rank.

The enemy footmen scrabbled back down the path leaving a tide mark of dead bodies. The Numidians jeered at them, some hurling stones along with their curses.

Isan turned to Varro with a satisfied smile. "If they had sent more men, then we would have sixty dead. As it is, perhaps it is forty dead."

"That was a fine display." He peered over the top of the barrier and scanned the dead and dying. Isan's estimate seemed appropriate. But of course they had plentiful targets in a small area, so that killing anything less would be a shame.

Varro watched the rebels regrouping and heard the angry

shouts from their companions. The footmen vanished into the ranks of horsemen now swelling together.

"I think they sent those footmen in to soak up our javelins."

"Tanan is a shrewd enemy," Isan said calmly. "Too bad he is a rebel. The King could use such a man."

"They're preparing a cavalry charge. They're going to try to smash through the barriers."

"Reckless," Isan said. "But they have no other choice if they want to take this position."

Varro nodded in agreement, then stepped back onto the stone to review the developments. The rebel horsemen looked much like his own troops had, except more than double their numbers. It was an impressive sight to see so many mounted men compacted into a tight formation. They would have the weight of numbers to complete their push into the camp. But it would cost them much. Whatever they expected to gain by capturing this place, they must also expect it to bring reinforcements to their cause. Otherwise, it would be an empty victory.

Then Varro saw an enormous shape emerge from the throng. It was a rider on a black horse taller than all the others. His arrival hushed the chatter among his own. The rider was a hulking brute and dwarfed his horse. He was bald and wore no helmet. In fact, he wore no protection or carried no shield. The longsword in his grip seemed no bigger than a gladius.

"I think the one called Djebel has come to the front."

Isan nodded without concern. "Yes, he is their legendary Roman warrior. A man they say who cannot be killed by a mortal weapon. Whatever might be true of that, I know he is a fearsome fighter. We should prioritize killing him."

Varro, still standing on the stone, looked harder at that giant rider. He felt familiar in both profile and demeanor. Perhaps it was because he was Roman, he thought. But as the figure edged his horse closer to the line of dead footmen, the sun fell across his bald head to deepen the shadows of the cratered scars there.

"This cannot be," he said to himself. "I killed him."

But the giant rider seemed to be glaring at him across the distance. And Varro could not deny he was looking at his former kidnapper, Lars.

22

Lars searched up the slope. His vision had never been the same after his head wound. The Roman and his Numidian lapdogs had constructed barriers of wood planks and sharpened stakes. It was all a vague smear to him. But unlike Tanan he did not care what riches were in the camp or how many tribesmen would feel avenged for the loss of their sons. He was within charging distance of his entire reason for living.

Up that slope, cowering behind those feeble barriers, was Centurion Varro.

A burning thirst raked Lars's soul and could only be quenched with the Centurion's blood. He would drink it from his pumping heart, and crush the last pulpy bits of it in his fist before eating it.

"Bellus, I avenge you this day."

He spoke Latin but it was the most complex thought he had been able to articulate since joining with Tanan. Every night he consumed a draught of bitter liquid that was to keep Bezza's poison from reasserting itself. It seemed to work, for Lars felt the return of boiling rage and a lust to kill. Under Bezza's concoctions, he was always tired and sleepy. Healing is what he called it. His leg was fine now. Bezza had just been keeping him down like a pet dog.

But he tore the old men to shreds, with great patience so that he could enjoy the suffering. It was good practice for Centurion Varro.

"Djebel, you will lead us to victory this day!"

Tanan had broken the silence in the ranks. He spoke cheerfully as if that victory was in hand already. Lars was not certain. There was a large pile of dead between them and the camp. He knew not to underestimate Centurion Varro. But his mind could not settle on one thing, but leaped from visions of bloody murder to Bellus's dead face and then to other violent images that made no sense to him. He would have no peace until Centurion Varro died.

"I will."

Such a simple statement was a cause for celebration among Tanan's people. They now began to whoop and shout, raising spears and swords as their horses snorted for release. Lars felt the sides of his own mount rising and falling as it too anticipated the battle.

"Then we shall not delay," Tanan said as the cheers subsided. "A fortune in captured Carthaginian goods awaits us, and freedom for our oppressed brothers."

Tanan said other things, but Lars did not listen. Instead, he fought with his vision to pick out the Centurion. He would be wearing a fine bronze helmet and carrying a big shield just as he himself had. But that was a decade ago. Today he rode a horse with the Massylii and carried one of their long swords. They called him one of their own. He supposed he liked that. But so had his former citizens and look what they did to him?

He only trusted Bellus and now he was gone. The urge swept over him and he felt rage shaking in his arms.

"Drink your potion," Tanan said, quietly offering him a small bladder of the bitter liquid. "We need all your fury to break through those barriers."

Lars stared at the bladder as Tanan's crooked fingers pulled out the stopper. That so-called potion gave him incredible strength, but it fogged his mind. If he drank it, he might forget his purpose was to kill Centurion Varro.

"No, I don't need it. I will kill Centurion Varro."

"Djebel," he said with a false smile. "The people look to your strength to carry them to victory. They have already lost some of their heart after seeing so many killed. We cannot risk it."

"I said no." He set his eyes on Tanan and his focus came clear. That seemed to cow the man, and he stuffed the bladder into this tunic again.

"As you wish, Djebel. I just hope Bezza's poison does not return during the fight."

He wanted to curse the man and tell him his fears and dreams meant nothing to him, and that he cared for revenge alone. But he could not make such a statement, at least not without a long time to think about how to speak it aloud.

"It won't."

Tanan now turned to the others and began to rally them for the charge

Lars felt his focus returning. He could see better now, but not far. There was a gleam of a helmet from behind a tall board. The hint of a large shield showed through gaps in the planks. That was the Centurion. That would be the point of his charge.

Something sharp and cold struck his cheek. He touched it, finding a clear raindrop on his thick fingertip. He looked up. The wind had been blowing all morning and the sky darkening. At last the rain would come. But even if no one else charged alongside him, he would still take the Centurion for himself.

"No one kills the Roman. Only I do."

Tanan turned from his speech, his expression caught between a fake smile and irritation.

"Everyone knows your desire, Djebel. The Roman is yours to do with as you wish."

Not waiting for the call to charge, Lars urged his mount forward. He had to build up speed to leap the bodies in the way. He was not sure if his horse could manage with his weight. He felt its fighting spirit under him. It was afraid of the barriers, but it trusted him.

Tanan shouted for the rest to charge alongside him. As if the gods were listening, the clouds opened up in the same moment.

Rain splattered over Lars's head. It darkened the yellow ground before him as if it were showing him the way up the slope.

He did not fear enemy javelins. Such weapons might hurt him, but could not kill him. There was no pain or injury that would keep him from killing the Centurion in battle this day.

The horse cleared the bodies easily but now slowed as it landed among uneven and rocky ground. Lars let out a bellow of frustration. The footing was terrible for a charging horse, and even the most loyal mount could not be made to run through it.

Yet others surged around him now. Their mounts were burdened with less weight. Most of these tribesmen were little better than reeds compared with himself. Tanan pulled up beside him as they all met in a line to plug the road toward the barriers.

"They flee before us!"

Tanan was right. It seemed they were falling back from the barriers. He tried to focus on the Centurion, but he had vanished behind his wall. No matter. He would smash it aside and lay Varro bare under the sky before killing him. There was no place for him to hide that Lars could not reach.

The battle cries of men and the thudding of hooves on the rocky ground filled his ears. The horses would not charge but still carried them forward. Tanan said the horses would batter aside the boards and create an opening to the camp. Lars guided his horse toward the wall where he expected Centurion Varro to hide. The many stakes and other sharp sticks limited the paths open to them. But Lars insisted he be first in and no other tribesman would challenge him, not even Tanan. He rode at Lar's right, a head-length behind him.

"Destroy the barriers, Djebel!" His shout was hardly audible over the rain, shouting, and snorting from the densely packed horses. "They have no more javelins!"

It was true, he thought. By now they would be filled with javelins if the Numidian lapdogs had any to throw. So he urged his mount and it lurched ahead of Tanan.

The sharpened stakes and sawhorse barriers funneled them to a point. Lars suspected this was deliberate. But a lusty rage controlled him now that his enemy was so near. In the deepest part of his brain, he recognized something about the layout. The barriers and stakes were arranged much like marching camps he remembered from long ago. But what did it mean?

Then his horse screamed and crashed headlong into the ground. Caught by surprise, Lars flew over its head to slam onto the stony earth.

Rain scoured his face and between its slashing into the ground and the thunder of hooves rumbling through the earth, he heard nothing else. He lay dazed, staring at the dull glare of the sky and the steady line of rain.

But larger shapes tumbled out of the glare.

"Stones!"

Someone shouted the warning. Lars at last looked to his horse laying still at his feet. Its tongue and teeth were exploded open beneath a huge stone. The rest of its skull had been shattered to spray blood and brains that melted into the puddles of rain.

Men screamed as huge stones fell from the sky. Horses screeched and crashed hard on their sides. Massive rocks fell straight down, blasting into the ground to create a new barrier for the horses.

Lars stood. He had lost his sword. But he rose above the madness and found a churning mess of men and beast and scores of huge rocks that had pounded them into bloody mash. Rain lashed them like a scourge of the gods.

A stone struck his shoulder, staggering him onto one knee. It had skimmed his head, and he fought to stay erect. Now something coppery mixed with the rain flowing into his gaping mouth.

Rain and blood blinded him. He fought to his feet once more and roared his frustration.

"Centurion Varro! I will kill you!"

Tanan was screaming for retreat. Rocks fell around him, large and small. Water rushed underfoot, sluicing sludge and blood down the slope. The massive press of horses, unable to turn, kept men bottled under the stone barrage.

Lars lurched forward toward the wood barrier.

He slammed both hands on it and with all his strength he unmoored it. The wood cracked and snapped as he hauled it aside like peeling the shell off a turtle's back.

Two men faced him, both in shock at the sudden loss of their protection. They were smeary blots in his burning, swirling eyes.

One seemed to scurry back. The other picked up a large shield, or what looked like it, and leaped at him.

"Centurion!" Lars screamed with joy. Only the Centurion would be brave enough to charge at him.

Lars knew the punch and thrust technique of the legionary too well. No matter how much of his past he had abandoned, he could never forget what had been drilled into him.

He stepped back with the punch, draining it of its power so that the heavy shield strike was little better than a tap. Expecting the stab of the gladius, he stepped aside for it. When it darted from behind the shield, he slapped his gigantic hand around the Centurion's wrist. Crushing down on it, he felt the racing pulse.

"For Bellus!"

He twisted the arm and the Centurion gave a howl of pain. It was dull and unsatisfying under the driving rain and cries of panic and pain.

So he yanked the Centurion out of hiding and flung him like a child's doll into the bloody mud outside the barriers.

He heard him cursing as he rolled down the slope into a dead horse, but Lars could hardly see.

Someone flickered out of the barrier and stabbed his leg. The bright pain reminded him of the danger of standing amid this chaos. He slapped aside the spear in his thigh, then punched his attacker in the head, sending him flying back into the destroyed barrier.

But the man was not deterred and rebounded at him. Now boiling with rage at this bug of a man, Lars stepped out of the spear thrust and grabbed the enemy's head. It was hot under his palms and twisted easily on the man's shoulders. The thin crack of bone satisfied him, and he let the enemy fall into the rainwater rushing over his sandaled feet.

Turning back to the Centurion, he found him struggling up with his sword arm hanging limply. He was like a drunk, and only half upright.

Another rock struck Lars in the back. It hurt, but he did not flinch. This one might have been thrown at him rather than dropped from above. But as he watched his enemy slip and fall into the mud once more, he realized he could never enjoy proper revenge while being harassed on all sides. All his companions were fleeing back down the slope. The cheering of the Numidian lapdogs meant they had won this round of battle.

Lars kicked Centurion Varro in his stomach as he once more tried to rise up from the mud. He flipped atop a dead horse. But with rain and blood flooding Lars's eyes, he could not even enjoy the expression of pain in his enemy's face.

"You come with me, Centurion."

He scooped him off the horse then threw him across his shoulder. Centurion Varro was strong and struggled hard. His hand searched for another weapon, finding his pugio and drawing it with a dull hiss.

"Not again, Centurion."

Lars slammed Varro onto the rocky slope with both hands. His scream cut short on the impact. While Lars could barely see, he knew his enemy had been stunned into silence. His hands opened and his pugio dropped into the mud.

"I will enjoy killing you," he said as he hefted his limp body over his shoulder again. "But later. You will suffer. Bellus would want that."

He tramped back down the slope like a farmer returning from a long day in the field. The rest of Tanan's men sped past him, eyes of both rider and horse white with terror. Hooves splashed mud on him as they dashed back to the safety of their line. The torrential rain did not abate. Maybe the gods had truly been angry with Tanan.

But they had not been angry with Lars. They had granted Centurion Varro, after all. The weight of his limp body on his shoulder was a comfort. No matter what Tanan might think about today, it was Lars's great victory.

The retreat finally halted when they reached the women and children, who had been left in the rear. They had not been idle and set up small tents for shelter against the rain everyone had anticipated. Tanan stood before these tents commanding his men to stop fleeing. Some listened, and others continued to ride.

"Djebel!" Tanan ran to him, his expression unusually panicked. "Make these men stop."

"This is the Centurion."

Tanan's expression immediately shifted from terror to shrewd calculation. "He's alive? Give him to me, Djebel! I will keep him safe for you. But you must stop the men from fleeing or we will have nothing left."

He stared hard at Tanan. Should he give him his prize? But Djebel could not see and his leg was hurting again. Bezza's potion must have been at work, for he was beginning to feel tired and weak.

"If the Centurion dies, you die too."

"Of course, Djebel. Rally the men!"

Tanan accepted the heavy body of the Centurion. He groaned as he took him onto his own shoulder. He then looked around as if searching for a safe place to hide him.

Now Lars turned to the men riding past. He roared out to those yet to reach the camp.

"Stop!"

Some men obeyed, such was the power of his booming voice. But others had been too terrorized by the carnage and tried to charge past him. One got by, but he easily plucked the next rider off his horse.

He crashed screaming to the ground, but Lars straddled him. He slapped both his hands to either side of his head.

"Stop or die!"

He twisted the man's head around on his shoulders. He kept twisting, and the skin and sinew tightened as he did. But the bones of the neck had snapped and Lars felt burning impatience translate into raging strength.

Twisting and pulling, the man's flesh tore with a satisfying rip and spray of blood. The head flopped to the shoulder, still attached to the body but clear enough to demonstrate Lars's intent to others.

He hefted the corpse up in one hand and displayed it to the incoming horsemen.

"Stop!"

Seeing his great strength, men came to their senses. They reined in their horses before him as he held the body aloft. Many said they had heard he had been killed, and so fled for their own lives. But Lars shook the bloodied corpse at them.

"He is dead. I am alive."

The rain did not abate, but Tanan's men came to their senses. Their panic ebbed, and so did Djebel's strength.

"Damn you, Bezza."

He dropped the corpse and stomped off toward a tent. Three men were crowded under one. But at Lars's approach they scurried away. He slipped out of the rain, wiping blood and water from his eyes.

He looked at his leg. The old wound that Varro had given him and Bezza had burned shut seemed to be pulling apart. A line of beaded dark blood showed there. On the back of his leg, a deeper wound from that enemy spear bothered him. But it was nothing a bandage wouldn't handle. The pain meant nothing to him.

He waited a long time as Tanan organized his men. He made a bandage for his leg out of a strip of his own soaked tunic. No one approached him and he asked for none to come. The wait tired him and he felt like sleeping. He caught himself nodding forward twice.

But soon the rain slowed and Tanan seemed to be making a camp. Horses were counted along with injured. Lars could see it all from his position, but most important was Centurion Varro's tent. Four men stood around it so that he could not escape from any side of it.

At last, Tanan crossed the muddy ground to find him.

"We have lost many men, and many more have fled."

Lars stared at him, uncaring.

"But we have the Centurion, and so we have a hostage worth trading. Djebel, can you wait to kill him until after we used him to bargain? We will have another chance to capture him again. We know right where he is."

The rage returned and Lars sprung to his feet, knocking the low tent off its poles. Tanan retreated out of the tent, pleading with him.

"Djebel, you must see reason. The Centurion's life can be traded for the camp and its riches. We need that to replace what was lost. What have so many died for if we retreat now?"

"No!"

His roar could have flattened every tent in the camp. Tanan fell away as if a gale had swept him into the air.

Lars now stalked across the muddy ground. His hands began to itch and his arms quiver with the anticipation of tearing Centurion Varro to bits.

Tanan chased after him, spouting more words that Lars did not hear.

The men guarding the tent were wide-eyed and frightened, pulling back from his approach.

He tore away the entirety of the small tent and threw it into the wind.

"I will kill you, Centurion."

Now his eyes were clear and focused.

The man exposed under the tent was not Centurion Varro. It was another man, bigger and with a heavy brow that was drawn down into a frown.

"You fucking traitor," the man said in a voice that was not Centurion Varro's. "You can try killing me. But I'll be feeding you your balls for breakfast, you dumb shit."

"Where is Centurion Varro?"

But before the man lying at his feet could answer, he felt a burning prick at the back of his arm. Hot blood rolled under his bicep and he turned around.

Tanan stood behind him with a thin-bladed knife that gleamed in the dull light. Something bitter wafted up from it.

"I am sorry, Djebel."

"I cannot die from a mortal weapon."

But his sight was already dimming and his head felt heavy.

He crashed to his knees and held his temples.

Tanan knelt beside him.

"Not killing, just calming you. It is for your health, Djebel. You are bleeding."

"I will kill you, too."

But then Lars fell back into blackness.

23

Varro stood atop his rock once more to survey the results of the barrage. Rain raked across the battlefield where scores of rebels lay in mangled heaps. The Numidians on the cliff walls and along the barriers cheered at the retreating rebels. Even the cavalry within the camp cheered.

"Had the weather been better, I'd have ordered the cavalry to clean them up." Varro smiled at Isan as he stepped down. "I think the rebels are broken."

Isan looked equally satisfied.

"The bad weather helped to drive them off, and would be just as treacherous to us as them." The captain glanced back to the camp. "But I would still expect them to outnumber us unless more men desert Tanan after this defeat."

"I expect more will," Varro said. "And if we do not act fast, they will escape. We must bring Tanan to justice with all speed. Then we can turn to Baku and my men over the border."

"Yes, sir." But Isan's tone spoke more than his words. He did not hold any hope for the captured men, for the Carthaginians would treat them as ordinary brigands. To treat them otherwise would actually open up more troubles with Numidia. A wise commander would simply proclaim them as outlaw raiders and execute them with haste rather than have to admit Numidia and Carthage were skirmishing at the border.

"I must try," Varro said. His voice was lost in the pelting rain, but Isan nodded again. "Now, let us see how our side fared. There was a small breakthrough in the center, from what I saw. But otherwise, hardly a man reached us before they fled for safety."

He and Isan picked their way toward the center. This was where Lars had led the charge, following the path that would place the enemy in the right position for the rock trap. It still seemed impossible that Lars had somehow survived what should have been immediate death. Yet he could not deny it was him riding up the slope. Fortunately, it seemed he died after all when a rock landed atop his horse. Varro did not see more from his vantage, but finding his crushed body would settle any doubts.

Yet as he approached the center, he saw Curio running back and forth through the gap in the barriers. One of the main wall boards had been wrenched aside. Fortunately, a large stone plugged the gap or the enemy could have broken through to the lighter defenses in the rear.

But he did not like the concern he read on Curio's face. Rain plinked off Varro's helmet as called him over.

"Falco's gone," he said. He held up his palm, and a naked pugio caked with mud shined in the rain. A silver owl's head was inlaid on the pommel.

Varro took it and frowned. "What do you mean? Why do you have his pugio?"

"I mean he's not here," he said, looking down the slope. "I can't figure it out. The man on guard with Falco is dead."

They both looked to a body sprawled over the destroyed barrier. Rain caused his tunic to stick to his corpse. He had no blood, but his face was completely blue and head spun around on his shoulders. A broken spear lay at his feet.

"That's the work of Djebel." Isan crouched beside the man and closed his wide-staring eyes then lowered his head.

"Lars?" Varro whispered the name under his breath. It could not be, but then he held Falco's new pugio. "Where did you find this?"

"Just beyond this breach," Curio pointed to a dead horse. "It was laying on the path next to that horse, shining like it was calling to me. Rainwater was piling mud over it. It'd have been buried soon."

Varro examined the spot, but it was all muck. The horse's head had been crushed and spilled gallons of blood around it. Between that and the rainwater, there was nothing to read in the mud.

What he did not find was more instructive.

"Lars's body is not here." Rain pelted his helmet and his chain shirt as he stared down the slope at the confused retreat. He could not see the giant through the gray sheets of rain between them. "I think Falco was captured."

"I can't get the story out of these men," Curio said. "They all retreated when the rocks started falling. I did too. I guess Falco stood in place."

"He probably wanted to hold the center against a breakthrough," Varro wiped the rain dripping off his helmet into his face.

"But one of those rocks could've landed on him."

Curio's words fell away as he shared a knowing smirk with Varro.

"He wouldn't be afraid of falling rocks. Our friend is too stubborn for that. He stood his ground and kept that man with him. Lars broke through, killed Isan's soldier then captured Falco before fleeing."

Isan had moved down the line, and returned while Varro and

Curio stared into the sheeting rain where the enemy had fled. He confirmed Varro's guess with reports from others. In the end, Falco and his companion had been the only casualties.

"I'd call it a good day if it weren't for Falco's capture." Varro shook his head. "Now I've got to rescue that stubborn fool."

"Sir, I know he's your friend, but a counter attack now would be dangerous. If Djebel is still with them, and it seems he is, then they will rally for a new fight."

"So your advice is to wait until they have recovered fully and are rested for the night? That will be more advantageous?"

Isan's noble face darkened and he titled his head in reply.

"With respect, sir, we now have all the advantages. We've thinned their numbers, broke their morale, and this downpour will refill your cistern. We can hold out until King Masinissa sends a relief force. And that might not be needed if they attempt another attack. Why put so many in danger for one man's life."

Varro blinked at Isan and felt his neck throbbing with rage. Curio stood straighter beside him as well.

"Captain Isan, I am in command. If I order a counterattack now, then that is what we will do."

"I understand, sir. But I question your reason for it. You want to save your friend. But if you do not even allow Tanan to bargain for his life, then he will just kill him the moment you send in the cavalry."

Trying to conceal his frustration, he looked back toward the enemy camp. It was a dark smear in the distance.

The rain pelting his helmet filled his ears with metallic echoes. Rainwater poured down his body, turning hot with his quivering rage. With a professional cavalry against demoralized rabble, he would expect an easy victory. There would be inevitable casualties, but his mission to maintain the peace in the region would be achieved. Fulfilling his orders should be his highest priority.

But the bonds of a deep friendship pulled at him. Isan's words had the intended effect. He now wondered if such an attack would ultimately lead to Falco's death. Surely, if this Tanan was any kind of leader he would understand he could bargain for something to show his people their attack was not a complete failure. But if Varro demonstrated disregard for Falco's life, then the next best thing to appease his men would be to have revenge on their enemies by killing Falco.

"Do you think they will try to trade him for something?"

Curio asked the question, breaking Varro's pensive silence.

"Of course," Varro said. "I don't even need to know Tanan to guess that is his plan. It would be mine if I was in his position."

Isan's dark face finally cleared. "Not all the enemy are dead. We have prisoners to question. We can learn what motivates Tanan."

"It's not just this camp that he wants," Varro said. "That was a determined attack for ground they do not need to take. Find out what they really are after, and we go from there."

As Isan left to organize a party to retrieve prisoners from the wreckage along the barriers, Curio grabbed Varro's arm and drew close.

"What's the real plan? We're going in after him, aren't we? We're not just going to sit up here and wait on the enemy?"

"I know what they want," Varro said with a heavy sigh. "At least what Lars wants. He thought Falco was me. I killed his brother and thought I had killed him as well. So he wants revenge."

Curio grumbled. "If that's true, then we've got to get to him now. Dribble might be a giant brute, but he'll be smart enough to know torturing Falco is a great way to torture you."

"He doesn't know our relationship." But Varro felt a chill touch his heart. Maybe Lars was too stupid to take anything but the straight path, yet this Tanan character might test for Varro's weak points.

"Falco wouldn't sit by if it was you."

"I'm not sitting by." Varro's shout rose above the slashing rain, but no one was near to hear him besides Curio. "I'm trying to figure out how to get him back without everything going to shit. I've already lost one entire command. I can't lose another. There are men probably being tortured and killed right now because of my actions. And now I've got Falco to deal with. Just work with me, Curio."

Curio stepped back and nodded. "Alright. Falco's a tough one. They might slap him around but he can take that. We just can't let them get bored or they're going to look to Falco for entertainment. We killed a lot of their friends and Falco is right there to provide some revenge. What if they want us to surrender this camp? Why do we care if they have it?"

"For one, we just taught them how to defend it, and we'll be the ones to dig them out of it. Isan and his men would probably rebel if I agreed, in any case. I might be in command, but it's just you and me here. How easy is it for Isan to tell King Masinissa the enemy killed us?"

"Well, let's hope the rebels want something else."

It hurt to turn away from the line, knowing Falco was a short ride down the slope and in the hands of his enemies. But he had to count on Tanan to recognize the value of his hostage. In any case, he would not wait long to take action regardless of what Isan and others felt.

He and Curio met at Isan's tent, which was Baku's former tent and the largest one in good condition. They dried off as best they could and helped each other wipe down their mail. Rain was notoriously destructive even with the best oils to repel it. They would need professionals to scour off the rust, which was never a problem in the Roman army. But out in the mountains of Numidia, Varro expected his armor might be ruined.

"Did Baku keep anything to drink in here?" Curio asked, looking around.

Varro shrugged and glanced around. The contents of his chests and bags had been thrown in a corner. His tunics were slashed up and bits of freshly broken wood were all that remained of some chests. In the end, they waited on their thirst and sat in companionable silence.

Isan joined them in the tent after the rain had tapered off to a steady drizzle. He looked enviously at both of them as they were now drying off and seated comfortably on stools. He wiped water from his face before reporting.

"I've figured out what they want. You raided a Carthaginian caravan a month ago? They have heard you have a fortune in captured goods here."

Varro's mouth opened but he said nothing. Curio spoke instead.

"So that's all they want? Can't you give it to them?"

"We didn't capture a thing," he said. "We never made it back with the goods. We just barely got back with our lives."

"Well, that is not the story they have heard," Isan said. "And the prisoners we set free earlier are likely going to tell them we don't have a stockpile of Carthaginian goods up here. So I expect Tanan is going to be in a rage for sacrificing so many men for basically nothing."

Varro looked at Curio, and he knew his friend had the same thought.

"Then he's going to kill Falco out of frustration." Varro stood up from his seat. "We need to act before he learns the truth."

"But that's not all of it," Isan said. "He also wants to drive us away to impress the locals and bring them into his rebellion. This camp was to bring him wealth and fame. He can still get the fame if he defeats us."

"That won't happen," Varro said. "He no longer has the men for it and he let us get a messenger out before he sealed us off. He will understand this."

"We've got to get Falco." Curio stood beside him. "Even if it's just the two of us. We can't let him be killed for this piece of shit hill in the middle of nowhere."

Varro expected Isan to protest, but instead, he grew strangely quiet and his eyes turned to the side. Varro narrowed his own eyes at the captain.

"Nothing to say about that, Isan? Curio and I will ride down and free our friend with Jupiter at our shoulders, throwing thunderbolts into our foes?"

"Well, I didn't think the gods would be joining us." Curio rubbed the back of his neck.

"Sir, there was one last thing all the captives mentioned. It seems Djebel has also learned you are here, and your life is what he desires above all else. They say he has declared he will rip you into pieces with his own hands."

"Yes, he told me that last time we fought. Djebel, as you call him, can die like any other man. I thought I had killed him, in fact."

"But you did not," Isan said, almost with a hint of reverence. "And so the tribesmen see him rise once more from a mortal wound. You also thought you had crushed him beneath a stone. But he lives to thwart you still. He has his reputation for a reason, sir."

"He's as lucky as I am," Varro said with a humorless smile. "And I believe Fortuna is right now trying to decide which of her favorite sons she wants to see live and which to die."

"Well, it's going to be you," Curio said. "Dribble makes the goddess look bad, being just a stupid pile of muscle."

"Don't underestimate him, sir. Djebel is a legend not only for surviving deadly injuries but also for battle victories."

"I don't doubt his rage will be enough to destroy me with one punch from his giant hand. It's Falco I fear for more. What do you know of Tanan? Will he act rashly when he learns his prize is not here?"

Isan shrugged. "He is newly risen to leadership. His name has never been a factor in any reports I've received. But he has a great amount of charisma or he could not have come this far. He killed his relative to take control of his tribe and knows to use Djebel's reputation to boost his own. He's a schemer, but I have no idea how well he tames his emotions."

Varro returned to his stool and rubbed his temples as he considered all that he heard. Falco's danger increased with every hour in the enemy's hands. Isan refused to risk his men in an immediate attack or at all, and Varro had no real way to enforce his authority. He was a commander in word only. However, he had one clear choice that might solve all his problems in one stroke.

"Captain, send an envoy to Tanan. Explain to him that I wish to exchange myself for Centurion Falco. We will not surrender this camp under any circumstances. Be sure to have him believe I will command a greater ransom than Falco, who is merely a junior officer."

Isan's brow furrowed. "Sir, that does not achieve anything."

"It gets Falco out of trouble, puts Tanan on notice that he cannot take this camp, and promises wealth for his sacrifices. My ransom will be paid by the King, of course. Which removes them from the area." Varro glanced at Curio, who smiled knowingly. "And it gives me the opportunity to kill Lars like I should have done before. From what you've described and what I've seen, he will come for me right away. Even Tanan won't be able to stop it unless he wants to kill Djebel."

"That's madness," Isan said. "Djebel will kill you."

"He will try," Varro said. "And Tanan will see him threaten his ransom money. If he takes me into his camp, we will have done more to disrupt him than if we risk a direct attack. It would seem half of

Tanan's strength comes from his alliance with Djebel. He'll have to let him fight me and hope that I win so he can collect his ransom. Or will he denounce his so-called immortal hero and kill him before his men? That would dissolve this loose rebellion and destroy his reputation with the tribesmen. Either way, he is diminished in some form. If I die, he loses his ransom. If I win, he loses his greatest ally. If he refuses the offer, Lars will create chaos trying to reach me."

Captain Isan shook his head. "Can't we just say Falco is a senior officer and offer to ransom him instead?"

"The prisoners we released will know who is in charge," Varro said. "Plus they've had my name all along. Lars wants revenge and won't stop trying to kill me. Falco means nothing, but if we leave him in their hands too long then I'm afraid the next time I see him it will only be his head on a pole. I'm not waiting. It's this plan or an immediate attack while they're disorganized. The former saves everyone from danger, except me of course."

Curio scratched his head. "If Tanan is so shrewd, then won't he realize all this himself?"

"Probably," Varro said with a smile. "But he has demonstrated ambition and greed in excess of common sense. His power has been shattered, and he needs something to boost his fame again. He probably believes he has some control over Lars, and would risk claiming me for ransom. In the end, he's just a brigand looking for wealth and fame. He'll take that if it's dangled before him."

Both Curio and Isan nodded in appreciation, and Varro repeated his order to send an envoy at once.

"As you command, sir." Isan inclined his head then shook it. "You would risk your life for your friend?"

Varro tilted his head. "And you would not?"

"Not while I command nearly a hundred men. They would be my first concern, sir. But I understand your heart. I will organize a group and deliver the message myself. You should rest if you think you will face Djebel soon."

Varro simply nodded and watched Isan leave the tent. Curio cleared his throat.

"He's got balls to criticize you like that. Who would want to follow him with that attitude?"

But Varro sighed. "He might be right. But he doesn't understand friendship. Now Curio, there's another part of this plan I did not tell him. I'll need your help to make sure Falco and I both walk out of that enemy camp. I have a feeling that good Captain Isan might be fine if neither of us returned alive."

He gave a boyish smile in reply.

"Let's hear it."

24

"Tanan has accepted the offer."

Captain Isan looked solemnly at Varro as if he already counted him dead. They stood in the cool evening air, outside of the large tent Baku used to occupy before his capture. Varro's mind flickered to him, yet another friend in need of his aid. He hoped his plans today did not lead to Baku's death. He loved Falco more but had come to see Baku as a mentor. His demise would forever weigh on him.

"Then we make the exchange tonight," Varro said.

"We agreed on tomorrow at dawn," Isan said. He looked sideways to his men, who were already settled into their tents for the night. A humid mist hung in the air, fading them into shades of gray.

"I didn't specify a time," Varro said. "And since we are trading Falco for me, then no harm will come to him. How long before that relief column arrives?"

Isan looked up in thought. "The messenger left this afternoon. He will be at Cirta by tomorrow. The palace will organize a response and send men. Maybe two days?"

Varro shook his head. "Two days too long. Well, once the exchange is made I will have nothing but time to wait. Did you see Falco?"

"He was tied to a stake in the center of camp. They said it was like the one you used to flog your men. You flogged your men, sir?"

"Of course," Varro said, staring disinterestedly at the high cliff walls. "That is the punishment for disregarding protocol in the Roman army."

"Well, it seems some of your men have sided with the rebels because of it."

"That doesn't usually happen in the Roman army," Varro said, folding his arms. "Everyone understands its a worse fate to desert than to just behave like a good soldier. Those so-called men I was handed to command had no idea of discipline."

Isan seemed to consider this and shrugged. "They were mostly criminals and vagrants. And now they are rebels. A flogging is the least of their worries. Sir, your plan surrenders command of the men. I should be appointed commander in your absence. Before you leave, you will make that known."

"Was that an order or request, Captain?"

"My orders were to obey you or Baku and after tomorrow neither of you will be capable of giving orders. Please, sir, I am known to the men. Falco and Curio will remain in their advisory roles. But neither are cavalry leaders."

"I suppose not," Varro said, rubbing the rough stubble on his chin. "So I will appoint you temporary commander in my or Baku's absence."

With arrangements concluded, Varro and Curio both returned to their tent.

"Good thing it's tomorrow," Curio said. "I've not been able to get everything settled yet. I can tonight."

"Get your rest," Varro said as they entered their small tent. "There's time still."

"You're the one going over to the enemy. You better rest."

It was wise counsel and Varro took it. The path to sleep was full of sharp fears of the day to come. He was letting these legends about Lars feed his imagination. But he had his plan for the coming day, and soon he found rest.

The next morning Isan assembled cavalry and infantry, all packed shoulder to shoulder in the parade ground. Varro explained the situation and Isan translated. Some of the men did speak Latin, though not well enough to understand all that was said. So Varro spoke deliberately for the parts he hoped they would understand.

"Captain Isan is in command until you receive other instructions from me or either of my subordinate officers." He gestured to Curio, who had earlier protested the reference to being a subordinate, but now simply nodded in agreement.

Isan's translation stuttered, and Varro's understanding was insufficient to know if he repeated everything verbatim.

He wore his full war gear, intent on riding to his enemy with dignity rather than as a prisoner. Isan and a half dozen cavalry would accompany him to the exchange. But Curio remained behind as arranged earlier.

With a new day on the horizon, the black clouds had vanished and left only bright skies above. The ground remained muddy and long puddles reflected the orange sunlight. Infantrymen had cleared the slope of bodies, which were thrown at the foot of the path up. Crows and vultures had been to work early on the feast, leaving the bodies stripped of flesh and eye sockets emptied. The entire area smelled of rot.

"They didn't even collect their dead," Varro said as they passed. "And yet they think being flogged is enough reason to rebel. How about being discarded for vermin? That doesn't bother them?"

Isan grunted but said nothing. He wore a deep frown, which Varro could not tell from disgust or worry.

Tanan had come forward with his own party. Behind him, less than half of his original numbers lined up at the edge of their camp. The camp followers made it seem as if he had more than his actual fighting capability.

"I don't see Falco," Varro said mildly. "We're to exchange me for him."

Again Isan only grunted, and now Varro confirmed his captain must have made a different arrangement than what Varro had explained. He gave his own silent nod in answer.

He never thought Isan would overtly act against him. He seemed to believe in his own sense of honor. But Varro had handed him the chance with his idea of an exchange. Now Isan could work within that framework to further his own agenda. He spoke Latin with incredible fluency, and a note of contempt that Varro had learned to hear over the years. He was glad his instincts had not failed him. Isan was selling him out and probably thought Curio a small problem because of his stature.

Varro hid his smile.

The one called Tanan sat atop his small horse with his light blue tunic pulled tight across his chest. Having only seen him at a distance, Varro was surprised to see that he had an open, almost affable face. He seemed in high spirits despite his defeat, smiling as Varro's own party drew closer. He had a faint red scar that marred his otherwise handsome features and eyes like the pale amber of the mountain grass. Varro could see how he stood apart from the common man.

Lars was nowhere to be seen, and his bulk could not be hidden.

Tanan had a slave who stood by his horse. He was a shrunken old man who seemed permanently twisted in a defensive posture. Otherwise, he was surrounded by other tribesmen of about the same cut as the men Varro had once led.

"Where is Centurion Falco?" He looked to Isan to translate, and he gave a brief nod.

His reply was quick and clipped, and Varro was fairly certain he said something like, "Here he is."

"Isan, what treachery is this? Are you handing me over to the enemy?"

He spoke with deliberate calm, and it had its effect. For Isan looked back at him wide-eyed and shaking his head.

"Not at all, sir. But they cannot release Falco until you are secured. You understand that, of course."

"And I will not be secured if Falco is not produced. You said you saw him yesterday. I'm not surrendering if Falco is already dead."

The slave at Tanan's side seemed to translate, as his master interrupted the response with his own answer.

Varro managed to determine Isan had agreed to hand him over in exchange for Tanan's retreat, not a swap for Falco.

"You will face the consequences," Varro said mildly, without even looking at Isan. "You are a coward, Isan. I'd have more respect for you had you stabbed me in the back."

"Surrender your weapons, sir." His voice was quiet and low. "They mean to pit you against Djebel. No matter what your original offer was, he planned to kill you. But be warned, they also mean to force you to watch him kill Falco first."

"Am I to consider that some sort of attempt at aid, or are you taunting me?" Varro at last turned to Isan, being careful to not express any emotion. "You would let these rebels escape just so you can get rid of the Romans and assume command for yourself? Is it so hard to gain promotion in the Numidian calvary that you would stoop to this?"

Isan stared cooly at Varro, while his men looked on with raised brows. Across the short gap, he heard Tanan chuckling at the slave's translation of their exchange.

Varro removed his gladius and then his pugio, handing the harness and holding both over to Isan who accepted it wordlessly.

"Of course, it's not personal," Varro said. "You don't like Romans, but you wouldn't murder one. However, you would be glad to see dead anyone who wants to rescue Baku."

Isan recoiled as if struck. Both Tanan and Varro laughed aloud at his reaction.

"He has kept you down, hasn't he, Captain Isan? What fortunate news to learn Baku is captured and facing death, and how dismaying to meet a commander so intent on his rescue. At first, I thought you wanted to reassert command by removing me. But why would you need to? After this mission, you would go back to being the leader. So what was it, I wondered. Then I saw how you had quietly defaced so many of Baku's belongings. When Curio and I were resting in his tent, I found the evidence but said nothing. I wasn't certain of your actions, but now it's clear. You're sending me to Tanan to ensure that your rival at court will die."

The color had fled from Isan's regal face, but his expression hardened as he realized Varro figured him out.

"He's common scum who has the ear of the King. He has no right to his position."

"Unlike the noble-born Isan, eh?" Varro slipped off his helmet and handed it over. "Well, it seems you will have everything you want. I would not trust Tanan to keep his word to you. You better hope that the relief column is on the way. I suppose you've detailed someone to handle Curio? He'll have lots of questions when you return with no one."

Isan did not answer, but accepted the helmet and handed it off to another. Varro still wore his chain shirt, but Tanan waved him down as he tried to remove it. It seemed he understood its value and would have it for his own. Varro was glad he had not put any effort into a proper cleaning of it.

"I am sorry, Centurion," Isan said. "You did a fine job building the defenses around camp. I'm not afraid of anything while inside it. There is no relief column, by the way. I've sent news of your deaths and Baku's execution. I'll simply await my orders to withdraw."

"I must commend your confidence," Varro said. "I go on to my fate, and you to yours. One day, I will see you in Hades and there will be a reckoning."

Isan tilted his head. "I don't think we will go to the same places in the next life. This is it, Centurion. I'm sorry it ended like this for you."

Varro slipped off his horse and Tanan snapped his fingers at two men who lowered spears and collected him from Isan. He was encouraged to see the surprised faces of the men surrounding him. But they were well trained to obey their captain, and since Varro went over without protest they likely assumed this was all according to plan.

He scanned past Isan and his men but saw no one else among the rolling grass plains.

Tanan's horsemen closed around him, and without looking back he was led toward the heart of the camp. People emerged from their tents and cursed him. Curses were some of the first words he learned from the tribesmen, even without any formal instruction. They now flowed freely at him, calling for his death.

The slave at Tanan's side staggered along with Varro.

"Sir, are you still on active duty?" The slave spoke with a feeble voice and he winced as if expecting to be swatted for speaking out of turn. But Tanan simply glanced down.

"I'm on a special assignment," he said. "I don't have a century at the moment. I did command the Tenth Hastati of the First Legion against the Macedonians."

"We went to Macedonia?" The slave's haggard face brightened, and Varro looked carefully at him. He was not as old as he seemed.

"We did, and we won. I don't suppose you get much news. Who are you?"

"I don't remember my name," he said. "I think it was Strabo. I was captured at Zama, and have lived to this day a slave of the tribes."

"But we won at Zama?"

"Some of us lost, sir. Before he silences me, the monster you will fight. I dare not use his name. They feed him magic potions to make him sleep or make him rage. He is always confused and angry. Maybe that will help you, sir. Because you're going to need it."

"Thank you. If I can free you, then I will."

Strabo laughed, a snorting, wheezing laugh that drew Tanan's ire. He kicked the slave in the head and shouted at him. He fell back and did not speak again.

They now came to the center of the camp, and Tanan dismounted with his men. He chattered at Strabo, nodding toward Varro as he did.

While his captor decided what happened next, Varro scanned this camp. It was erected in a large circle and with horses picketed at the edge. The camp followers and remnants of Tanan's rebels had come out to reinforce the circle, which is where Varro expected to face Lars. Tanan might be a barbarian but he understood the value of spectacle. After losing half his men in battle, what could be more satisfying than watching the leader of your defeat be torn to shreds by one of your own living legends? It was a calculated play to make himself seem more competent to his people than he was.

Falco was tied to a post at the far end. Varro met his eyes, though at this distance he was a mere shadow. He saw him shaking his head slowly, as his body was wound with rope.

For the moment Varro was surrounded and the center of camp's attention. Yet the men guarding him and Tanan himself were preoccupied with their shouting. It seemed his guards were important to Tanan, perhaps being his relatives or inner circle. Varro could not determine their argument other than it seemed to be about the timing of events.

While he remained encircled, he thought it best to start his plan now.

Feigning despair, he sank to his knees and held his face in his hands. Looking through his fingers he saw that he got nothing more than sneers from his captors and the rest of the camp jeered. So he leaned forward as if to collapse from his stress. But instead, he reached high into his tunic where his own pugio was strapped to his thigh. Curio had helped bind it there this morning.

It was an unsheathed blade and the edge of it had left minor cuts on his hip that burned as he worked it free. But now it fell to the muddy ground, and he shifted over it. He then forced it into the soft earth and slathered mud atop it before standing again and placing his sandaled foot over it to press it deeper.

Tanan had settled his decisions. Strabo was shoved forward to explain his fate.

"Sir, they are going to fix you to a post like your friend. Then they'll wake up Djebel and let him rip that one apart. For finale you will be given to him for the same fate."

Despite the confidence in his plan and Lars's predictability, Varro worried that Lars would simply kill him while tied to the post. This was the one variable he had not explicitly planned for. But Curio was near, even if he could not see him. He just had to avoid serious injury before Curio could intervene.

So Varro was taken away and had his chain shirt removed, folded, and then carried off. He had to wait while they pounded his stake into the soft ground. Tanan had left for another tent with most of his guard.

At last, he was forced to the stake and tied with rope. He tested the bond and did not find any give. But he was certain Lars would solve that problem for him. He simply stared at Falco across the way. They were set up like two practice dummies. Falco shook his head again, but Varro only smiled in reply.

Tanan re-emerged from his tent and then addressed his people. It was a long-winded speech and Varro guessed he spoke about revenge, the favor of their gods, and other things that made their predicament sound better than it was. The audience cheered, looking between their two captives.

At last, with a flourish, he announced Djebel to the crowd and the cheers and stamping feet shuddered through the ground.

Lars stumbled out of a large tent. His leg was wrapped in a bloody bandage and his eyes rolled like a mad horse. He drooled on himself and staggered around, screaming and roaring. He had no weapons, only two huge hands that swiped at the air.

Varro swallowed hard. Lars was senseless and mad, and probably beyond understanding anything said to him. But Varro had to try.

Tanan's men shoved Lars toward Falco, and he screamed out, "Centurion!"

Then he charged across the mud, both hands extended to rend Falco to shreds.

25

Lars's strides shuddered the ground like the tramping of an elephant. He did not see Varro as he shot toward Falco, who began to squirm in his bindings as his head turned desperately from side to side.

Varro drew his breath down deep into his lungs. He had always been a loud child. His mother said his crying as a baby could be heard around the world. As a Centurion that sharp, brilliant shout served him well in the chaos of battle. He summoned it now.

"Lars, you fucking idiot! I killed Bellus! You stupid beast!"

But he charged past as if he did not hear.

"I am Varro! Your brother died like a coward! You dumb shit! I killed him!"

The giant bulk stuttered to a halt, drawing groans from the crowd. His bald, cratered, head swiveled across his massive shoulders to look back at Varro. His eyes were so red, they seemed to bleed. The smoldering hatred paused Varro's shouting, as Lar's drifting eye moved sickeningly into focus.

"Varro!"

"That's right, your idiot! You fucking fool!"

"Don't call me that!"

Now he swung around, hunched forward as if he were going to launch himself off the ground. The crowd hissed in protest. But Varro's eyes fixed on the mad gaze of his mortal enemy.

He thundered across the mud, his mouth opened in a roar as spittle fell onto his chest. In two bounds he had closed the gap, and then he launched himself at Varro.

His massive bulk collided with him and the pole, slamming both to the muddy ground. The tremendous impact drove the air from his lungs and turned his vision white. The heat of his body was like a furnace and the blast of his breath smelled bitter and foul.

But the toppled post had loosened his ropes and the moment he recovered from the impact he easily sloughed away his bindings, though he was still trapped beneath Lars.

"You're brother was a fool!"

Lars sat up and roared.

"Don't say that!"

He clamped both hands to Varro's throat and began to crush down. His windpipe sealed and the pressure behind his eyes made it feel as if both would pop free. But he forced his panic back and worked his hand over to the wound in Lars's leg. It was easy to find, with the bandage leading him to the spot. Even as Lars choked the life out of him, he dug his fingers into the bleeding hole and then plunged in deep.

To no effect.

Lars did not even flinch where another man might pass out from the agony.

Varro's vision turned white again and his fingers slipped out of the bloody wound. His miscalculation would cost his life, for Lars seemed unable to feel pain.

However, the giant seemed to realize he was killing Varro too soon. So he released his grip, but still kept him pinned under his prodigious weight.

Varro gasped and sucked in air. His neck pulsed as blood flushed back into his head and sent his vision spinning.

Getting up with a grunt, Lars grabbed Varro by the hair and yanked him to his feet. He now ran on the tips of his toes as Lars swung him around. The crowd responded with a massive shout of approval.

"I'll tear you to bits!"

Even in his raging stupor, Lars handled Varro as easily as a javelin. He clapped both hands onto his shoulders and crushed down so that lightning pain shot through his arms. Then he hefted Varro overhead as the crowd cheered him.

Next Varro knew he was flying through the air and landing hard on his shoulder. He rolled up against something and realized he was at Falco's feet.

"By the gods, do you have a plan, Varro?"

"I'm working on it."

He got to his hands and knees in the mud, but Lars was on him again. He seized his collar and heaved him off the ground. He hung before the brute in both his hands, feeling like a half-drowned cat just pulled from a river.

"This is for Bellus!"

He released one hand and cocked his arm, but had overestimated his own strength. Varro fell out of his grip as one mighty fist missed destroying his face.

Varro was up and running before he understood what had happened. He staggered and spun his arms to keep his balance, for if he fell now the raging Lars would surely destroy him.

"I'll kill you!"

Lars now ran after him, but Varro knew he was out of his mind. As long as he could maintain his own panic, he would easily win.

He dodged into a crowd of women and children who were

laughing a moment ago. The crowd flipped from jeering to scattering in terror. Tanan did not have enough guards to maintain such a wide circle, and Varro exploited it.

Lars came charging after him, but Varro was knocking away women and kicking over children as he pressed to reach the other side of the circle.

Armed men came after him now, trying to cut him off from escape. There was not much distance for them to cover. Varro doubled back into another part of the crowd, punching and kicking any man or woman, adult or child, who blocked him. But he encountered none deliberately trying to stop him.

However, when Lars saw that armed men were threatening Varro, he had a predictable reaction.

"He's mine! You fucking bastards!"

Lars grabbed one of the spearmen by his arm and wrenched it out of its socket. Varro did not see what happened next, as he had fought his way back into the circle, but he heard the horrified screams of agony.

While Lars wreaked chaos amid the crowd in his blind fury, Varro staggered back into the circle. He could not truly escape, at least not escape and save Falco. But he did not want to. He had to finish what he had begun months ago.

"I'm here, you fool!" He flashed a quick smile to Falco. Even under the shadow of his heavy brows, the whites of his eyes shined with shock.

Lars relented on the guards. A wide gap formed around him, and two bodies lay heaped at his feet and fresh blood splattered his bare chest.

Varro backed up as Lars began to gather steam. He was not far from his hidden pugio.

As Lars charged for him, he slipped down to snatch the weapon out of the mud.

And came up with a clod of dirt in his hand.

Lars hit him like a battering ram. Varro screamed as he flew back and crashed into the mud again. A black shadow enveloped him as he lay on his back facing the sky. His head swam and limbs trembled. He saw a flash of yellow teeth gnashing in that blackness that descended on him.

"First your ears," Lars shouted.

He clasped his hand over Varro's right ear but found it hard to grip it in his blood-slicked fingers. He pinned Varro with his knee on his torso and his other hand on his shoulder.

When Lars at last grasped the top of Varro's ear, he twisted and tugged hard. Varro felt pain like he had never experienced before. It was as if the side of his head would tear off.

But he also felt hot fluid running onto his stomach. He knew what it was, for it was the same leg he had cut before.

He reached down with his hand and felt the blood running freely along a seam in Lar's thigh.

His fingers plunged into the gap, finding hot and slick flesh and muscle.

With a grunt, he pulled up and out, tearing open the long line of the old wound.

No matter what potions he had been fed, Lars recoiled at the horrific pain. Blood gushed from his leg as he hopped back.

The crowd fell utterly silent, with only Lars's manic roars echoing through the camp.

Varro rolled over, dizzy but flush with rage of his own, and rebounded to his feet. At the same moment, Lars collapsed like the column of an ancient temple finally giving way.

"Now I kill Djebel!" Whether anyone understood his shout in the tribesmen's tongue, he did not care. Instead, he pounced atop Lars.

He worked his hand into the reopened wound and began to tear up the skin like ripping up rotten floorboards.

Lars stared in horror, unable to fix his eyes on anything, one drifting out of focus as his blood poured in sheets beneath him.

Varro groaned as he pulled the wound open to the crotch.

But this was not enough. Lars would die, but his people needed to see him not only dead but utterly defeated.

He drove his thumbs into both of Lars's eye sockets. The resistance was surprisingly hard, but he pressed until both plunged into the thick, bloody soup behind his eyes. Lars gasped and his head fell back in death.

Varro leaped up, raising his gory fists to the sky.

"He is dead! Dead! I killed Djebel!"

Tanan began shouting at his men, but many were already peeling away in fear. The silent crowd erupted into horrified shrieks at the sight of Varro placing his foot on the mighty Djebel's lifeless corpse.

Then the cavalry charged the camp. Curio had arrived late but as planned.

Now everything dissolved into madness. Tanan fled as did every other rebel, each one looking to their own safety. The surprise charge obliterated them. As Varro had hoped, he put all eyes on himself and Lars while Curio positioned the cavalry to attack. Captain Isan had probably already returned to an empty camp and was now fleeing for his life.

Varro smiled back at Falco, whose calm was incongruous with the havoc unfolding all around him.

Trudging to where he thought he had buried the pugio, he made a closer search of the mud. He had done his job a little too well in hiding it. He was off by several feet when he pulled it up.

Even as rebels and cavalry swirled around him, he walked slowly across to Falco with the pugio in hand.

"I'm not sure what your plan was," Falco said. "But that was fucking dramatic if you don't mind my saying so. Did you plan the part when he threw you across the field like an old stick or was that just improvisation?"

Varro waved his pugio generally back at Lars's corpse. "I just did whatever came naturally."

"Like sailing through the air and choking out?"

"Don't make me rethink cutting you free."

"Say, your ear's looking pretty bloody. I'd help you out, but since my arms have been numb for about a day you'll have to figure it out yourself."

Varro touched the side of his head and the pain was immediate. "Is it still attached?"

"Can you free me so I can get a better look?" Falco scanned past him and bent his mouth in appreciation. "Looks like you've ended the rebellion at least."

After cutting Falco free, he only glanced at Varro's ear and instead began massaging his dangling arm. "It's on there," he said of the ear. "But it'd be no big loss to you. You never listen to anyone, anyway."

"I need it to hold my helmet up."

And after all the pain and fear, both he and Falco burst into laughter. Even as men screamed and died, run down by merciless, blood-thirsty cavalry, they continued to laugh until Curio trotted up on his horse.

"What happened to your ear?"

Varro gingerly cupped his hand over it. "Nothing really. Just a memento of Fortuna's sorting out her chosen."

Curio blinked and looked at Lars's corpse. "I said she favors you more."

"But she hasn't been doing his looks any favors," Falco said, now seated on the grass and rubbing his calves with his one good arm.

"Did you run into Captain Isan?" Varro knelt beside Falco and examined his arm which appeared dislocated at the shoulder, doubtless Lar's handiwork.

Curio shook his head. "Not sure where he is, but your silver was enough to buy most of his men. They were ready to fight and didn't understand why their captain was so hesitant."

"I think Isan acted entirely on his own. The men are innocent of any scheming."

Falco's heavy brown furrowed. "What's this about Isan?"

"It's a bit of a story," Varro said. "But I figured out he wanted me gone so that Baku would be left for the Carthaginians to execute. I was too forceful about rescuing him, and Isan was too happy that he was in danger. So I knew he would find some way to make sure I could not interfere with Baku's demise."

"I think he would've tried to kill you,' Curio said. "I mean, if you didn't come up with this plan."

Varro nodded. "If I tried to use my authority to rescue Baku, then he maybe would have."

"So you paid all your silver to his men?"

"Everyone got an equal share," Curio said. "Paid in advance too. These Numidians have a deep sense of honor to whoever is paying them the most."

"Well, it's not like we asked them to charge Hannibal's elephant line." Varro looked appreciatively at the mopping up of Tanan's rebels. "They got a handsome payday for destroying an already broken and underpowered enemy."

Falco scratched his head. "Well, good thing the rebels shit in your tent. That was probably a better guard for your coins than anything else. But now you're a poor man."

"But I'm alive, and so are you." Varro handed the pugio to Falco. "This one is yours. We're not supposed to be leaving them around for anyone to find."

Falco took it into his hand and began working the mud out of the recesses. "I'm starting to feel like you now, losing my pugio and having to get it back."

"Isan has mine," Varro said with a thin smile. "I'm sure I'll have it back from him."

"You're not going to kill him?" Curio asked.

"I'm not even going to speak of this, never mind threaten him," Varro said. "We don't know who he is, or how he fits into the politics of this place. It's just the three of us out here. We got caught in palace politics, despite being packed off to a mountain hideout. Let's learn something from that. Isan might never trouble us again, but what might his family do if we took justice on him?"

"That's stupid," Falco said. "But it's probably right."

"It is right," he said, then looked east. "And for all my coin, I think I've paid enough for the cavalry to deliver me to the Carthaginian outpost. I've got a friend to save if I can."

26

Varro sat in the cool shade of the palace garden. Falco and Curio sat with him, sipping sweet wine from silver cups. Cirta was the hub of Numidia and all the best wines and foods flowed through it, particularly in the royal palace. As both his friends sat to his left, he could not hear their murmured conversation through the bandage on his ear. But it sounded like Curio was moaning about reading lessons again.

Purple flowers waved in the wind as women in white stolas passed behind them, servants on some urgent duty by the way they shuffled hurriedly through the shadows of the surrounding garden walls. He watched the garden gate for nearly an hour, and at last, Baku arrived.

As he entered, his halo of frizzy hair caught the sunlight and seemed to glow. He smiled as he saw Varro and made directly for him.

"Glad to see you in better condition," Varro said, rising to his feet. Both Curio and Falco stopped their conversations and joined him.

"My joints still ache," he said. "And my sleep is troubled. The

Carthaginians know best how to injure a man's mind as well as his body. But I am alive and so are you."

Varro lowered his head. The day he rode into Carthaginian territory on the heels of his victory over Tanan, he had found a dozen severed heads mounted on the walls of the outpost fort. Their faces were unrecognizable, but their head covers marked them for his men. He had feared Baku's was among them. The Carthaginians of course recognized his name and verified his claim, sparing him death. But everyone else had their heads struck off, and Baku had been made to witness it.

"Do not regret what happened," Baku said in a soft voice. "There could have been no other resolution."

"And King Masinissa?" Varro looked hopefully to Baku. "How bad was his displeasure?"

"He was more confused than displeased," Baku said. "After all, he had word of our deaths just before we arrived with a new story."

"What did he say of me?"

Upon return to Cirta, following Isan's promised withdrawal order, he had been sent to have his ear stitched and tended by doctors. Baku, who had been badly beaten, was also taken to an infirmary. But the King had only sent word that he was glad for their survival. He had not summoned Varro for a report and instead conferred with Baku alone.

"Perhaps we should speak in private?" Baku's tired eyes looked to Falco and Curio.

"It's time to get back to your lessons, anyway," Falco said. His arm hung in a white sling and would remain so for several weeks. "Let's see if we can find more of Varro's reports to read again."

Curio moaned. "Don't drink all that wine while I'm gone. It's delicious."

Both he and Baku watched them exit the garden by the gate.

When it clanked shut, Baku sat down and gestured Varro to do the same.

"Loyal friends are a rare gift."

Varro glanced at the gate where they left. "I would say friends alone are hard enough to come by. Friends like them are one of a kind."

"Well said." Baku swirled a small leather bag around that had been slung across his back. He now produced Varro's pugio from within it. "This is yours. All your gear has been recovered and placed in your room. I wanted to return this to you directly."

Taking it in both hands, Varro rubbed his thumb across the leather sheath. He stared at the silver owl head, the symbol of Servus Capax. "Thank you for this. How is Captain Isan?"

"As quiet and small as you might expect. We won't hear anything from him." Baku gave a deeply satisfied smile. "But I will ensure that turd suffers. Just give me time."

Varro set the pugio to the bench, tucking it against his leg.

"So what will the King do with me? I lost all his men. I did not keep the rebellion down as he commanded. It seems I have failed in every way."

"On the contrary, you did better than expected." Baku reached into his bag and produced a roll of papyrus with a broken wax seal. Varro recognized it as Flamininus's letter to the king. But he simply held it gently between two fingers as he continued to speak.

"You burned wide stretches of Carthaginian farmland, and have caused them to rethink their border defense strategy. You have destroyed Tanan's rebellion and ended this furor over the return of Djebel to the tribes."

"Djebel is dead, but Tanan escaped."

Baku shook his head.

"He is a spent force. He led the tribes to defeat, something unforgivable on its own, but also squandered a legend in the bargain. No one would follow such a man. I know this, as these are my people too. Tanan must travel far from here to outdistance his shame, but it will find him wherever he goes."

"Everyone in my command was killed or deserted."

"Such a cheap price for so much." Baku closed his eyes. "Those men were never meant to be tamed but instead spent. And their disquiet was meant to bring out the rebels around you. The king was eager to see what you did with them and cared not one whit for their lives. They were scum and criminals, men who took from society and offered nothing in return. Many were marked for death, and so died in a small service to Numidia. He does not weep for them, and neither should you."

"They were not all as bad as you say." Varro tried to think of a specific example, but his words fell short.

Baku chuckled. "You have a warm heart. That is admirable in a doctor, but not in a Centurion. Here, I'll let you read this. It will explain some things, and maybe create new questions. I'll leave you to think on what you read. Tonight, we will eat together. You and I will talk more then."

He extended the papyrus to Varro, who took it gingerly in hand. Bellus's grimy prints were still on the page.

"Besides this," Baku said. "King Masinissa will repay all the silver you lost and more again. Consider it a reward for sparing me the horrors of a Carthaginian prison and for your dedication. My cousin is generous to those who serve him well."

"Cousin?" Varro leaned back on his seat, a twisted smile on his face. "I'm glad you only told me that today."

He waited for Baku to leave by the gate, then unrolled the papyrus sitting on his lap and angled it so a patch of sunlight lit the page.

It had been torn in half so that some of the letter was missing. Yet, the parts Varro needed to read were left intact in Flamininus's careful script.

~

NOW IN REGARDS to Centurion Varro, I intend him to be of great value to you. I do not relinquish his services in Rome easily, for as I hope you will learn he is a resourceful man. You may put him to use in any military capacity you deem fitting, and I shall be surprised if he does not exceed your expectations.

However, even as Centurion Varro shall be at your disposal, I ask as both formal ally and friend that you develop not only his skills but also his character. There are no better cavalrymen than the Numidians, and so I would have him learn what he could not learn here in Rome. Nor is there a better teacher of guerrilla warfare than the Great Masinissa.

You will find that the Centurion is a conscientious person and given to moments of self-doubt and hesitation, particularly in regard to spending the lives of the men under his command. While laudable, we both understand this trait does not serve a commander well. As he is learning from you, so must he learn from bitter experience. There is no better instructor. Place him in situations where it is impossible to not sacrifice his men. He must not be made to believe he can avoid this fate. Just as Sisyphus must forever roll his stone uphill, so must Centurion Varro find his desire to always spare his men an equally vain effort.

I commend him to your command and discipline. Our other arrangements will be kept as agreed.

~

THE FINAL LINE of the letter was struck out with black ink. Varro stared at the letter after re-reading it twice more. At last, he rolled it up and set it beside his pugio, then folded his hands on his lap.

"Well, one lesson completed."

HISTORICAL NOTES

Masinissa was a young chieftain of the Massylii tribe at the time of the Second Punic War and was allied to Carthage. He fought admirably against Rome, until the end of the war when he realized that Rome would prevail. He then switched sides and proved to be a key ally at the Battle of Zama in 202 BC, where his cavalry had a major role in the defeat of Carthage.

For his great contribution to Scipio's victory, he was awarded the Kingdom of Syphax to the west of his own kingdom, which had been an ally of Carthage. This created the vast Kingdom of Numidia under his leadership. He then married Syphax's wife, Sophonisba, and made her his queen. He accepted that she had been forced to marry Syphax and that she had no real desire for him.

Unfortunately for both, the new queen's loyalty came under Scipio's suspicion. After all, she had been one of Rome's enemies. Sophonisba had been betrothed to Masinissa prior to his turning to the Roman side. Yet this did nothing to quell Roman suspicion. Scipio demanded that she be displayed in the thanksgiving celebration back in Rome. Rather than subject her to such humiliation, and knowing he could not free her from Roman captivity, in the end, Masinissa gave her poison. Maintaining her regal bearing, Sophonisba drank the cup of poison but not before chiding Masinissa for making their marriage so short. Masinissa then presented Scipio with her corpse.

Numidia and Rome would thereafter become strong allies, with the loyalty of Numidia never in doubt. Masinissa united the Massylii and Masaesyli into one kingdom. Modern-day Berbers trace their lineage back to him and his legend enjoys an iconic status among many of them.

The semi-nomadic lifestyles of the tribes needed to be modernized in his view. He knew Numidia was capable of becoming an agricultural powerhouse. However, the tribes were not prepared to handle this level of production under their traditional structure. He settled their nomadic ways and enforced Carthaginian-style agriculture among the people. This was an incredibly successful strategy, if not without its struggles along the way.

At the same time, he was able to encroach on Carthaginian territory thanks to the hand-binding, antiwar treaty Rome enforced. As long as he had Roman permission, Masinissa could continue to put pressure on Carthage across its long borders.

Masinissa is famous for his lifespan as well as many other military and political achievements. But as that is for the future in the timeline of this series, I leave it for you to discover on your own.

NEWSLETTER

If you would like to know when my next book is released, please sign up for my new release newsletter. You can do this at my website:
http://jerryautieri.wordpress.com/

If you have enjoyed this book and would like to show your support for my writing, consider leaving a review where you purchased this book or on Goodreads, LibraryThing, and other reader sites. I need help from readers like you to get the word out about my books. If you have a moment, please share your thoughts with other readers. I appreciate it!

ALSO BY JERRY AUTIERI

Ulfrik Ormsson's Saga

Historical adventure stories set in 9th Century Europe and brimming with heroic combat. Witness the birth of a unified Norway, travel to the remote Faeroe Islands, then follow the Vikings on a siege of Paris and beyond. Walk in the footsteps of the Vikings and witness history through the eyes of Ulfrik Ormsson.

Fate's Needle

Islands in the Fog

Banners of the Northmen

Shield of Lies

The Storm God's Gift

Return of the Ravens

Sword Brothers

Descendants Saga

The grandchildren of Ulfrik Ormsson continue tales of Norse battle and glory. They may have come from greatness, but they must make their own way in the brutal world of the 10th Century.

Descendants of the Wolf

Odin's Ravens

Revenge of the Wolves

Blood Price

Viking Bones

Valor of the Norsemen

Norse Vengeance

Bear and Raven

Red Oath

Fate's End

Grimwold and Lethos Trilogy

A sword and sorcery fantasy trilogy with a decidedly Norse flavor.

Deadman's Tide

Children of Urdis

Age of Blood

Copyright © 2022 by Jerry Autieri

All rights reserved.

No part of this book may be reproduced in any form or by any electronic or mechanical means, including information storage and retrieval systems, without written permission from the author, except for the use of brief quotations in a book review.

Printed in Great Britain
by Amazon